Meet Your New Roommates

ALWAYS DREAM BIG!

Lucky Number Four

Amanda Jason

Cover design by Sarah Hansen of Okaycreations.com
Four Leaf Clover title illustration by Robert Kunz

444

For my friends and family, who have all been my biggest supporters through this entire process. Without them I would never have been able to follow my dream of writing my first novel.

First Printing

ISBN-13: 978-1494783822 (pbk)

ISBN-10: 1494783827 (pbk)

C.A. Kunz, LLC
Orlando, Florida

Acknowledgements

Where do I start? I guess at the beginning with my Mum and Dad, because if it wasn't for them I wouldn't be here. Their love and support have helped me make it through all the bad times, and they've always been there to help me celebrate the good times.

Very special thanks to my husband, Bob, for all of his love and support throughout this entire process. Oh, and of course without him there would be no Stephanie (my daughter), Adam (my son), or the twins (Amanda and Jason).

Big thanks should go to my son Adam. He came to me in the spring of 2010 to ask me if I wanted to write a Young Adult/Middle Grade book, and I immediately jumped at the chance. Writing a book was number one on my bucket list, and he knew that. We've written three books together under the pen name C.A. Kunz, but then took a break to write our own novels. When I decided to write Lucky Number Four, Adam was behind me one hundred percent, and even though we weren't writing it together, he was there any time I needed to vent about where the story was going, and I'm ever-so-thankful for his help. What else can I say about my son, Adam? Well, he's my rock, he inspires me to carry on, and he's my hero. I'm truly blessed to have a son like him! Thank you, son, for giving your Mom her dream.

On this journey I've met some truly AWESOME people, people I hold dear to my heart, and it would take a whole book to name them all. So, THANK YOU everyone that I've met on this journey, and yes, this means YOU!

I do have some special people that I really do need to mention. These ladies gave up their time to help me with extensive editing and suggestions. They are Megan Bagley, Misty Provencher, Hollie Westring, and Raine Thomas. A thank you is truly not enough for what you've all done for me and I cherish each and every one of you.

I started my dream late in life so I have words of wisdom for you: FOLLOW YOUR DREAMS, DON'T WAIT…DO IT NOW!

In closing, I LOVE YOU ALL, and I sincerely hope you enjoy my debut novel, Lucky Number Four.

BIG HUGS AND SMILES,
-Amanda Jason aka Carol Kunz aka half of C.A. Kunz

Contents

"Oh my God, I can't wait anymore! Please, please, harder, harder. Deeper, deeper. I'm almost the fuck there. Ooooooooohhhhhhhhhh."

No, I'm not watching porn. In fact, I'm lying here in my semi-dark room listening to one. Actually, it's the sexual antics of my two very best friends, who were only married a month ago.

"Oh, baby, I think I'm gonna …. Ahhhhhhhh yeaaaaaaaah."

"Yesssssss, I feel it. Harder, harder!"

By the sound of it, you would think this was their first time, and really, I can't believe they're being so inconsiderate. I mean, the walls aren't soundproof. I left them alone for a month after the wedding, trying to give them alone time as a newly married couple. All the while I was suffering—I mean, spending "quality time" with my family back home.

Oh, thank heaven. Now all I can hear is muffled voices. Maybe I can finally get some sleep.

One hour later…I'm still not asleep.

I haven't heard any more noises through the wall, which is good thing, but now my throat is dry and I'm thirsty. I swear if it isn't one thing, it's another. Jumping out of bed, I listen at the door for any movement. Hearing none, I make my way to the kitchen. Turning the corner, I find the fridge door open and a naked Kevin Browning, the newlywed, standing there. I'm frozen as he bends over and moons me. I must have made a noise because he suddenly straightens and turns. My eyes immediately focus on his nether region.

"Hey Dora, can't sleep either?" His voice penetrates my brain, but I don't look up. "A little different from when we played 'you show me yours and I'll show you mine' when we were seven, huh?"

Mortified at being caught staring, my eyes fly up to meet his grinning mouth. "Geez, Kev. Couldn't you have at least put your boxers on?" I say as I swivel and take my hot (I know it's totally red) face back to my room. I cringe as I hear him laughing behind me. "Jerk. Hope it rots off," I mumble, making him laugh harder.

Slamming my door, I fall back on my bed and fume. I really don't want his penis to drop off. He and Julie are my best friends, and I don't want her to have a dickless spouse. I'm not that mean.

I hear them talking through walls and then Julie laughing. Putting my pillow over my head, I pray for sleep.

444

The next morning, work is hectic, of course, not giving me a break because of my lack of sleep. Seven mornings a week, I work as a barista in a wonderful coffee shop a block away from our apartment. Five afternoons of the week though, I'm stuck in classes at the local university.

Today is Monday, and after my five-hour shift, I have three wonderfully boring classes back-to-back. I feel like I've been in college all my life. I'm jealous that Julie has graduated early, gotten married, and has secured a real job. But I'm stubborn. I could've had my maternal grandmother pay my way, but the price had been too high. What normal girl goes to "finishing school" the summer she graduates from high school? Nope, couldn't and wouldn't do it. What the hell is finishing school anyway? Isn't that like an ancient practice?

So, because of my stubbornness, I'm a year behind in terms of graduating.

Sadness floods me as I realize I need to move out of our apartment. The newlyweds need their space, and I don't need a nightly reminder of my sexless existence, just another thing to add to my feel-sorry-for-me list.

444

Shopping is usually an escape for me, unless it's for boring groceries. Why can't we just skip eating? I mean, I could afford to lose a pound or two. But no, it's my turn to do the shopping, and I have to do that often because I hate to cook. Thank goodness Kevin is a chef and it's his night off. With his deliciously wicked meals, I'll gain two pounds instead.

Entering the local supermarket, I grab a cart and glance over at the colorful announcement board. Nestled among the ads for items for sale, dating sites and such, I spy a flyer with numerous perforated tabs at the bottom.

REALLY! DESPERATELY! WANTED! ASAP!
A ROOMMATE!

MUST BE HOUSEBROKEN AND WILLING TO SHARE
WITH THREE OTHERS TO MAKE A LUCKY FOUR!
AWESOME LOFT APARTMENT! YOUR OWN BED AND

FULL BATHROOM! YOU WON'T BELIEVE THE RENT, AND THE UTILITIES ARE INCLUDED!

Wishing they had put the unbelievable rent amount on the flyer, I grab one of the little slips of paper and decide it's worth a shot. I have nothing to lose. Tucking the slip into my purse, I put my backpack in the cart and start my journey with grocery list in hand.

A mouthwatering smell greets me at home when I arrive with two full grocery bags and my ever full backpack. I hear Kevin humming in the kitchen and he pops around the corner, apparently hearing me coming down the hallway.

"Ah, she has arrived with the rest of the ingredients for tonight's cuisine." He grabs the two bags from my aching arms and plops them down on the counter. "Hey chick, you look tired. You know you should really get more sleep."

I want to wipe that grin from his face, but I can never stay mad at Kevin for very long, I just can't.

"Julie called. She'll be late. The slave driver wanted an impromptu office meeting. Dinner will be ready in about an hour. Why don't you take a nap?"

"I wish. I unfortunately have homework that won't do itself. Your day must have been good since you're so happy and all."

"Every day is an awesome day," he says. "I have a job I love, a woman I love, and a roommate I adore. What else could a man ask for?"

I shake my head at his dimpled cheeks as he smiles. Growing up in a small town, Julie, Kevin, and I were like the Three Musketeers. Our parents were good friends and we went on family camping trips and vacations together. It was like having three sets of parents, which was fun until we got into trouble, and then it was a nightmare.

Kevin was goofy looking when he was younger, and majorly awkward when he went through his growth spurt until he reached his final height of six foot three and a half. His parents encouraged him to play sports and he excelled, winning a scholarship to a college out west. His dark brown hair, good looks, height and adorable dimples had panting females following him everywhere.

In contrast, Julie is blonde, fair-skinned and, like me, short. We had a growing contest as kids and to our delight, we grew to the same height of five feet four inches.

We would never be mistaken as twins, though. She always looks put together and I always look thrown together. I think she's far prettier too. Her natural light blonde hair is straight and falls like a waterfall down her back. Well, when she doesn't have it up for her job as a social worker. Mine is a red, curly mess. It's as long as Julie's, but mine could never be described as a waterfall—more like tangled vines. I don't tan, but Julie can and used to. Now she shies away from the sun since her dad was diagnosed with skin cancer. Her skin is blemish free while mine has a few freckles—okay, so I have more than a few. Sun kisses, my dad calls them. We both have curves. Not fat, but not skinny and no cellulite yet.

When Kevin and Julie graduated last winter and he moved back, they fell in love. They had tried to hide their feelings from me because they didn't know how I'd react, but I knew. I'd just ended a three-year relationship, and being the awesome friends that they are, they didn't want to upset me. I had known these two all my life. I love them both and told them I couldn't be happier for them. That night, we celebrated and ended up with massive hangovers the next day.

"Earth to Dora. Come in, Dora!" Kevin's voice jolts me from my musings. "Not thinking about last night, are you?" he jokes, his dimples dancing in his cheeks.

"Yeah, I was," I say, watching him stand taller and push out his well-defined chest. "I was thinking it hasn't grown much since I saw it last."

I giggle and quickly exit as he throws an oven mitt at me.

444

Later that night, while finishing up my homework, I remember the slip of paper from the grocery store and pull it out of my purse. Grabbing my cell phone, I quickly dial the number. A female voice answers.

"Hello?"

"Uh, I saw your ad on the board at the supermarket, and I was wondering if the rental is still available, and if so, could I come by and look at it?"

"Yes, it is, and yes, you can! How about tomorrow, say around one?" her bubbly voice replies.

"Sure. I mean, that would be wonderful." I grab a piece of paper and write down the address and then thank her. She tells me her name is Emily. We say our goodbyes and disconnect.

I breathe out a sigh of relief. Well, that was easy, and she sounds so nice. I'm not going to tell Kevin and Julie just yet. It might not work out. I know they'll be upset, but I have to give them some space for my sanity … and theirs. I've only been back two days, and soon they'll realize they need to be alone.

I hear Kevin yelling my name as the front door opens, announcing that Julie's arrived home. I tuck the address in my backpack, put a smile on my face, and exit the room to greet her.

444

Smoothing down my hair, I ride up in the spacious freight elevator. When I found the building—or, should I say, giant warehouse—I'd become more excited. I watch those home improvement channels and I've seen what people have done with warehouses. There are four floors, and the address I'm looking for is at the top.

The wide steel doors open, and I pull back the old-fashioned gate. I step out and look to my left, where I see two blank doors. The same on my right. In front of me is an ornate double door with the number four hundred above it.

My excitement turns to nervousness when I wonder if this whole floor could be the loft. No, it can't be. I mean, really, it would be so huge!

I hesitate and shake my head. *Just do it, nothing to lose. It's just a rehearsal for looking at future apartments. I want to see what this place looks like. The rent is probably so out of my league anyway. So buck up, Dora, and march on.*

While I'm doing this dialogue in my head, my feet have made the decision for me, and I find myself standing in front of the door. There's a button to the side and I press it, hearing a muffled chime sound from inside. I paste a smile on my face as I hear the lock being disengaged and the door is flung open.

Oh, my sweet sexy heaven, my brain thinks as my eyes ogle the sight of a tall, beautiful male standing before me wearing nothing more than a skimpy pair of silky boxers and a smile. I take a quick glance at his face before examining his body, which is tanned and totally amazing—with twelve-pack abs. I swear, honest truth. I give it a twelve out of ten for definition. His hands rest on his hips and my eyes are drawn to *the* area.

"Do you like what you see?" his husky voice asks, bringing my embarrassed face up to meet his laughing eyes.

"Uhhhh, I'm looking for Emily?" How moronic can I sound? I know my face is a "wish a hole would open up in the floor and swallow me" cherry red.

"Emily, you have a visitor," Mr. Dreamboat's loud voice echoes in the hall.

"Geez, Drew. What would our grandmother say if she saw you answering the door in your boxers? Move your bubble butt out of my way," a feminine voice, the one I recognize from the phone call, pipes up from behind the black-haired god.

A tall, black-haired girl emerges as she pushes gorgeous Drew to the side. "Hi. I'm Emily, and you must be Pandora. Come in. I swear, this boy never learned manners."

Besides the hair color and the height, they don't look like siblings. Maybe I heard her wrong. She's very plain until she smiles and then her whole face lights up. I instantly like her and wish I could afford to live here just to have her for a friend.

The whole time I've been thinking this, she's been chatting to me and I notice Drop-dead Gorgeous has ignored her suggestion and made himself comfortable on a deep brown sectional in the middle of the room. And what a room it is. It's like my apartment living room times ten. My favorite fall colors of rich browns, oranges, and reds fill the room. It looks like a room right out of one of those popular design magazines.

Emily leads me to the sectional, ignoring Drew, and sits on the opposite side of him. "Please sit, Pandora. Would you like something to drink?"

I shake my head and try to ignore the eyes that are watching me. I will my face to quit turning red, but does it listen? Hell no.

"So how did you hear about the apartment?" Emily asks.

"I saw it on the board at the supermarket. I just live about a block away from here."

"Damn that Liam. We'll never hear the end of it!" Drew's rich voice interrupts. I wonder who Liam is.

"Shut it, Drew. You guys and your juvenile games." She looks at me. "They each put an ad in different places, and so far, Liam has had more nibbles from his ad. Now Pandora, let me tell you a little about the place. There are four bedrooms, each with its own bathroom and a sitting room. There's a games room complete with pool table, big screen TV, etcetera, a kitchen, of course…oh, and an indoor garden complete with a lap pool. Any questions?" Emily sounds like a real estate agent trying to get a sale.

"Well—" My brain seems to have forgotten to signal my mouth, as I find it hard to speak. This place is a freakin' palace. Like I can afford it.

"She'll take it. Look, she's speechless." Mr. Dreamboat interrupts again and Emily taps her foot, looking at him with disgust.

"You wanted me to do this, right? Well, let me do it," she says to him. "My flight leaves in three hours and if I miss it, you'll be in big trouble." She turns to me. "Pandora, what do you think? I think you'll be a perfect fit."

"It's beautiful, but I don't think it's in my price range. I mean, I'm a college student and I work, so…" I shrug.

My eyes are drawn to a billboard outside the window with a picture of a male model in his underwear. The model is Drew. I swear by my twenty-twenty vision it's the same grinning guy who is presently sitting across from me. I look out of the corner of my eye and see him look at the window and then he chuckles.

"Yeah, it's me. The others are jealous, but what can I say? Fame, baby, fame."

Emily rolls her eyes and glares at him. "Conceited much? Pandora, look. You can afford it. Our dad owned the building, and he gave it to Drew for his birthday last year. Yeah, I know he's a spoiled brat, but I have to love him—it's in the family contract." A pillow flies across the room and hits her in the head. "Anyway, money isn't the problem. It's whether you're a fit, and I have an overwhelming feeling, you are."

"So you live here with Drew and another roommate?" I ask when it finally sinks in this is his apartment.

"Oh. No, I don't live here. I just popped in for the weekend. Drew and two others live here," she says. I get the feeling she's not telling me everything. "Why don't I show you what would be your room?" Emily gets to her feet, pulling me up as she does.

"Who are the two others?" I ask. A feeling of dread lies heavily in my stomach.

"Oh, just two guys who are model friends of Drew," Emily says quickly as Drew laughs.

"I'm the best-looking one, of course," he quips.

"Drew, you are not helping. Go to your room," Emily's voice echoes in the vast room.

"Okay, okay." Drew stands and moves closer to us. "All kidding aside, Pandora, you are the one. When can you move in?"

"God, Emily. What is all this racket?" a male voice with an Australian accent sounds behind me.

I turn to see a brooding, masculine blond guy in a robe, pajama bottoms, and bare feet. I can't believe my eyes! Julie and I drooled over him in a magazine last month as we were being made up for her wedding. A few feet away from me stands one of the most famous models in the world. This must be a dream.

"Hey, Liam, come meet our new roommate, Pandora," Drew says cheerfully as Liam scowls more.

"I need coffee. I was up all night, and I get no respect for my rest," he mumbles as he exits the room.

"Ignore him, Pandora. Liam pulled an all-nighter for a shoot last night, and if Drew had behaved himself, Liam wouldn't be as peeved as he is. Liam really is a sweetheart. As is Colin. He's from England and is a love." Emily grabs my hand as if she knows I'm ready to flee this place. "When can you move in? Oh, I forgot to show you your room, didn't I?"

I pinch myself—no, not a dream. It's time to go. I have enough drama in my life with school, work, and my crazy family. No way am I living with three giant *male* models. I figure the third one is tall too, because geez, there are no short models.

"Thanks, Emily, but I have to run or I'll be late for class. It was nice meeting you and Drew, but I think I'll have to pass. I know you'll find someone who'll fit in here. This place is a little too big for—"

"If it's about cleaning the place, don't worry. They have a housekeeping team who comes in three times a week. It's included in the rent. Oh, and the cable, and the phone," Emily says in a rush and then smiles as if she just sealed the deal.

She still has a hold of my hand, and I give it a light pull. She lets go as I grab my backpack and move past her before she can react.

"Sorry, I must run. Nice meeting you," I say as I walk to the front door and tug it open—only to find a tall, sandy-haired, drool-worthy man attempting to put his key in the lock.

SHUT THE FRONT DOOR.

His smile is killer, but it turns to puzzlement as I push past him, saying a quick hello. I do have manners after all. I sprint to the elevator, thankful it's still on the floor, and collapse against the wall as the doors close.

444

Thinking back, I don't really remember much about my classes today. I was distracted all day with my mind returning to the events at the loft. I had imagined what it would be like to live with three, drop-dead gorgeous, complete eye-candy guys. Not that any of them would have the slightest interest in my Medusa hair and me. I'm sure they date tall, beautiful female versions of themselves. Oh, well. I guess it's going to be a fun night of scouring the want ads on the interwebs when I get home.

The minute I step into the apartment, I feel the vibe—the "we're not having sex in our bedroom" vibe.

I quietly close the door again and back away from it when I hear, "OOOOOOOOOOOOOOOOOOOOHHH, YESSSSSSSSSSSSSS, Kevin! More!"

Homework in the apartment lobby it is then.

We have to convince her to move in. That small amount of time with her made me feel something....again. Now to convince the others

that she is our LUCKY NUMBER FOUR! She is the perfect package, and we must treat her delicately so she doesn't run away. What if she won't move in? What if I never see her again? No, that can't happen. A few phone calls will take care of this. I can't wait to see her again.

Two

My eyes feel like they're full of sand, and the incessant ringing of my cell is giving my headache a headache. Groaning, I squint, looking at the brightly lit screen, and moan (yes, it's different from a groan) after seeing who it is.

"Hi, Mom!" I say, trying to sound awake, alert, and happy.

"Dora, sweetie, what's wrong?" my psychic mother asks. Yes, she really is a psychic, medium, or dead talker … or whatever you want to call her really. Luckily, she can't read immediate family members, so I'm safe. She's relying instead on mother's intuition, which is usually right on target. One of the reasons I want to be a therapist, counselor, or psychologist is because I'm an empath, which means I feel other people's emotions. It took me a few years to perfect "my gift" to the point I wouldn't walk around depressed all the time. It hit as I embarked on the wonderful journey they call puberty, and with the crazy hormones and the emotional bombardments, I was an utter mess.

Luckily Henry, my mom's spirit guide, informed my mother of my condition and she helped me deal. When I was younger, I used to walk up and hug random strangers and end up with wet shoulders on a daily basis from their violent shedding of tears. Try explaining that to your friends. Julie and Kevin were the first to know, but our other friends, well, they took a while to come to terms with the fact that I was different. More different than being redheaded, left-handed, unable to tan, and having the ability to play connect the dots with my freckles.

"Nothing is wrong, Mom. I just woke up," I reply, hoping that will be the end of her prying.

"Just woke up? People die in bed! It's after eight. Aren't you supposed to be at work? You're sick, that's it! I will be right over with chicken soup—"

"Mom! Mom, listen I'm not sick. I don't have to work today. Steven wanted one of his shifts covered, so he took mine today. And I haven't slept past eight since I was nine," I say rolling my eyes, then focusing on an ugly brown stain on my ceiling. Where did that come from? What the hell is it?

"So I've had this feeling since yesterday that something really rattled you."

Shoot, I missed the first part of her sentence while I was pondering the ceiling. I hope she believes I'm not sick…at least, not yet. Maybe that stain is some kind of fungus.

Oh hell, I've missed more. Concentrate, Dora, concentrate.

"Are you listening, Dora? I'm going to drive into the city and pay you a visit if you don't answer me," my mom threatens.

It's a threat I take seriously, especially since my mom doesn't drive well in the city. Last time, she flipped off a policeman who cut her off, laid on her horn, and ended up with a ticket. I mean, red lights on a police car mean *pull over*. I don't care who you are.

"Yes, Mom, I'm listening. I'm fine, yesterday was fine, and tomorrow I'm sure I'll be fine. Now give my love to Dad and the grandparents. I have to get up and get ready."

"Get ready for what? You're off today. You're sick, I knew it. I'll call your dad at work and tell him I need the car—it's an emergency," my mom's worried voice comes through louder.

God, I wish I had listened.

"Mom, I still have school this afternoon, and I'm going to look for…" I say, almost telling her I'm apartment hunting, which until I find one, is not going to be told to anyone, especially her. "A new coffee pot … I kind of broke ours."

"Are you sure you're telling me everything?" she demands.

"Yes, Mom. I've got to go and beat Kevin for the bathroom. Love you!" I hang up before she can answer, and drag myself out of bed.

I really need to get a good night's sleep soon. I laid awake for hours last night going over the events at the loft. I'd acted like a complete moron, like I'd never been around such beautiful men before. Most of the night, I pondered what my life would be like living with the three of them. Then the thought of a foursome got into my head, and I stayed awake longer, trying to forget the image I created. I finally went to sleep, only to dream a totally screwed-up dream involving three sex-crazed zombies that looked suspiciously like the three drool-worthy models, but dead looking.

I kept yelling at myself in the dream—okay, someone who looked like me being chased by these creatures—to run, run for the hills. But would she listen? No, she slowed down so much that they grabbed her. Then my phone woke me up. Damn, it was right at the good, or bad, spot, I haven't quite decided which. Maybe something to ponder in the shower while naked—no, not there. Maybe on the subway to school.

I hear Kevin whistling, and I beat his ass to the bathroom by seconds, shutting the door in his shocked face.

444

Calculus—a total waste of mine and my professor's time. When will I ever use this in the field of psychology? I want to be a counselor or a therapist, someone who helps others figure out their problems. Not work with math. Okay, so I may use basic math for doing my checking account, the percent-off sales on my favorite shoes, and other mundane things, but Calculus? When the hell would I ever use this?

I feel a nudge on my shoulder. "Are you as lost as I am?" Karen, a fellow student, whispers.

I nod my head in response. The door to the room is suddenly flung open and a girl who looks to be a freshman runs in with a note in hand. She delivers it to Dr. Parker, the professor.

"Pandora Phillips, you need to report to the office immediately," booms Dr. Parker, his eyes picking me out of the crowd.

My stomach churns. What's happened? An accident? A death? Has my mom come to the city to check up on me?

I look down at my cell, and though it's on silent, it has a signal and there are no new calls. Surely someone would have tried my cell … unless it's really bad news.

"Pandora, did you hear me?" Mr. Parker's voice seems louder.

I pick up my backpack and walk in a daze to the exit, following the energetic freshman down the hall. By the time I reach the office, many horrible scenarios have flashed into my mind, and I feel like I'm going to hurl any second.

The first thing I spy in the office is the staff standing in one corner staring at a space that's blocked from my view by an empty bookcase. They look my way when the perky freshman, who is holding the door open for me, announces my arrival. The four middle-aged women look at me in shock, dazed, in fact, as if in a trance, but with tiny smiles on their faces. They turn their attention back to the space I can't see, and I walk around the sight-blocking item, seeing immediately what is causing their zombie stares.

There I go with zombie references again.

They look like three mouthwatering trees—yes, trees, as they all tower over my five-foot-four self like trees. Drew, Liam, and the third hottie stand before me. Drew and the third one are wearing huge grins, while Liam looks bored.

"Dora, sorry we interrupted your class, but we had to see you. We want you! Don't we, boys? Oh, and this is Colin. I don't think you were properly introduced yesterday," Drew says with a heart-stopping, mischievous grin.

I hear sighs from my right and turn to see all four women and the freshman smiling like fools while fanning themselves. "They want her," I hear one of them whisper.

"For Christ's sake. They mean they want me for their roommate," I practically yell, and still the five act like they don't hear me. "Outside, now." I point to the door and watch in awe as they obey. I turn back and see the eyes of the silly women and girl following their retreat. "I swear, you'd think you've never seen male models before," I say before following the cutest denim-clad butts I've ever seen.

A slight autumn breeze swirls leaves around my feet as I stand before the gorgeous trees. "What the hell are you three doing here? How did you find me?" I demand, and then feel smug as I watch Colin's and Drew's smiles slip a little. Liam, his arms crossed, still looks bored.

"It wasn't easy," Drew says. "You told us your name, and my dad knows some people, and we … well, we tracked you down to your apartment. Your friend was very friendly, but I think she went through a shocked and then angry phase for a few moments when she found out you were looking for another place to stay. Kevin calmed her down. He's a pretty cool guy."

"And you bigmouthed behemoths forced my whereabouts from them after telling my secret. What the hell? I didn't ask for this," I exclaim. I watch two sets of faces have the grace to look embarrassed, but Liam…you guessed it. Bored. What possessed these three mega famous models to track me down? I know most women would jump at the chance of sharing a space with them, but not me. Look at those silly women drooling over them with their faces plastered to the window. I don't want my life scrutinized under a microscope by reporters and ending up as some new tabloid fodder. No, I want low-key. I want to finish my degree and find a nice sensible man to settle down with—*normal,* that's what I want. I take a deep breath before continuing. "Okay, so the secret is out and I'll have to make amends, but what is your deal? Why me? There must be a million people you could line up to move in with you guys."

I watch as Colin takes a step forward. "Pandora, I humbly apologize for our intruding. Drew is stubborn, and when he makes up his mind and then ultimately makes us make up our minds, well…" he says, spreading his arms out and shaking his head. His English accent has me mesmerized, and all anger flees my body. A warmth starts to build inside me. "We would really love for you to consider moving in with us. But it will have to be your decision," he finishes and steps back as Drew opens his mouth.

"Yeah, what he said. Besides, we really like Julie and Kevin, and we asked them to move in too. Oh, not in our apartment," Drew hurries, seeing my confusion. "No. Remember I own the building? We have several lofts empty, so we offered them one."

Colin rolls his eyes and Liam shakes his head. What the hell? I feel my anger returning.

"Okay, so you bribed my friends with a dream loft just to *force* me to move in with you. What kind of freaks are you? I'm sure they turned you down. They did, didn't they?"

From the looks on their faces, even Liam's, I realize I don't need an answer. Of course they didn't! The silence is deafening. We stand there awkwardly with Drew being the only one looking me in the eye.

"Pandora, I'm sorry. I can be a little pushy." The two beside him make sounds in agreement. "But I felt we had a connection yesterday, and we will make things as easy as we can for you to say yes. Please say yes." He gives me puppy-dog eyes and Colin smiles, which makes my legs a little weak, and even Liam is now wearing a ghost of a smile.

"I guess I'm stuck. If I don't give in, I'll be homeless." My voice is weary.

"Fantastic!" Drew moves forward, but stops as I put my hand out. I have no idea what his intentions are, but I'm not in the mood to find out. "Here's your key! Let's go, guys," he says, handing me an antique-looking silver key. "Oh," he says over his shoulder as he hustles the others across the fallen leaves covering the dying grass, "the movers are at your apartment right now, so just meet up with us at our apartment." His last words float on the breeze as they quickly round the corner.

Sons of bitches. How dare those conniving behemoths assume I would consent to move in? I've been played. I'm perfectly happy with my life the way it is, now it's going to have so much drama. I don't like drama. Why me?

Turning around, I see the five female faces still pressed against the windows with those silly dreamy looks still present and accounted for. I huff as I storm off back toward my class. I'm pretty sure my blood pressure is sky-high at the moment.

I don't pay attention in the remaining few minutes of class. I can't wait until I can leave. By tomorrow, the whole campus will find out what happened to the short, plain, little redheaded Dora. I know most women would love to be in my position, but all I want to do is finish school, get a job, and find a sensible man to settle down with. Is that too much to ask? No.

Three

I take a deep breath as I prepare to enter the building. A young, fresh-faced guy behind a desk quickly stands up and smiles. "Ahh, Ms. Phillips, so happy you're joining us. I live here too. Drew—I mean, Mr. Johnson—rents me the apartment here on the first floor," he rushes. "I man the desk when I'm not in school. I believe we both go to the same one."

He finally takes a breath and I return his smile. It's not his fault I've been ambushed.

"Call me Dora. And you are…?"

"Brad. Bradley Mason," he replies.

"Nice to meet you, Brad. Well…" I hesitate.

"Your stuff has arrived and your friends are in their apartment. If you need anything, just ask."

"Thanks, Brad. I better go up and unpack. Later, okay?" I say, my teeth clenched as anger flows through me again. Brad presses the elevator button and it dings, the doors open and I step inside.

"See you around, Dora." Brad grins as the doors shut.

It seems like forever until the door opens again. I feel my hands tingling and look down to realize I've fisted them and they are stark white from the pressure. I relax them and step into the hallway. It's quiet and kind of spooky. I walk to the huge front double doors and go to knock, only to remember the key in my pocket. I quickly insert it and am slightly surprised when it clicks and I push the door open.

The huge living/dining room is morgue quiet. All the doors off the room are closed except for one, and I move forward to peek inside. The room is as big as my mom and dad's living room, and that's pretty big. A familiar queen-size pedestal bed is centered on one bright white wall, with the other three walls a light tan color. My feet sink into the rug that matches the walls as I walk across the room. The rest of my bedroom furniture, which isn't much, is dwarfed by the room. I look around, but spy no boxes.

Off to the side of the bedroom is a sitting area with a couch, a couple of chairs and a large, closed armoire that probably hosts a TV. There are two doors in front of me, and I open the first and inhale deeply at the sight. It's a bathroom, but not like any bathroom I've ever used. It's massive and looks like something out of a high-end magazine. The tub is so huge it could hold at least four people, maybe more, and the walk-in shower is amazing.

There's even a bidet. Yes, I know what that is. My grandmother has one in each of her bathrooms. But that's a story best left for later.

Exiting the luxury bath, I open the other door and my jaw almost hits the floor. It's a closet. At least, I think it is since my clothes are hung up inside of it on two long metal rods. Built-in drawers and a massive, oval-shaped mirror hang opposite the door. My shoes are placed in little cubby holes built into the wall.

"What the hell?" I say to myself while plopping down on the bed, overwhelmed by it all.

I know the story of Pandora from Greek mythology very well. She was so curious she opened a box (it was really a jar) which she was told never to open. Of course she opened it and allowed evil to fill the world. At the bottom of this jar was hope. So that's how we have hope. I'm not saying I've opened Pandora's box and now have evil in my life, or anything. It's more like I've opened a freaking can of worms…and I hate worms, like, really hate them.

I jump as my phone buzzes from my backpack. Pulling it out, I see it's Julie.

"Hey," I say, testing the waters.

"Hey, yourself. So, first, I almost fucking dropped dead when I opened the door and saw not one, but three of the hottest guys I've ever seen. I swear, Dora, my heart actually leaped out of my throat," Julie whispers before her voice picks back up. "Okay, honey, see you in a few." She must be talking to Kevin. "He's gone. Dora, what the hell? I'm so pissed you didn't tell me you were looking to move. We've been friends since diapers, and I had to find out from…three totally fuck-worthy, gorgeous male specimens," she blurts. "I swear, I almost wet my pants. And then they asked about you and told me your little secret, and next thing I knew, Drew is offering Kevin and me an apartment at a fucking unbelievable amount a month. I thought I was hearing things. Then the movers came in and moved all of our shit—I mean, stuff. Kevin said we moved uptown so I have to watch my fucking cussing, but hel-lo, I feel like we won the lottery! But you are not off the hook about this secret, and we will most definitely be having a little chat about that soon. Now, go take a bath in that ginormous fucking tub, and I'll see you at dinner."

"Dinner?" I say.

"Yes, dinner! Drew invited us to come over at seven. I'll have to have a snack before then, or I'll pass out from hunger. Did I tell you how the movers did everything? There must have been ten of them, and they were finished in no time at all."

Moving to lay on the bed, I prop up the phone so I can listen to her ramblings. After a lengthy description of where she had the movers put everything in my room, and then how they went down to hers and did the same thing, she finally comes to an end with a "see you later" and hangs up.

I feel like a hamster on a wheel and I can't get off! My eyes feel gritty, so I rub them and attempt to get some shut-eye.

444

"She looks like a sleeping princess," I hear a familiar voice say.

"What princess have you seen wearing jeans and an old sweatshirt? I admit, the hair could pass," a dry Australian accent replies.

"Should we be in here? We might scare her, standing at the end of her bed staring at her like this," a proper English accent whispers.

"What part of privacy do guys not understand?" I blurt out, opening one eye, and I'm so satisfied when I see them jump a little.

"Ah, well, we just wanted to let you know it's almost seven and dinner is ready," Drew says loudly, as if I'm deaf.

"Sorry, Dora, I tried to stop them, but—" Colin shrugs his shoulders, looking apologetic. Liam just stands there with his arms crossed, rolling his eyes. Without a word, he walks out of the room. I close my eye again, wishing the others currently in the room would take the hint.

"Okay, I'm getting up, so you two can leave now," I say when I realize they're not budging.

"Great," Drew says. "You can come as you are, no need to change."

"Good, because I'm not planning on it," I snap, opening my eyes again and watching as Colin pushes Drew out the door.

I punch my pillow. I hate feeling angry. The last time before today I was truly angry was when I found my so-called madly-in-love boyfriend in bed with a bleached blonde.

Now is not the time to relive that. I need to calm down and go eat, but arrive fashionably late. Yes, I'll be late, as it's ten minutes past seven.

I open my door to find the dining room table full of people who all, as if on cue, turn to look at me. I wish I had changed. At least my hair is decent, I guess. It's still a mass of curls, but these curls are as tame as I can make them. I spy an empty chair and slide into it, not meeting anyone's eyes. Everyone starts chatting again, and I take a peek at Julie, who is sitting opposite me. She grins and takes a bite out of a chicken leg. To my right is Colin, and I meet his eyes to find them smiling back at me. My heart does a little flip as I quickly grab the dish he's holding, thanking him and plopping a spoonful of heavenly-looking mashed potatoes on my plate.

Throughout the meal, I look around the table and notice that beside the three models, everyone looks average(ish). I thought models only hung out with other model types, but it seems that might not always be the case. I'm enjoying the convos around me. Every time Colin's dreamy British accent hits my ears, my heart skips a beat.

Drew sits at the head of the table, and when I look his way, he winks at me. My heart only does a half-flip, thank goodness, as I know he's a party boy from all the stuff I found out about him, and the others, when I Googled them this afternoon.

My eyes finally land on Liam. He nods, sans smile, and no heart skip/flip happens. So why only Colin and Drew? What the hell am I thinking? These guys are my roommates. Also, they are way out of my league. Most importantly, I'm not looking for a relationship right now anyway. My focus is on finishing school and working. That's ALL.

Nothing else.

So, heart, I'm warning you, stop it now.

Dammit, cheeks, don't blush.

Geez, for the love of cauliflower.

"So, Dora, what do you think of your room?" Julie's voice interrupts my inner thoughts and I look up.

"It's okay," I say before putting a forkful of mashed potatoes in my mouth. Hopefully she'll get the hint that I don't want to talk. She raises her eyebrow at me and goes back to eating. Thank you, gods, I can eat in silence.

I have to admit, I'm enjoying this evening. The girl sitting to the left of me is in college and works too. She tells me her name is Tess and she's known Drew since they were in elementary school. I keep talking to Tess, partly because Colin is causing my blood pressure to rise. His leg is so close to mine, I can feel the heat radiating from it. What is up with my internal thermostat? I think it's broken.

"Tess, is it hot in here to you?" She shakes her head, so it's just me.

How will I survive?

444

I wish she would look my way more. There's something about her. I just can't put my finger on, but she has me intrigued. I need to get to know her, and the other two better keep their distance. I have to think this one through. I don't want to screw it up. I'm tired of all the phony women I've met and continue to meet on a daily basis. They're so shallow, only wanting me for what I can give them—more exposure. Dora is like a breath of fresh air in a stale world. Will she ever think of me as something other than an annoying roommate? Time....I just have to take it really slow, even though it's hard.

Before fighting it, I wish I would've known how easy it was going to be to live with three HOT guy models. I haven't seen them in more than a week. The day after our dining experience, I found a note on the kitchen island informing me they were working on a gig together, and would be gone for a little while. It's been so wonderful having the place all to myself, and boy, have I taken advantage of it. I've stayed away from their rooms though. Okay, so I may have peeked, and was shocked by how neat they were. Of course, that could be due to the cleaning team overseen by Harriet, the little, round woman, who I met on Monday afternoon since there weren't any classes. I love her already. She is truly an organized bundle of energy.

She works for Drew's father and has been part of the family since before Drew's birth. Drew's mom left them after Emily was born and Drew's dad has looked for Ms. Right for years. I gathered that he had been married several times, though Harriet didn't tell me how many. "Liam isn't much of a talker," she said. She also told me he's the reason for them needing a fourth roommate. She says four is his lucky number, and he's known to obsessively buy four of the same thing to not tempt fate. She says she's very fond of him but feels he's tormented by some secret. She hopes one day he will tell her so she can help him. I waited patiently while she went through the first two, and then she finally expounded on Colin.

Colin has known Drew for years. He was an exchange student who one of Drew's stepmoms invited into their home when they were ten. They became instant friends and kept in touch, and when Colin became a model in America, Drew suggested they move in together. Poor Colin dated this other model for several years. I got the impression that Harriet despised Judith, his ex. "Witch with a capital B" is how Harriett described her. One day, Judith just dumped him out of the blue and left Liam and Drew to pick up the pieces. Harriet said that was nine months ago, and he seems to be back to his old self, thank goodness.

Damn. So Colin's heart has been broken too. Just another reason to tell my heart to stop it.

I have no desire taking on someone else with a broken heart. When it came time for Harriet to leave, we had already bonded so well, and it felt wonderful when she hugged me and told me I was what these boys needed in their lives.

Confession time: I haven't told my family about my move yet. In fact, I swore Julie and Kevin to secrecy when we all went for Sunday dinner with the fam, which is quite the story within itself. No time to tell now. I'm enjoying my last day of being by myself in this mansion in the sky. Poetic, aren't I?

444

Saturday morning comes too quickly. Today, the 'three' are supposed to return, and I plan on making myself scarce. First work, and then the afternoon in the library, and finally dinner at Kevin and Julie's with a night filled with movie watching.

Work is as hectic as usual on a weekend morning, and the library is a refreshing calm after the thundering storm. Sitting at my laptop, I feel someone staring at me. No, I'm not psychic. I see a face in my screen as my computer turns off. Closing it up, I turn to see the face more clearly, and the object of my attention smiles.

Good lord, it's Drew. What the hell is he doing in the library? From what I can tell, he's causing a scene as I look to my left and right and see women, girls, and even some guys staring as if they're seeing a movie star. Well, he's not in the movies yet, but I guess you could say he's famous. He's in every effing magazine and on almost every billboard in the world.

Pushing my laptop in my backpack, I grab it, and slowly rise from my seat. I watch as he gets from his, still grinning like a smexy idiot. Yes, I said *smexy*. Well, he is, but boy does he know it. He starts forward and I move quickly to the exit, walking as fast as I can in a library. I swear I can feel his breath on the back of my neck, but I keep going. Pushing open the door, I'm temporarily blinded by the bright sunlight. I look way up at a frowning Drew after he gently takes hold of my arm and spins me around.

"What's your hurry?" he asks, finally cracking a smile.

"Oh, hi, Drew. I didn't see you. What are you doing here?" I ask as innocently as I can.

"Yeah, sure. You looked right at me. How could you have missed me?" he asks, pointing to himself.

"Well, I did. But you didn't answer me."

"I've come to pick you up," he says. His killer-watt smile makes a girl walking by trip over her own feet at the mere sight of it.

"What makes you think I need picking up? I have plans."

"Well, if your plans are with Julie and Kevin, I guess things have changed." He loses the smile and tries to look serious. "The guys and I chipped in to give them a present for their wedding. Kevin and Julie are going out for a night on the town. You know, limo, dinner, and a sold-out play that tickets magically appeared for. I guess you're stuck with us."

We keep walking toward the parking lot and guess what? Standing by a huge luxury car are Liam and Colin, the rest of the "us" Drew was referring to, and they don't look too happy.

"So you knew where she was the whole time … yet you sent us on a wild goose chase anyway?" Liam's dry voice matches his stern look.

"Like you two could've convinced Dora to hang out with us? This plan needed my touch," Drew says with confidence.

"I never said I was going to hang out with you," I announce as I stare at Drew, trying to make him feel uncomfortable. It doesn't work. He just grins at me.

Infuriating.

"Now, Pandora Phillips, how can you pass up an evening with us? Okay, so Liam may not be as friendly as Colin and me, but give him a few drinks and he loosens up."

As I look at the two grinning faces of Drew and Colin, my mind begins to betray me. I glance at Liam and even he's wearing a half smirk. My mind makes its choice for me, and I decide I'm stuck. I need to eat, right? And my two so-called friends have dumped me for a better gig, which I don't blame them for, but still.

"Okay, I'll hang with you guys, but I make all the decisions, okay? That's the deal, so take it or leave it," I cross my arms and wait for their negative replies.

"Okay," Drew quickly agrees.

"Sure," Colin readily says.

Liam nods.

We pile into the car, and I get stuck in the front next to Drew, who's driving. "All right, so we're going to my favorite eatery," I say and then quickly rattle of the directions while Drew pulls into traffic.

I love the looks on their faces as we enter a part of the city I'm sure they've never stepped foot in. I point to an empty parking spot a block away from our destination. Drew looks a little nervous about leaving his car, but he locks it and we make our way down the darkening street. A few streetlights pop on, but most seemed to be burned out. We turn a corner and there it is—Papa's. Its warm glow from within lights up the pavement in front. Opening the door, a flurry of delicious smells hit us and my stomach rumbles, reminding me that breakfast was a zillion hours ago.

"Pandora Phillips, my little angel! Such a gloriosa day this is, gracing us with your beautiful presence." Papa's voice makes me giggle, something I do every time I hear his cheesy line.

Papa is a big man, not tall, but round. He reminds me of that famous chef on the cans of spaghetti I ate as a child. He wears a huge apron and a tall chef's hat. His Italian accent completes the image. He strides forward and embraces me, swallowing me up in his arms.

"Where have youa been my naughty girl? We haven'ta seen you ina months! Where is thata young man of yours?" I see him peering over my head, looking for the SOB.

"Papa, he's history," I say flatly.

"Good, bella, good! Never liked him. You are a princessa and deserve a prince." He finally lets me go and I turn to introduce him to my escorts.

"Papa, I want you to meet three new friends of mine." I see the three smiling widely at my statement. I'm shocked that even Liam's smile looks genuine. After the introductions, Papa sternly looks them up and down.

He puts his arm around me and glares at them. "This is youra only warninga, one not lightly made. Any of you breaka my Pandora's heart, it will be your lasta day on Earth. In fact, her lasta one is now on my hit list. I have connections, if you know what I mean." All three nod their heads, which is pretty funny as they tower over the short rotund man.

"No, Papa," I say. "We're just friends, and as for the other one, he's not worth your anger. I'm so over him."

"Okay. So I will let it go, just because we lovea you. Now, Giuseppe, get the special table ready. These people are hungry."

Giuseppe is Papa's nephew, and I've always thought he should be a model. His dark, Italian looks are one of the reasons I've had a major crush on him forever. He comes up to me, bends over and kisses my hand, and my heart flips as usual. Yes, I know my heart flips at the attention of beautiful men, except for Liam, which I will have to analyze further. Giuseppe then takes my hand and leads us to the best table by the kitchen. Out of the corner of my eye, I see the three

"Modelteers" frowning at the gesture. So much testosterone in one space. *Awesome.*

Dinner, to my surprise, turns out to be a wonderful affair. The food is delicious as always, and the company keeps me laughing with the tales of the life of a male model. Even Liam chimes in, telling us of his photo shoot with an amorous kangaroo. I haven't laughed this much in years. I suddenly feel so comfortable with these guys.

Papa's equally rotund wife joins us at one point, and with the wine and the company, I really don't want this night to end.

On the ride home, Drew turns on the heat, and with the wine and the smooth ride of the car, I feel my eyes closing. The next thing I know, I'm being carried from the car into our building. The arms hold me snugly, and my eyes are so heavy that I keep them shut. I hear voices, but I'm too tired to answer. My bed feels wonderful when I'm placed gently on it. I feel lips touching mine and then I feel myself drift off.

444

I loved having her in my arms. Tonight I wanted her complete attention. She is so amazing—warm and giving. Watching her with the people at Papa's makes me believe I can feel again. I wonder how long she was in that relationship Papa mentioned. Who ended it? Does she have a broken heart? Will she even give me a chance? I felt so much jealously when that Giuseppe guy kissed her hand. I would love for her to look at me the way she looked at him. I need her. God, I sound like a stalker. It's been such a short time, but I feel...she makes me feel alive.

I haven't seen the guys in a few weeks, and I still don't know who put me to bed that night. I can still feel his lips, and then *nothing*. I'm not going to go there. Life is hectic with my classes seeming to stretch for hours, and work, well, let's just say it's work. It seems like I'm always rushing, like right now to go meet Julie. She's waiting by her car, and I can tell by her face she thinks I'm late.

"It's about time. You're late," she quips as she hits the button to unlock the doors.

"Yep, three whole minutes," I respond, loving the scowl she sends my way. "Turn that frown upside down. We're going on a big adventure. Oh, how I love Halloween!" I watch as she tries not to smile and then rubs her hands together, breaking into a huge smile.

"I want to be something totally different this year. I'm tired of vampire teeth and zombie stuff," she says as she backs out of the parking spot.

"I thought you looked awesome last year. You had that dead look down!" I say.

"I know, I was pretty hot as a zombie babe, huh? But different is what I'm going for this year. This party's going to be epic, don't you think? Drew says they rented out that whole floor, and that anybody who is anybody is going to be there."

"Then why are we going? We're the biggest nobodies I know," I reply with an eye roll.

"They won't know that since we'll be in costume. They'll believe we're famous," Julie argues with a grin.

Now don't get me wrong, I am excited about going to the party. I guess I just have reservations about feeling out of place. I don't like feeling insecure, and since my life's upheaval in September, that feeling has crept up on me more than I would like.

"We're here!" Julie's excited voice interrupts my musings as we pull in front of the biggest costume shop in the city, aptly named "Biggest Costume Shop in the City." So unique, huh?

The store is like a decorated two-story haunted house with racks of clothing separated into sections. They have a werewolf section guarded by the biggest stuffed werewolf I've ever seen. I swear it's more than fifteen feet tall. Then there's the vampire section with—yes, you guessed it—a fifteen-foot bat. You thought I was going to say vampire, but no, it's a humongous, jet-black bat with glowing red eyes. Creepsville, for sure.

I already know what section I'm heading for, so I leave Julie pondering while I enter the Victorian section. I know. Lame. But I feel like I belong back in that era. My mom says I must have lived there in a previous life. Anyway, here I am, surrounded by long, flowing dresses and low-cut bodices that would make any woman feel feminine. I spot a light lavender dress with fake pearls patterned on the bodice and make a beeline for it, praying it's my size.

"May I help you?" A voice stops me in my pursuit and I turn to find a small, even-shorter-than-me female dressed as Little Red Riding Hood, basket and all.

"Yes, this dress." I move forward and place my hand on it.

"Beautiful, isn't it? We just put it out yesterday. It comes with a mask. Let's see what size it is."

I cross my fingers. Spying the tag she pulls out from the sleeve, I know it's too big.

"I venture to say this is tooooooo big for you," she says in a singsong voice. I guess she's getting into character.

"Damn. I mean, crap, it's the one I want."

"Don't worry. I'll check in the back. We have a couple more sizes in this one." She takes off and disappears behind a partition in the section after I tell her my dress size.

Looking around, I see an elaborately dressed footman, like you see in Cinderella stories, guarding this section. He's standing on a pedestal and looks to be about six feet tall and very lifelike.

"Good afternoon, madam," the footman says, making me jump.

"God, you almost gave me a heart attack," I say a little more loudly than I should have. But damn, he almost scared the pee out of me.

"I beg your pardon. I did not mean to startle you." His tone is very solemn, but the gleam in his eye gives away his lie.

"Guess what? We have it in your size. If you follow me, you can try it on back here." Red is back and takes one look at my face, which must be pale, because she goes up to the footman and smacks him on the leg. "You creep. Get down from there. Next time you'll scare the wrong person and be in big trouble."

"Geez, Red. I was just shaking things up a little. I'm tired of walking the floor. She looks too young to have a heart attack. I do pick my victims well." The handsome, even with the white wig, footman gracefully jumps down and bows low to both of us.

"Ignore him and follow me." Red takes my arm and guides me to a bank of dressing rooms behind an elaborately painted scenic backdrop of a Victorian ballroom. "Here we are. Now the corset comes with it, so you'll need help with that. If you want to disrobe, we'll get to it."

Red puts down her basket and waits for me to undress. I'm praying my underwear is up to par. She laces the corset tightly, which makes my waist even smaller and pushes my boobs up. I must say, I have magnificent cleavage. I pull the dress over my head, and it flows down my body, fitting perfectly. Okay, so the bodice is a little low, which is okay because my family won't see me in it. No worries. So what if I want to look a little slutty? Everyone should, once in their lifetime.

I put on the lavender mask Red hands to me, and then she turns me around so I face the full-length mirror. I can't believe it's me, but it is because Red is standing beside me, grinning like the Cheshire cat.

"You look so beautiful, and your red hair is perfect for the lavender color. It's like you just stepped out of a Victorian painting," she gushes. Watching her eyes, I know it's not just a sales pitch. She means it.

"Thank you, I'll—"

"There you are!" Julie says as she walks up. "I swear some fucking idiot dressed like Cinderella's hand boy just scared the daylights out of me. Oh my, Dora, you look…well, you don't look like you, that's for sure! You look fucking great!"

"She does, doesn't she?" Red nods her head in agreement.

"Now get out of that so we can go find me something just as fucking awesome!" Julie says as she exits the fitting room. I look at Red and apologize for the language.

Several frustrating hours later, we make it home. Julie's costume is, well, it's Julie, and she's happy with it, but I can't wait until Kevin sees it. The loft is quiet when I enter the front door. There's a part of me that hopes the guys are here because I want them to see my costume I'm carrying in a see-thru bag, but I'm glad they're not. I kind of want them to see it on Halloween.

444

"Will you effing stand still so I can pull this tighter? I swear, it's like dressing a toddler."

Julie's frustrated tone makes me want to laugh, but I know if I do, I'll be finding someone else to lace me up. We're standing in front of my mirror and I'm trying not to look at Julie, who looks like a high-end streetwalker. If her outfit was any tighter, she might get arrested. I thought my cleavage was over the top, but she has me beat by a mile. Her blonde hair is piled up on her head in a messy knot. Her makeup is overdone, with thick black eyeliner on her top and bottom lids. Her eye shadow is a hideous teal color, and her cheeks, lips, fingernails and toenails are the red of all reds.

Her outfit, what little of it there is, is a jet-black leather halter top with a leather micro mini skirt. Nine-inch—okay, so maybe I'm exaggerating—red, fuck-me—her words, not mine—pumps complete her outfit. They're so tacky, but hey, it's Halloween. When she smiles, which she hasn't since arriving at the loft, she has realistic vampire fangs, which would scare away any john in a heartbeat. But she loves the look, and it's not like any of her co-workers will see her, so that's all that matters.

Kevin, who at the moment is in the main living room, is dressed as Frankenstein. He's Frank and she's Frank's vampy slut. A perfect match.

"Earth to Dora! Step into the fucking dress." So much for her effort in curtailing the language.

"Slutty Julie, language, please?"

"You would make anyone cuss. Let me button you up. They could have put a zipper and put fucking fake buttons on top. There must be a hundred," she complains.

Now some people would think from Julie's tone that she hates to do things for me, but no, she loves me. She just shows it in a different way than most people. She's kind, giving and a sweetheart,—oh hell, who am I kidding? She's a pain in the butt.

"There, done. You can handle your shoes, right?" she asks as she walks into the bathroom and shuts the door.

I found the perfect shoes to match the color of the dress. They're not Victorian, but they won't be seen, as the dress sweeps the floor when I walk or stand. But they match even though they're hidden. Mine are not "nine" inches, but a sensible two. Walking out into the common living room, I take a seat by Frankie waiting for the slut to finish in the bathroom.

444

We can hear the music as soon as the elevator opens on the top floor of the majorly upscale hotel. A long hallway with burgundy—sink-your-heels-in plush—carpet leads up to a door at the end of the hall.

We're late—half an hour, to be precise. All because Julie rubbed her eye and her fake eyelash fell in the sink. Kevin, aka Frank, had to run to their apartment and get the glue to put it back on, which for some reason was harder for her to do the second time around. But it's fashionable to be late, right?

So here we are, and all I want to do is turn around and go to a normal party where people are only known to each other. Julie's radar picks up on my hesitation and she grabs my long, white-gloved arm and pulls me down the hall. The walls are mirrored, so I glance at myself and then relax as I remember I'm masked, and thus anonymous. I gently touch my hair that I was going to leave down, but Julie pulled it up for me and produced a tiara, which is nestled in the middle. I feel like a princess.

As we approach, the doors magically open, and I look up and see one of those security cameras in each corner above the door. No magic, just someone manning the cameras. As we enter, the party is indescribable, a definite system overload. Yes, appropriate scary music, decorations and a mass of dressed-up party-goers. Even the waiters are dressed up in Grecian togas, sandals and laurel headbands.

Within seconds, Julie loses her grip on my arm and Frank and Slutty Vamp are sucked into the crowd. Great, just great. Maybe an escape should happen. I turn to leave right before I feel a hand wrap around my wrist, and I'm pulled onto a marble dance floor. I turn back and find myself facing a topless construction worker with eighteen abs, or maybe twenty. He's wearing dark sunglasses and tight jeans with pristine work boots that completely make his outfit seem phony. Anyone knows a construction worker doesn't have dirt-free and scuff-free boots. It's a slow dance, so he pulls me closer and starts humming in my ear. His cologne assaults my nose, making me want to sneeze as my eyes water. I definitely need unpolluted air right now, and just as I think it, it happens. I'm pulled away from construction man and into the arms of a vampire, whose devilish grin and wicked teeth make me shiver. His cologne, thank goodness, is subtle and his arms feel comfy.

"Do you come here often?" His corny fake Transylvanian accent whispering in my ear makes me giggle. "I vant to drink your blood. Your neck is begging to be bitten."

He continues his corny lines, making me laugh loudly, which unfortunately for me, happens at the same time the music stops. I feel a thousand eyes staring at me. Geez, who knew laughing was prohibited at a monster's ball? The music starts up again and I turn my head to find that Mr. Vamp has disappeared and has been replaced by a half-mummy, half-zombie. It's kinda cool, and since it's a fast song, I get to look all I want.

The costume must have cost a pretty penny. It looks like someone really cut an actual mummy and a zombie in half before fusing them seamlessly together. Out of the corner of my eye, I spy my last dancing partner, Mr. I Want to Drink Your Blood, pouting with his arms crossed, staring straight at me. Is it wrong of me to feel a little satisfaction at him wanting little ol' me? I think not.

The music ends and a hush falls over the crowd. They all look at the entrance to the huge room. I stand on my tiptoes to see what's causing all of the commotion. The crowd parts, and I see three identically dressed, all in white…Musketeers? I say this because of the tight pants, elaborate white capes with a crest on the left side, high black boots, realistic swords, a blousy undershirt, and cavalier-looking white hats with a huge black feather sticking out the back. Their faces are covered with a full cloth mask with only their lips and eyes showing, definitely creepy and theatrical at the same time.

"Great, the Modelteers are here. The party's finally started!" a voice yells.

The crowd roars. Yep, light bulb goes on as Julie stands beside me, grinning.

"Aren't they something?" She moves in closer so I can hear.

"Show-stoppers for sure. These guys love to perform. Maybe they missed their calling and should have chosen acting."

"I know I would pay to see them in a movie." Julie seems to have missed my sarcasm and has gone over to the dark side with everyone else in the room.

"I'm off to pee."

Julie just nods her head.

"Excuse me, could you direct me to the bathroom?" I ask a waiter juggling a full tray of drinks.

"Hallway at the back. Turn right and you can't miss it." He smiles and then moves on—delightful butt, muscular arms, and all.

It takes a few minutes to reach my destination, dodging clusters of gyrating bodies. When I had tried on my costume, my first thought had been how I would actually go to the bathroom. But low and behold, the skirt is velcroed on. I quickly peel it off and toss in over the door. The slip I'm wearing underneath is easily raised and I finish in record time. Leaving my skirt on the door, I wash my hands, not having to touch anything while doing so. Modern technology amazes me. When the towel machine dispenses its prescribed item with a wave of my hand, I wonder why we don't have them in our loft. I grab my skirt and go to put it back on when the bathroom is suddenly filled with a group of Amazon women in various costumes and a cloud of obnoxious expensive perfume.

I exit the room and stop in the hallway to put my skirt back on, but before I have a chance, I look up and see one of the Modelteers standing in front of me. He bows and then takes my left hand and kisses it. He straightens up and his mouth pulls up in a grin.

Then I'm gently pushed up against the wall. My skirt falls to the floor and his mouth meets mine—oh lord, he tastes like peppermint—but that thought quickly disappears as his arms pull me closer. My heart can't beat any faster without giving out. I try to keep my eyes open, but they fall as his lips place feverish kisses around mine. His body is hard against mine, and I feel his tongue lick my lips. I moan and his tongue plunges inside my mouth. My whole body goes into a total meltdown. I want to wrap my legs around his waist as his tongue wildly mates with mine, but my legs are like jelly, and I know his arms are the only way I'm still standing. His hands roam up and down my back, pulling me so close I can feel his apparent desire as another moan rips from his throat.

Colin. It has to be him. I grab his waist and hold on as wave after wave of hot desire washes over me. If only our clothes could magically disappear…

What am I saying? I'm in a hallway—dark, yes—but still with enough light for anyone to see us, and I can hear the women in the bathroom still chatting away. The door opens and I push him away as the Amazon women walk back into the hallway. His breathing is as heavy as mine as he stands in front of me, his head bent as if trying to gain control.

Suddenly, I realize I don't need this, don't need him. I'm attracted to him, but I'm not willing to be a one-night stand, and with all the women drooling over him, that's what I could only expect. As the voices fade, he looks their way and I sigh, glad that they were so wrapped up in their conversation that they didn't even see us. I reach down and grab my skirt and quickly move back into the bathroom, leaving him standing outside. My face is flushed and my hair is gently mussed. I don't remember him touching my hair. All I can remember is our tongues making love and his body making mine feel like a boneless mess. Splashing cool water on my face helps a little, but the feeling of loss fills me. What would it be like if I was a model, tall and beautiful, and having Colin filling my passionless body every night?

Get a grip, Dora. He's so out of your league.

"There you are. I've fucking looked everywhere for you. Are you feeling okay? You look feverish." Julie's voice startles me, and I see her forehead worry line appear.

"No, just a little warm. Enjoying yourself?"

"Kevin is. We'll probably have to drag his ass home. That boy can't hold his liquor for shit. Are you sure you're okay?" She puts the back of her hand to my forehead and shakes her head. “No fever. Maybe we should call it a night. It’s packed out there, and frankly, this isn’t my scene.”

“Yeah, I feel the same way. Let’s get drunk boy and head home.” I need to get the image of my encounter with Colin out of my brain.

We make our way into the crowd, searching for an inebriated Frankenstein, and after some pushing and shoving, I catch a glimpse of a Modelteer. I push farther from him. Julie squeals as she spots Kevin gyrating by himself to the music. We each take an arm and make our way to the front door.

“Why are you movin’ me sooooo earlier,” Kevin mumbles out.

“You’re going to have a major fuckin’ hangover as it is. Any more liquor and you’ll be in bed for days, that’s why.” Julie sounds pissed off, but I know her. She’s gloating that Kevin will suffer for his stupidity.

“I’m totackly in charck of my facials.” We both laugh at his attempt at being coherent.

Thirty minutes later, we’re home, and Kevin, minus his costume, is tucked in bed.

“Want something to drink?” Julie yells from the kitchen.

“No, I think I’m going to head upstairs and pour myself into bed. It’s been a long week and I have work tomorrow.”

"Something happened tonight. Spill." Julie's radar is up and spot-on.

"I'm just tired," I say, and Julie pegs me with a glare. "Okay, quit looking at me like that. It's creepy. If looks could kill, I'd be dead." Julie smiles. "I had a little encounter before you found me in the bathroom."

"An encounter? Well, hurry up and share. Inquiring minds need to know." She sits opposite me, her elbows on her knees and her head in her hands. A perfect picture of sluttiness.

"It was Colin. I came out of the bathroom and was ready to put my Velcro skirt back on after peeing."

"For fuck sake, Dora, get to the juicy part." Julie's frown line is so deep it looks like it might stay permanently.

"Well, he came up to me and had this super smexy grin, and he pushed me up against the wall—gently, of course, because he's a gentleman—and then he kissed me. Geez, Jules, I could have jumped his bones right there in the hallway. My ex never made me feel this way. I was a total hot mess. I wanted to wrap my legs around his waist, but my legs were like limp noodles. That man can start a blaze." I close my eyes, remembering the feel of his hard body pressed against mine and the frustration of the clothes between us. Yep, I was a totally wanton woman. "Then we were interrupted. I remembered where we were and who I was and the fact that I don't run in the same circles, and I stopped him. It wasn't easy, but I did it. Jules, I should have been dressed as a slut tonight, because I totally felt like one after."

"Dora, what the hell are you talking about? You're not a slut, just a horny woman who's desired by an equally horny, hot man. I think you should go upstairs and wait in his bed." She pauses to put a red-nailed finger to her chin in contemplation. "Yes, I think that's an excellent idea. Get your ass up there and go for it. He fucking wants you. You know you want him too." Julie reaches forward and grabs my hands to emphasize her point.

"Nope, not going to do it," I say before standing up quickly and making my way toward the door.

"You won't forgive yourself if you don't. You'll always wonder what you missed. I'm betting you're missing a whole bunch of fast, slow, dirty, sweaty sex. Makes me wet just thinking about it." Julie flops back in the chair.

"Night, Jules," I say loudly as I close the door behind me and head for the stairs.

444

I glance over at the clock again and cringe at the realization that it's one a.m. and six in the morning is going to come really quick, and the coffee shop is always packed on Saturdays. I've been thinking about my encounter with Colin, his sizzling kisses, his rock hard body, and something else that was rock hard too.

A sound interrupts my musings. I hear a muffled voice coming from the door that leads to the living room. Creeping out of bed, I put my ear up to my door and hear Colin, Drew, and Liam's voices, several more male voices I don't recognize and a mess of female ones too.

Great, they brought the party home. How the hell am I supposed to sleep with Colin and a bunch of women in the next room? Okay, so maybe they aren't with Colin, but maybe my rejection turned him off. What the hell? I don't want him. He doesn't want me.

Irritated, I leave the door and flop down on my bed. It's going to be a long night.

444

I am so wound up. She's just on the other side of the door. I shouldn't have kissed her tonight. At first I thought she was enjoying it, but pushing me away made me think I made a huge mistake. I want to knock on her door and apologize, but I'm really not sorry. She was just as I imagined, so giving, and she made me realize she is who I've been searching for. I will let things calm down a couple of days and then maybe approach her. I can't screw this up, I really can't. She is it.

Six

The next few weeks fly by, and the weather has changed drastically. I haven't seen my roommates since Halloween. The Sunday before Thanksgiving, Julie, Kevin, and I find ourselves on the way to my parents' house for dinner. I had been able to avoid it for weeks, but the threat of my mom driving to the city to see me convinces me to go. I finally broke down and told them about my move, and my mom seems okay with it.

The traffic is light and it doesn't take us long to get to the house. Both of my grandparents' cars are parked outside, which is no surprise since unless they're in the hospital or majorly sick in bed, they're always here.

My family is dysfunctional, just saying. My mom is like I said before, a true medium/psychic. My dad is pretty normal, considering he's put up with my mom all these years. My fifteen-year-old sister is a self-absorbed teen—always texting, concerned about boys, hair and clothes, in that order. My seventeen-year-old brother is a popular jock—always surrounded by a crowd of admirers. Luckily, he doesn't let it go to his head, and is a really nice guy. I know it's weird that a sister describes her brother as nice, but it's the truth.

Now the grandparents…where do I start? My mom's parents are…well, my granddad, George Anderson, is a normal quiet guy. He usually lets Alice, aka Grandma, do all the talking, which she does too well. She's so outspoken that sometimes it can be downright embarrassing. My dad's mom, Beatrice Jones-Phillips, is snooty. She's materialistic and looks down on others not of her status. My grandfather on my dad's side passed over five years ago from a heart attack, which many, including my mom, believe my grandmother caused. I'm not saying my grandmother—yes, we call her Grandmother—is evil, she just lives on another realm, above ours. She's the one who wanted to send me to that finishing school.

"Are we going in, or are you going to sit in the car and daydream all day?" Kevin's voice interrupts my thoughts.

"Yeah, let's get this over with."

Julie opens the passenger door as I open mine.

The front door is flung open by my brother Mike, whose tortured look says everything. "Where have you been? It's been hell in here. Mom says I can leave as soon as we eat, so let's get eating," he says, accepting my hug.

"Hey, dude, lighten up. We're here," Kevin replies, ruffling his hair. "It can't be all that bad."

"It's more than bad. Grandma and Grandmother are really at it today, and Dad is MIA. He went to the store more than an hour ago. Wish I had gone with him."

"Where's Bridget?" I ask, not wanting to go into the house now.

"She's in her room, where else? Said she won't come down until the food is being served. I made the mistake of being thirsty and snuck down for a drink and got caught up in the mess," Mike groans.

Julie giggles, grabs his arm and pulls him into the house. I follow, closing the door, ready for the battle.

"Oh, here they are!" My mom, Sarah Phillips, is a vision of beauty, not a hair out of place on her blonde head and her makeup is done up perfectly. She moves her slim form forward and gives us all a hug. My mom is a major hugger and she gives the best and warmest hugs.

"Pandora, have you put on a little weight?" Grandma Alice looks me up and down and then envelops me in an overpowering perfumed embrace. She is as short as I am, that's where I get my height. My siblings were blessed with the tallness of my father's side. Andersons have a slight weight problem, whereas on the Phillips side, extra weight wouldn't dare show up. "You look better with a little more fluff around the middle. You were too skinny a couple weeks ago. Your boobs even look a little bigger. Don't they, George?"

My poor granddad looks like a deer caught in the headlights, obviously not knowing how to respond. You would think after all these years, he'd be prepared.

"How crass, Alice, really?" Grandmother Phillips, tall and willowy, has her say. "Is that any way to talk to our granddaughter? Except for her wardrobe choice, she looks fine."

"Beatrice, don't you think it's time to get that stick out of your high and mighty ass for once?" Grandma chuckles, and we all cover our mouths to hide the smiles that appear at her words.

"Now, Mom and Beatrice, we'll be having guests, so I want you to be on your best behavior, please!" Mom interjects sternly, knowing it's no use. They'll behave the way they want to and nobody will change that.

"Guests?" I ask, looking at my mom and then past her to the dining room table, quickly counting the number of plates and silverware laid out. Three extra?

Three?

Oh no. Tell me it's not true.

The doorbell rings and my mom gives a sigh of relief and pushes past us to open the door. Why am I not surprised? There stand my drool-worthy, bodacious roommates, smiling as if they know they're giving me heart palpitations.

How could Mom do this to me? I mean, things have been going just fine, and then my mother takes it upon herself to invite them to Sunday's Hell Table. Yes, I said "hell" on Sunday. Sue me. I'm only speaking the truth. Just you wait and see.

"Well, hello. It's so nice to finally meet you boys," my mom gushes.

Boys? Freakin' hell, they are definitely not boys.

Their grins get bigger and Drew pulls a bouquet of red roses from behind his back, presenting them to my Mom. She's actually blushing, which I've never seen before.

We hear a car door shut, hailing my dad's return. The next few minutes are chaotic, and I can't and won't begin to describe it. The introductions are finally over and we sit at the dining room table, surrounded by my mom's mouthwatering food. Everyone is here except for Bridget, and when Mike is asked to go and get her, he pulls out his cell and calls her. We laugh and he just shrugs.

We hear the thud of feet on the stairs and she finally appears. Bridget is tall and willowy with blonde hair, just like Mom's and Mike's. No, I'm not adopted. In his youth, my dad had red hair just like me, but in his twenties it went a brownish color. Now the red only shows up in the sun.

As she walks to her seat, Bridget's fifteen-year-old mouth is hanging open and her eyes are wide. Her cell, which is her whole world, falls to the carpet, taking a bounce.

"Honey, close your mouth and come sit so we can introduce you to Dora's new roommates."

Like a zombie, she moves and sits next to our dad, mouth still open like a baby bird waiting to be fed. Dad reaches over and pushes her lower jaw up, which seems to shock her back to reality. She frantically looks down at her hand, and then heaves a sigh of relief as Mike hands over her cell.

"Put that away. It's rude. Now this is Drew, Liam, and Colin. And guys, this is Bridget, our youngest," Mom explains as Bridget stares, but at least her mouth is closed.

I can tell she wants to call her "posse," as she refers to them, or at the very least film the three models in front of her in order to post the video to her Vine account. I thought only guys had possees, but she quickly informed me a few years ago that I was wrong. The food starts to be passed around, and I think maybe my family might actually behave for once.

"So, what's it like to be queer nowadays?" Grandma asks, plopping a mound of mashed potatoes on her plate. I choke on the sip of water I've just taken and turn bright red as my dad, who is sitting on my right-hand side, thumps me hard on the back. I don't want to raise my head. I wish a hole would just open up in the floor and swallow me whole.

"Well, Mrs. Anderson, it's better for us gays in today's world. We still can't get married in every state, but I see that happening one day soon," Drew says smoothly with a straight face. The straight face doesn't work as well for Julie, who's laughing so hard she's turning redder than I have ever been.

"That was a rude question, Alice. As usual, you have completely lost your manners, what little you started with," Grandmother says, sticking her nose in the air.

"Oh, come on. You wanted to ask them yourself. You know you did, but that *stick* prevents you."

"Mom and Beatrice that's enough. You're embarrassing our guests, and I won't have it. Now shush and let's say grace." My poor mom, I bet she wants a hole to open up beneath her too.

"We might offend the q—gays if we do that. Do you guys say grace?"

At least she said "gays" this time. Drew, Liam, and Colin look at each other and then, as always, the other two leave it up to Drew to answer.

"We're fine with grace. In fact, we go to church every Sunday and say our prayers at night."

Julie has tears freely flowing down her now purple-looking face, which she quickly hides in her hands. Kevin is trying hard to keep a straight face—get it? *Straight.* Mike is grinning. The other men, my dad and granddad, are looking at the two grandmothers like they can't believe their ears.

"Well then, Dora, please say grace." My mom looks at me and mouths the word "help." Feeling sorry for her, I comply.

The prayer seems to calm the table. At least Julie is getting her old color back and has quit her silent, laughing fit. Bridget hasn't said a word and is still in her star-struck world. Mike is grinning and shoveling in his food, and the rest of us are just eating.

"It must be exciting being models and traveling all over the world," my mom says to the three across from me.

"It's a lot of hard work and not as glamorous as everyone thinks," Colin replies. I so love his voice. "Sometimes we're on set for hours at a time. We're all lucky to be free until after the first of the year. This is the first break we've had in more than a year. It's nice to relax and do what we want."

I'm surprised at his revelation that they're all going to be hanging around for the next few months. My classes end the second week of December, and I was hoping I would have the whole apartment to myself. They'll probably have wild parties every night, and though I like parties just as much as the next person, there's no way I'll fit in. Yes, I enjoyed the first night at the apartment and was shocked at the normal people they had over, but a party … I'm sure that will be different.

"Earth to Dora," Grandma says loudly, and I cringe at being in the spotlight, knowing anything could come out of her mouth. "Great, now that I have your attention. I was a little upset when I heard you'd moved in with three men. I don't believe in single people of the opposite sex sharing a space together. But when I realized they were, how do you say? I heard it on a talk show the other day. Batter up? No, that's not it. It has something to do with bats though. Now, what was it?"

"There you go again. Do you even think before you talk, Alice? I swear. I, for one, don't approve of her living with these…men. Even though they're different. It's not what a proper young lady should do." Grandmother is on a roll.

"I know what it was!" Grandma yells, ignoring Grandmother. "It's called 'bat for the other team,'" she says smugly, as if she's just answered the final *Jeopardy* question and won all the money.

Mike and the three hot stuffs can't hold back their laughter. Suddenly, we're all laughing, except for Mom and the Grands'. Poor Mom. What did she expect? Having the minister from our church over wasn't even enough to stop the Grands', so why would she think this time would be any different?

"Okay, that's enough, Mom and Beatrice. Let's eat," my mom demands, and of course the two elders act so innocent. The food is delicious, and I finally start relaxing, hoping the worst is over.

I spend most of my time after dinner doing the dishes. I don't want to hear the conversation in our living room. God only knows what's being discussed. A reluctant Bridget and Julie join me—after I grab their arms and drag them into the kitchen.

"Gosh, D, how the heck did you end up with them? I mean, really, do you know who they are? They're famous!" Bridget takes the dish from my hand and absently begins drying it, a dreamy look on her face. "They're not gay, are they? Tell the truth. I swear I won't tell." She rambles on and Julie just stands there smiling.

"No, they're not," I say, handing Julie a dish to dry.

"Oh, wow. Wait until I tell the posse. It's not fair Dad took my phone. I mean, geez, did he think I'd call all of them and have them come over and share this with me? Well, I might have. I mean, who's going to believe they were here? I need a phone, D, please?" Bridget's blue eyes plead with mine.

"We don't need any more drama, but maybe I can take a picture of you with them. Okay?" I say, taking pity on my poor sis.

"OMG that would be so awesome!" Bridget's smile can't get any larger.

"I wish I smoked or drank," my mom's voice startles us.

"Mom, is that appropriate to say to your daughters?" I say, including Julie because she is my sister in every way, but in blood.

"Those two would make anyone go over to the dark side, I swear. I can't believe your dad and I are so normal," she says, opening the fridge and grabbing a soda and gulping it down like it's a shot. "Dora, I almost forgot. Henry wants me to tell you something about Jeff. His grandmother says he needs to study more for his exams. He's not prepared," Mom says before belching loudly.

"He knows, Mom. We're going to be study buddies for the next few weeks, but I'll tell him anyway."

Jeff is a guy I met the first week of school, and we hit it off. No, not that way. He's gay, not that you'd know it unless you really got to know him. He's been there for me through troubled times, especially when Brian and I broke up after I found the jerk in bed with that bimbo.

Oh, and remember Henry is Mom's spirit guide. He's her channel to the other side. Medium stuff.

We finally finish the dishes and join the others. The rest of the evening is fairly uneventful. Bridget got her picture, Mike stayed and hung out instead of trying to escape, and the 'three' captivated everyone. Even Grandmother and Grandma behaved for once.

444

How frustrating! I haven't seen Dora since the dinner with her family, and it's driving me crazy. She must be using her private entrance to her room. How can one little bundle of energy and fire cause such chaos within me? Several times I've knocked on her door, a made-up excuse to why, but she isn't there. Where is she? School is on break and, wait, the coffee shop. She works mornings. I could just happen to go by. Boy, I sound like a lovesick stalker, and maybe I am, but she brings out feelings in me I thought were dead. She makes me feel alive.

Seven

"Yes, I want a caramel latte with soy milk, whipped cream—no, wait, I want—no, that is what I want," the man standing before me rambles on. I wait, knowing he'll probably change his mind again. Ben comes in every few days, and it's always the same old indecisiveness. He's an accountant down the street, and even if I didn't know that, it would be my first guess, with his black old-school glasses and ultraconservative black suits and black tie. I wait patiently because I know he has a stressful job, and the line isn't too long right now.

"Oh my goodness, Sally, look! It's them!" a voice from a nearby table loudly whispers, causing me to look around my customer. I immediately groan at the sight of my three roommates standing in line.

"I'm sorry, Dora. I just had an awful meeting, and I'm mentally beat." Ben's voice causes me to whip my eyes back to meet his apologetic ones.

"Oh, Ben, I wasn't groaning at you. Take your time. It's what's behind you that caused it," I reassure him. Voices are getting louder, as the majority of the female customers have recognized the trio. Darn. If I desert Ben right now, he'll think I lied to him, but I want to know what brings the Modelteers to my coffee shop.

Ben finally gives me his order, and I pass it to June and ask Stephen if he'll take over for me. He does and I make my way to the side of the shop and watch as Larry, Curly, and Moe—yes, I watched *The Three Stooges* with my dad as a kid—get out of line and move across the room to me. I roll my eyes at the looks on the faces of the female audience. Colin's eyes meet mine, and my heart squeezes. I get a warmth that is so unnatural to me I don't think a thousand fans could cool me off. I drag my eyes away from his and meet Drew's laughing ones, but there's also a strange warmth in them.

"Hi, angel," he says. "So this is where you spend your mornings." His voice is smooth, too smooth for me to fall for.

"Apparently, since I'm here and wearing the shops' apron. Such a good guesser you are," I say, my smile more a grimace.

I wish he'd at least look surprised at my comeback, but that infernal grin stays on his face. I glance at Liam and his bored look is replaced by a smidge of a smile. I skip over Colin and move back to Drew. "So, what brings you guys in today?" I say sweetly, knowing the glare my eyes are giving him is anything but sweet.

"We came to escort you home and invite you to come out with us tonight. Right, guys?" Drew looks to his two cohorts and seems satisfied when they nod in agreement.

I hear a sigh from the table behind them and two young girls whisper loudly that they are available, which Drew ignores.

"I'm confused why you guys would want to spend time with boring old me when any girl or woman would jump at the chance to do so. Do you guys feel sorry for me? Because I'm happy with my life, and I do have one." I take a deep breath and wonder at the puzzled look on their faces.

"What makes you say that?" Liam asks.

"Because I'm probably your pet project to show poor little, plain Dora how the beautiful people live, and frankly, I'm really not interested," I say, trying not to burst into tears at the possible truth in my statement. Okay so it's that time of the month and I'm a little grouchy, crampy, and bloated.

"That's bollocks!" Colin's loud voice makes the room quiet down, and I realize everyone is hanging onto our every word.

Great. By tomorrow I might be front-page news: "Short, unruly red-haired barista adopted by generous star models, their way of making her life more bearable."

Out of the corner of my eye, I spy my boss pointing to his watch and mouthing "quitting time," which makes me relieved that I can escape this nightmare. Without a word, I grab my backpack from behind the counter and push by the trio, avoiding eye contact. Once outside, I take a deep breath and jog down the street. The tension I'm feeling is slowly replaced by the rhythmic pounding of my feet on the pavement. I absolutely love running, and I try to run whenever I can.

I hear quick and steady footsteps behind me, like the sound of men's dress shoes clicking along on the pavement, but I push ahead and reach the subway platform seconds before the train doors shut. I turn and watch as my followers reach the platform, looking a little out of breath. I wave as the train shoots past them, and then I'm lost in the tunnel.

I don't want to go back to the apartment and face the music. What if I'm wrong? What if they really want to hang out with me? No! They're just rich little boys with a new toy, and I wish I had my old life back. My feet eventually lead me back to the loft. Thank goodness Brad isn't on duty, so I make it to the elevator unnoticed. I use my key to enter my own door.

Tomorrow is Thanksgiving and I was intending to go home in the morning, but I begin throwing clothes in my overnight bag. I take the stairs instead of the elevator to my car in the underground garage. It's kind of spooky—one of the fluorescent lights is blinking and then softly explodes, plunging my car into darkness. Drew's parking spot is still empty as I pass by, quickly unlocking my doors. I shiver, but I don't think it's because of the cold. I think it's the creepy feeling I'm being watched. I hold my breath until I'm clear of the garage and on my way home.

444

Home sweet home … my safe refuge from this crazy world, well, kind of. Walking into the house, my sense of smell is ensnared by deliciousness and I follow the trail to the kitchen. My dad is standing at the sink, apparently dancing to something only he can hear. I hesitate, not wanting to scare him, and then I notice the ear buds. I wait patiently, giggling at his ungraceful moves. I sense a presence behind me and my mom puts an arm around my shoulders and gives me a side hug.

"I thought you weren't coming until tomorrow, but I'm so glad you're here. He's adorable, huh? That's why I married him."

"You married Dad because he can't dance?"

"Well, there's that too, but his all-around charisma. I mean, look at him. Any woman on the planet would just love to eat him up."

"Ewww. Mom, that's so wrong on several levels."

She laughs. My dad hasn't noticed us as he continues to awkwardly gyrate. The sun is shining through the window, highlighting the red in his hair.

"So?" my mom asks as she gently guides me away from the kitchen door and into the living room. Pulling me down beside her on the couch, she waits.

"So, I came home early." I watch her eyebrows go up and I know she's intuiting again. "Okay, my life is a mess. It used to be so normal. I worked, went to school, came home for dysfunctional Sunday dinners, and listened to my best friends have sex every night. Now I live with three famous male models, and one of them makes my stomach hurt. I know they just feel sorry for me. They want to take this pitiful, short, red-haired, average-looking dork under their wings," I groan while gesturing to myself.

"Oh, is that all? I thought something was really wrong. Honey, those guys really like you. You're funny, loving, and beautiful all wrapped up in a petite package. I know for a fact you make men drool."

"Yeah, right. Zombies maybe. And you're my mom. You have to say I'm awesome because it's in the parental contract."

"Let's get back to the one who makes your stomach hurt. It's Colin, right? Tell me I'm right. I so hate that I can't read family."

"Yes, it's Colin, but he's been hurt, and by a beautiful model at that. So what chance would I have?" I look at her, feeling so inadequate. Even when I caught that SOB ex of mine with his slut, I still didn't feel this way. Why does there have to be such perfect specimens in the world?

"Have you given him a chance?"

I shake my head.

"Well then, you don't know, do you? I have a couple of things to tell you about Drew and Liam. Henry had a long discussion with me the other night and made me miss my favorite show, *Rizzoli & Isles*. And your dad forgot to tape it or DVD it, or whatever it's called nowadays. Anyway, they both need your help. He said if you hadn't blocked them with your negative thoughts, you would see that. Honey, did you hear what I just said? No, of course you didn't. Now pay attention. Liam and Drew need you. So you need to tune into them and figure out what they need."

"Are you sure? I mean, is Henry sure? They're perfect. Perfect faces, perfect bodies, perfect life—"

"Those are facades. Look below the surface and you'll see."

"How long have you been here, Sweet Pea?" My dad's voice makes us turn our heads to see him grinning at us.

"Long enough to see your smooth moves, Daddy Dear," I say as we all break out into laughter.

"It's good to have you here early. Your job, as usual, is to keep your mother out of my kitchen," he says, taking my mom by the hand and pulling her into his arms and planting a kiss on her giggling lips. I swear, if I ever find a man like my dad, I will definitely marry him. Though in my short life experience, I know they are hard to find.

444

So far, Thanksgiving dinner has had no surprises. Altogether, there are twenty-five of us—cousins, aunts, uncles and the grandparents all gathered at several tables placed throughout downstairs. As usual, Dad's dinner is amazing, though he only cooks on Turkey Day and Christmas. I'm sitting at the kiddie table with Mike, Bridget, and several other young ones. Being the good cousin that I am, I'm keeping them entertained, even my one-year-old cousin Sally. She has hair like mine, poor kid, and the cutest dimples you've ever seen. She's wearing more of her dinner than ingesting it, but she's happy and that's all that matters.

After most of the house guests leaves, those that remain sit around talking about the day and the gossip we may have missed while sitting at separate tables. The grandmothers had been on their best behavior, which isn't saying much, but was a relief to my mom.

We're watching a Christmas movie when the doorbell rings and Mom says, "It's for you, Dora."

Everyone looks at me and I jump up, nervous because Mom would have told me if it was Julie. My palms start sweating as I reach the front door and dread sits heavy in my stomach at who might be on the other side.

"Dora, it's a little cold to keep them waiting," Mom's voice prompts me to grab the door handle and open it. It's the roommates, sans smiles…normal for Liam, but for the other two, not so much. They all look like someone just died.

"Hey, guys. Happy Thanksgiving." My greeting sounds so lame.

"Hello, Dora. May we speak with you?" Colin's proper statement and his adorable English accent send my stomach and heart into their crazy antics again.

"Sure, come on in." I open the door wide and turn to see my whole family staring at us. Bridget grabs her phone and her fingers move so fast it's mesmerizing.

"We're going into the family room, okay?" I say, not waiting for an answer but leading the way to the back of the house. The family room has a door so I can be sure that we won't be disturbed.

The guys eye the leather couch and they all plop down and wait for me to sit in an overstuffed recliner opposite them. Gawd, they're so beautiful. Such a shame. It's times like this I wish I wasn't an average person in an average body.

"Dora, we want to apologize for disrupting your place of business yesterday." Colin's proper English makes me weak in the knees—and yes, a stomach and heart flip happens, as well. The memory of his kiss makes me blush. "Sometimes we don't think things through before we do them. We made you uncomfortable, and we realize we caused you undue stress. Can you forgive us?"

"What he said," Drew quipped, and he sends me a slight smile. "Look, Dora, our lives are crazy, and most of the time, not in a good way. You might think it's all glamorous, but it's not. No, don't roll your eyes. We're surrounded by phony people who smile in our faces and talk behind our backs. When we met you, you were—"

"A breath of fresh air," Colin interrupts. "You're so grounded and we work in a shark pool. If we make one mistake, there is always someone else to take our place. So you are like a—" Colin stops as if trying to find the right words.

"Ray of sunshine," Liam says in a monotone voice, sans smile. I can't help myself. I start laughing. "Ray of sunshine" from Mister Warmth himself. They all look startled and then join in. Even Liam chuckles—yeah, he actually has the ability to laugh.

"Thanks, guys," I say, wiping tears from my eyes. My side hurts, but I feel they're telling me the truth.

"No, thank you, Dora. That night at Papa's was the best night we have had in … well, in a long time. We want you to give us a chance to show you that we are fun, good guys who just want to hang out with a wonderful, normal girl." Drew says.

"Okay, stop there. It's getting a little deep now. And if you think I'm normal, I may have to remind you of Sunday's dinner. Yeah, normal." I roll my eyes and more laughter erupts from all.

My mom opens the door and peers in at us with a huge smile. "Would anyone like anything to drink?"

"Yes," I say. "We'll get you guys a beer or something, and then if you want to spend time with a *normal* family, you can stay and watch a movie with us."

Three heads nod vigorously. Oh, boy … I'm totally going to pick a really *good* chick flick.

444

"Bye, guys. I'll be home tomorrow," I say as they all get into Drew's car.

Home. After tonight, it just might feel like home.

"Dora, I need to speak with you for a moment in private," my mom's voice drifts from the kitchen. She's frowning when I enter, and I know it's serious. "I just talked to Henry and he's being very evasive, which isn't like him. Normally, I can't shut him up. It has to do with you, but of course the pain in the butt won't tell me."

"Mom, do you think you should talk about a spirit like that?"

"Yes, when it's warranted. He tells me you're to help Liam and Drew and do it soon. He won't tell me why. He said you will know. I hate this 'I can't read for my family' crap. It's just not fair."

"I think it's great you can't read us. Just think how our lives would be, knowing our mom can see everything about us. Don't worry. It's probably not that bad. Henry loves to be a drama queen, right?"

"I hope that's all it is, sweetie. Really, I do."

444

As I'm lying in bed in my old room in my parents' house, I'm wondering what I could possibly help Liam and Drew with and why Colin isn't involved. Just thinking his name is enough for me to feel warm all over. I'm usually levelheaded. Even my last boyfriend, aka The Jackass, never had me feeling this way. In the beginning, we had some chemistry. We'd have to, right? Or maybe I was tired of doing school and work and needed a little extracurricular activity in my life. The sex wasn't too bad, and yet it wasn't all that great either. I wasn't a virgin. I lost that to Mark Stephens the night of homecoming my senior year. Yeah, that was memorable…not. But when I see Colin or hear his voice, I melt in my nether regions.

Stop it, Dora. Don't go there. Concentrate on Liam and Drew's so-called problem. Colin is out of my league—way out of my league—so just block those thoughts.

I know, I know. I talk to myself, but who doesn't? Now, when I start answering my own questions out loud, then I know I have a problem.

My eyes are getting heavy and I snuggle underneath the warm down comforter, planning to dream about anything but my roommates … yeah right, like that's being realistic.

She forgave us. How can she not see how beautiful she is? I couldn't take my eyes off her, and I have no idea what movie we watched. I finally told the others of my feelings, and they told me if I hurt her, I'll regret it. They assume she'll want to go out with me, but I'm not so sure. I think she still feels we're these carefree, jet-setting guys who don't really feel. Boy, is she wrong. God, I sound like a woman. Now to get up the nerve to approach her. Maybe I'll wait until her exams are over. Yeah, if I can wait that long. Those lips are calling me again …

Black Friday. It should be called Pushing, Shoving and Forget That Yesterday was Thanksgiving and We Should Still Love Each Other Friday, Right? No, it's a complete madhouse.

I didn't have to be at work until ten, as a few of my co-workers wanted the early shift, and I gladly switched to have a few more hours to sleep in. My mom is all smiles as I leave the house. She's going shopping today. She follows me in her car until we reach the local mall entrance and then I wave at her and watch from my rearview mirror as she turns. I have decided that this year, Cyber Monday is my day to shop. Yep, going to get everything online. I have great insurance, but I'm not willing to waste it on tending to battle wounds from insane shoppers.

Every table is filled in the coffee shop and the line is almost to the door. Exhausted-looking people turn to look as I enter. I smile and hurry to the back to put on my apron and return to help my poor coworkers, who are trying to keep up with all the orders.

Time flies and before I know it, it's quitting time. I realize I'm at loose ends. It's Friday night and I have no plans. Julie and Kevin are spending the weekend with their parents, and my other friends are either out of town or already busy.

I slowly make my way to my car to fight my way home. The only part of living in the city I hate is the traffic. I usually take the subway to avoid it, but on days like this when I come to work straight from my parents', I prepare for the traffic jams.

Brad's smile meets me from the front desk when I walk into the lobby. He's definitely a great addition to otherwise cold and vacant entrance to the warehouse apartment building. The elevator quietly takes me to the fourth floor and I hesitate before putting my key in the front door, hoping someone is home.

The first thing I notice is the heavenly smell, followed immediately by voices coming from the kitchen. Yay, I'm not alone. I quickly throw my overnight bag in my room and move to the kitchen, drooling at what might be cooking.

Colin stands at the stove, stirring a pot. Drew is leaning up against the island sipping a beer, and Liam is getting plates out of the cupboard. Drew notices me first and he smiles.

"Hey, look who is home. Hope you're hungry." He winks as Colin and Liam turn to look at me.

"We're having a good old English nosh—roast beef, Yorkshire pudding, roasted potatoes, and baby peas," Colin says proudly before turning back around to stir the pot.

"It smells absolutely delicious, and I'm famished. How long until dinner?"

"About twenty minutes," Colin says without showing me his beautiful face.

"Great. I'll go take a quick shower." I turn and practically run to my room, shut the door, and start peeling off my clothes.

At least ten people could fit in my shower. It has a massive showerhead that feels like I'm standing underneath a waterfall. The first time I used it, I didn't want to turn off the water. In fact, it wasn't until I remembered I had to be at work that I dragged myself away from it.

When I'm done showering, I dress in a pair of yoga pants, boot slippers, and a comfy, super-soft sweatshirt. I decide to put my wet hair up in lazy ponytail.

The table is set and they're just putting bowls of food on it when I walk in. My stomach rumbles and all three chuckle to themselves. Drew pulls back a chair and motions for me to have a seat. I grab the first bowl, and soon my plate is piled high with food. I look up, realizing the others have stopped scooping food onto their plates and are staring at my plate.

"I like a girl who enjoys her food," Liam quips and he smiles—yes, he smiles. A thousand-watt smile, at that.

I blush—yes, it's a fault of being a redhead—embarrassed that I probably look like a little porker in their eyes.

"He means it, love," Colin says, looking with concern at me. "The toothpicks we get the pleasure to be around wouldn't dream of eating all that. Oh, no. That's a good thing. Like I said, toothpicks."

He grins and everyone else vanishes from the table as I stare into his amazing, crystal blue eyes. My stomach grumbles louder, breaking the spell. I break eye contact and concentrate on my plate, as does everyone else when they realize my discomfort. No one talks for several minutes. Thank goodness, because my brain is so wrapped up in the incredible food.

"So, Dora, how was your day?" Drew asks and all three pairs of eyes focus on me.

"It was super busy."

"Ah, yes. Your Black Friday nightmare, which I must say I have tried once and that cured me for all time," Colin says, his eyes twinkling. I swear they are.

"I agree, Colin. No shopping for me. I'm doing my shopping like I always do, on Monday online. I will never understand why people stand in line for hours to save a few bucks."

"To some people, it's a business." Liam's voice shocks me, as he always seems like he isn't listening. "They buy cheap and sell to make a profit. Not bad if you have the patience. Which, of course, I would never have."

His Aussie accent is so adorable. What am I saying? Liam … adorable?

The conversation continues. I listen and interject every now and then with my comments. I love listening to them talk, each with distinctly different accents.

"Colin, that was so good. Thank you." I watch his face light up at my comment. Not again. I can't get lost in those eyes. I may end up doing something really embarrassing, like climbing onto the table and kissing him soundly. Instead, I get up, grab my plate, head to the kitchen, and open the freezer to cool off my heated face and thoughts.

Drew's voice brings me back. "No dishes for you, 'Ms. I've Worked All Day'. Go get dressed up. We're going out."

"Out? Out where?" I ask, forgetting I'm still holding the freezer door open.

"Out. To have a good time. You do like to have a good time, don't you?"

"Yes, but I'm not … I mean, my hair is … I'm just not up to going out tonight."

"It's Friday night and we're going out. No arguments. So hurry up and get ready." He grabs my arm and gives me a light shove out of the kitchen, where I find Liam and Colin grinning.

"But I was going to relax. I have to work tomorrow."

"No, you don't. We got you the day off. No more excuses. We could help you get ready," Drew says, leering at me.

"Yes, we could. We wouldn't look, of course," Colin says, chuckling. I hear a small laugh from Liam. I swear he's smiling too … or maybe it's a leer.

"Okay, okay. I'll go get dressed. It'll take me a few minutes. Do I have time to shave my legs?" I ask, then regret it as I see them all smiling like hyenas. "Gutter minds," I say loudly as I open my bedroom door. I almost slam it shut as I hear the wolf whistles aimed at my back.

Here I stand in my closet, looking at my pitiful wardrobe. Hey, I'm a college student, so don't judge me. And remember, I wear a freaking apron for work. I do go out at night, so I have a few passable outfits, and my little black dress is always a great standby. I love wearing black since it makes my hair seem more vibrant. Even I can be a little vain at times. My mass of curly hair and my blue eyes are my best assets.

I'm going all out tonight. Armed with my diamond necklace with matching teardrop earrings, I feel my confidence is an eight on a scale of ten. Subtle eye makeup makes my eyes bluer, and a coral lip stain and matching blush finishes the job. And, of course, my "eff me pumps", as Julie would call them. The black, five-inch heels feel strange at first, but I stroll around my huge room, getting use to them.

I grab my small purse, put on my jet-black winter coat with an appropriate hood, check once more in the mirror and open my door. Three sets of eyes meet mine before examining me from head to toe. My long coat hides my short dress, so all they can see is my head and my feet, which is how I want it.

"Wow," Colin says, his warm eyes meeting mine. My tummy does its normal somersaults. Yeah, I said "tummy." Sue me. Thankfully, for once in my life I don't blush.

"I second that. But, Dora, what's hidden underneath that coat?" Drew asks.

Liam snorts, grabs his jacket and opens the front door.

"Wouldn't you like to know?" I reply. "I guess you're giving us a hint, Liam? And, may I say, you guys don't look too bad yourselves."

"May I?" Colin puts out his arm. I grab it gently and he pulls me close so we can move through the door together. We ride down the elevator listening to Mick Jagger singing "Jumping' Jack Flash." Drew has a rock radio station piped into the elevator. My dad will love this when he visits.

Whether planned or by chance, I end up sitting with Colin in the backseat, which is absolutely fine by me. My tummy is still flipping its little heart out. We are sitting so close I feel the heat from his body, which, combined with mine, makes me want to rip off my coat and his clothes.

What the hell am I thinking? He's just acting like a gentleman … taking my arm, holding my car door open for me. We really don't need to sit this close since Drew's backseat is huge, but I can dream, can't I? I've seen him on posters and in magazines dressed only in briefs, so I don't have to imagine how he looks under his clothes.

"Dora," Drew's eyes meet mine in the rearview mirror. "What's on your mind? You seem preoccupied."

"Oh, nothing," I reply, frustrated that I was so distracted by Colin that I couldn't think of a snarky retort. I'm so glad none of them are not mind readers.

"Riiiight," he says with a small laugh as my eyes widen.

"Yeah, right. My head is completely empty," I say in a huffy voice and the three laugh at my statement. "Where are we going?" I'm a little nervous that they're taking me to some star-studded club where I'll be the only nobody.

Quit that, Dora. You are just as important as they are. You just make a lot less money and you're not as pretty. But you can hold your own.

Boy, would my psych teacher have a field day with this whole situation. I've never thought I needed therapy, even with my crazy family, until now. Where the hell is my self-confidence hiding? See, I must be nuts.

"We're going to a little place that has the best drinks, music and—" Drew begins.

"And some of the most mouth-watering tapas you'll ever have in your entire life," Liam finishes, smacking his lips.

"Yeah, this is Liam's favorite spot for cheese sticks, chicken wings, and pizza bites. Watch how much this Aussie puts away tonight. He'll have to do double time in the gym tomorrow," Drew teases.

"I have to start back on my exercise regimen too," I reply, thinking about how long it has been since I've gone for a good long run.

"Well, you have full use of the gym downstairs. We've shown you that, haven't we?" I see Drew's forehead lines deepen through the rearview mirror as he tries to remember.

"I don't do gyms. I just run. In fact, I was just thinking I haven't run in a few weeks. Since I'm off tomorrow, I think I'll go for my mid-morning jaunt through the park across the street."

Colin looks at me with concern. "I don't think that's wise. Maybe you should use the treadmill."

"I don't like machines, and it's not like I'm going to run at midnight. The park is safe, I'm sure."

"We're here," Drew announces as he pulls into an empty spot in a brightly lit parking area.

Colin helps me out of the car and takes my arm, nestling it in his as we make our way to a building with a large neon sign.

"The Raven? Sounds intriguing." I look at Drew, who is walking to my left.

"The owner is a big Edgar Allen Poe fan," he explains.

"The owner has good taste. I love Poe," I respond.

Seeing his wide smile, I realize it's his place. He opens the door and Colin and I follow Liam into a foyer that looks like a Victorian parlor. A voluptuous girl dressed in an old-fashioned dress, complete with generous boobs threatening to spill out, stands behind an old, bar-like counter.

"Good evening, Jen. How's business tonight?" Drew's dazzling smile would make most women faint, but she doesn't even bat an eyelash. I need to talk to this woman and find out her secret.

"It's going. Still early. Let me take your coats." She holds out her hand and the guys strip off their jackets.

Then all eyes are on me. Okay, so I'm not into strip teasing, but I slowly unbutton my coat and open it even slower. I peel it off my left shoulder and slip my arm out. Their tongues are hanging out—okay, so they aren't really, but it's good to imagine. I hand my coat over to Jen, who smiles and winks at me in an appreciative way.

Ah. Now I think I understand why she's not affected by the guys.

I make sure my dress is straight before I turn around and face my roommates. I watch their eyes enlarge as they see how short the skirt is and how revealing the top part is. My boobs aren't ginormous, but with my push-up bra, they pass inspection.

"Wow, Dora. You dress up nice!" Liam takes my arm and leads me down a hallway, leaving the other two standing like statues while still gawking at me.

"Thanks, Liam. It seems something has made them speechless."

"You, you're a little bundle of surprises. I'm usually the quiet one, as you may have noticed. It's a refreshing change to see them shocked."

"Why, Liam, I like this side of you."

"Oh, no. Now you'll pester me to act this way all the time. Don't get any ideas," he laughs as he opens the door at the end of the hallway.

We enter another world. The music is pulsating and the décor I can only describe as a Goth-Victorian-Poe-era vibe. Pretty much everything is black with splashes of red scattered around in the forms of paintings and chairs. I'm shocked it's not more crowded.

Liam leads me to a secluded corner booth and motions for me to slide in. He moves in after me. I scootch over to make more room, but instead I hit a solid object. Turning to look, I meet Colin's eyes. I swear, they're devouring me. His intense stare is making me burn as hot desire shoots along all my nerve endings. I've read plenty of romance novels, and now I know what they're talking about.

Liam nudges me, spoiling the moment. "What's your poison?" he asks, grinning from ear to ear.

"Surprise me, oh, but not beer though, anything but beer," I reply.

He gives me a sly grin as Drew pulls up a chair to sit in front of us. Drew reaches behind himself and closes an embellished, antique sliding door, drowning out all the noise from the rest of the club.

"So what do you think, Beautiful?" Drew asks, smiling wolfishly, his seductive eyes meeting mine.

"Are you talking to me?" I ask coyly—yes, coyly. Deal with it.

"You know it," he replies, but even though he is a utterly delicious male specimen, he doesn't float my boat like Colin does.

What am I saying? I'm not up for a relationship, even if Colin was interested, which of course, he's not. I'm out with three hot guys who are my roommates and my new friends. That's all!

"Dora? I swear, you disappear into your head a lot. Where do you go when you zone out?" Drew asks.

"Oh, I was just wondering why this place isn't jumping on a Friday night."

"It's on purpose. Not many people know about this place, and that's the way we like it. Right, boys?"

"Yeah, it gets old going to clubs and not being able to enjoy ourselves," Liam pipes up.

"Oh, you poor sweethearts. It must be really hard having all your adoring fans swooning at your feet," I say sarcastically. To my surprise, they all burst out laughing.

"You are truly a breath of fresh air, and we are so honored you agreed to hang out with us," Drew replies as the waitress slides open the door and pops her head in.

"Hey, Drew, ready to order?" she asks.

By her flirting demeanor, I realize she likes men, especially these three. I try not to feel inadequate because she is everything I'm not. But to my surprise, all three sets of eyes are focused on me and not her. Drew gives her our order without turning around, and she slides the door back, disappointment obvious on her face.

"So what do you think?" Drew asks.

"I think it's perfect. Poe would have loved to hang out here. The detail's amazing."

"Well, they should be with the money I've put into this place."

"Would you like to dance?" Colin's dreamy accent makes me shiver. No, not with cold, but with the thought of dancing with him.

I'm tongue-tied, so I just nod. He exits the booth and helps me up when I slide out after him. I suddenly find myself on the dance floor, but how I got here is a blur. The second he takes my hand and doesn't let go, my brain goes to mush. How can he be having this effect on me? I don't feel this way with Drew and Liam, and they're just as mega hot, but Colin makes me feel … well, he makes my blood sizzle.

As soon as we start to dance, the music changes to a slow, seductive beat and he moves in, putting his arms around my shoulders. I'm so happy I'm wearing my five-inch heels so I'm taller, and I gladly slide my arms around his waist. As my head meets his chest, I hear the strong beat of his heart. His sweet smelling cologne clings to my nose. He smells one-hundred percent delicious. Oh my heaven, I can feel his sculptured muscles beneath his silky shirt as we sway, and I hold back a groan as his hips move seductively against my overheated body.

Please, legs, don't fail me now, I silently plead as they suddenly feel like Jell-O and I wobble a little on my heels.

As if he hears my thoughts, Colin tightens his hold on me and we begin moving as one. At least, I think we're moving. I've never, ever felt this way before. I want to drag him into the nearest booth and, well, you know … feel every inch of his body with my fingers.

"It's my turn."

Drew's voice is like a bucketful of cold water thrown over me. Colin's warmth is removed and Drew takes one of my hands and places his other around my waist. His cologne isn't overwhelming. In fact, it smells pretty good, but it's nothing like Colin's.

He moves us around the floor as effortlessly as anyone I have ever seen, but I feel nothing. No blood sizzle, no Jell-O legs and no desire to rip his clothes off and have my way with him. The song ends and he lets go and places a hand on my back as we exit the dance floor. I notice several females eyeing him up and down and smiling. I look up at him and he seems oblivious to their invitations.

The first thing I notice when we reach the table is that Colin is absent. Maybe he's gone to the loo—a wonderful word the English use for toilet. I scoot in beside Liam and he grins at me.

"Colin had to split. Received an urgent phone call. Said he'd let us know later," Liam says, minus the grin.

"That's all? No details?" Drew looks puzzled.

"Nope. I told him to wait and we would go with, but he said he didn't want to spoil our evening."

My night has officially gone from overwhelming to a low simmer. For the next hour or so, I find myself dancing with Liam and Drew while ignoring the glares from most of the female population, and even some males join in on the hate parade. But my mind is pre-occupied with the emergency that made Colin leave so quickly without even a goodbye.

It's Monday, and I still don't know what made Colin leave the other night in such a hurry. Drew assured me it wasn't anything serious, but Colin has been absent since the club. The coffee shop helps keep my mind occupied, as Mondays are our busiest days.

By the end of my shift, I'm exhausted and dread going to class. I quickly change my work clothes and jump on the subway, not wanting to be late to my class lecture. The next few weeks will be filled with studying, studying, and more studying, since end-of-semester finals are rapidly approaching.

Speaking of finals, I've only briefly mentioned Jeff. His full name is Jeffrey Thomas Bain Bradford the Fourth, and he's about the sweetest guy you could ever meet. Julie and I met him our first week of college and we hit it off. His family is mega rich, but Jeff is no snob. He's really tall—okay, so anyone taller than me is really tall—and he would make any woman drool over his long dark eyelashes and jet-black locks. But the true killer is his smile.

Yep, his smile makes you want to jump his bones … which the female population would find impossible because he bats for the other team, as my grandma loves to misquote all the time. It's such a shame. My family loves Jeff and the grandmothers immediately thought he was my love interest. Not my mom, of course. Henry took care of that. When I brought home The Jackass, though, they all instantly disliked him. I wonder now why I dated him for three years. Why couldn't I see what they saw? I guess "love" really is blind.

Anyway, back to Jeff. Since the semester began, he's been busy interning at a law firm. He wants to be a lawyer. Not the sleaze-bag kind, but a lawyer that's not solely in it for the money. We see each other in class, but little else lately.

That will change starting tonight. He's going to be staying with me. We're going to be joined at the hip while preparing for finals. I haven't told my roomies, but I don't think they'll mind. I'm paying rent after all and it's not like we'll be in the way. My bedroom/sitting area is as big as most apartments in the city, so we shouldn't disturb them. If only Jeff wasn't gay, maybe he could take my mind off Colin. Last night, I had this dream, and nope, not going to tell you. But just FYI, it was pure awesomeness.

"Hey, Good Looking. Are you interested in a one-night stand?" a familiar voice startles me as I wait outside the science building for Jeff.

"It depends on what you're offering and how much you're willing to pay for this amazingness," I respond, motioning to my body.

"I was hoping you'd give a poor college student a break," Jeff says woefully, his beautiful eyes sucking me in.

"I'm just as broke, but maybe we can work out a deal."

He puts his arm around me and gives me a warm side hug. "So, Red, where are we off to?"

I smile at his nickname for me. Usually I hate when people call me that, but when Jeff says it, it's somehow different.

"We're going to my new place. Remember, I told you I moved. Where's your stuff?" I ask, seeing only his backpack.

"In the car. You know I hate driving, so I thought you could be my chauffeur. Besides, I have no idea where I'm going, and you know I hate that even more."

"Oh. So, is this a paid chauffer gig?"

"Yeah, of course. I'm going to give you a huge tip." His grin is so infectious that I reciprocate.

"Like, um, a huge expensive dinner perhaps?"

"How about an extra-large pizza?"

"As long as I get what I want on my half," I reply.

"Wouldn't have it any other way." Jeff hugs me again and we take off to his car.

444

"Wow, Pandora Ann Phillips, you have most definitely come up in the world." Jeff is standing in my bedroom taking in our surroundings. "Did your grandmother finally open her Coach clutch for you?" he asks me. One eyebrow rises as he waits for my answer.

"Nope. I actually found this place for cheap, like, insanely cheap. And Julie and Kevin live on the floor below us."

"I'm surprised you moved out. I thought you guys were like the Three Amigos forever, or something."

"Well, it was the almost constant loud sex noises, and penis sighting that made me realize it was time to get my own place."

"Oh, I have to hear about this," he says, lying back on my king-size bed. I lie down beside him and explain everything.

"It's not that funny," I say moments later as Jeff laughs so hard tears are running down his face.

"Oh, my friend, that's hysterical!"

"No, it's not. I mean, Kevin's my best friend, and I was eyeing his penis … and it's not fair Julie has one and I don't," I say.

His laughter intensifies and I can't help but join in. A pounding at my door makes us stop. We look at each other like children who've been caught doing something bad.

"Dora, are you okay?" Drew's worried voice comes through the door.

Sighing, I get up from the bed and unlock and open the door. Drew is standing there wearing shorts and a sweaty muscle shirt.

"Hey, Drew. I'm fine. Come on in and meet my friend, Jeff." I open the door wide and Drew steps in while eyeing Jeff on the bed.

"Jeff, nice to meet you," he says, politely extending his hand to shake Jeff's. He doesn't look too happy when he sees Jeff's luggage by the side of the bed.

"Sorry if we bothered you, Drew, but Jeff is spending the next few weeks with me. I hope that's not a problem," I say.

"No, of course not. It's your room. So …"

I can't believe Drew's at a loss for words. I know he's wondering about Jeff. I'm not going to explain, though. That would be too easy.

"Hey, you want to grab a pizza with us?"

"As long as it's Papa's." Drew looks smug, as if he knows something Jeff doesn't.

"God, I haven't been to Papa's in forever. Forget calling a pizza, let's go hang out there." Jeff's enthusiasm immediately squelches the smugness.

"Okay," Drew replies. "Give me a few minutes to shower. Dora, why don't you go ask Liam? I know he's not busy tonight," he says over his shoulder as he leaves the room.

"Pandora Ann Phillips is living with two guys?"

"No, actually it's three," I say, not meeting Jeff's eyes.

"Three. One being the famous model Drew Johnson. I'm guessing Liam Chandler has be another one. They're always in the news together with Colin Lawrence. What the heck, Dora? How did you just stumble upon then place?"

"It just sort of happened. I saw a roommate wanted ad posted up in a grocery store and answered it on a whim. Liam has this thing for the number four, and their fourth roommate had just moved out and they needed one. So, they picked me. I guess I'm a safe bet, as I don't gush over their awesomeness. I'm *normal* in their eyes."

"You, normal? Not a chance. I saw a little jealousy in Drew's eyes when he saw me. I think he's hot for the little redhead."

"Yeah, right. And pigs fly. I have no feelings for him or Liam. They're every woman's dream, but not mine."

"Oooooh, I didn't hear Colin in that sentence. OMG, you're crushing on him. I'm right, aren't I? You're *so* blushing."

"Stop it, silly. I have to go and ask Liam to join us, so behave."

"Can I come too? I mean, I want to see if his intentions are anything like Drew's."

I smack him gently on the head before strolling out the door. I have never been in the others' rooms, even when I was alone. I respect privacy. That, and I'd have a hard time lying to them if they ever asked me. The blushing would give me away instantly. I have a terrible poker face.

Jeff follows me like a little puppy dog as I move toward Liam's door and knock.

"Yeah, come in."

Opening the door, I hear strange noises and realize it's from a video game Liam is playing on a huge flat screen hung on his sitting room wall. "Brains, we need brains," a creepy voice says from the TV. I watch as an armed figure fires at the zombie's head, making it explode into a million pieces.

"Take that, you zombie bastards," Liam says before turning around.

"Hey, Dora, what's up?" Liam's eyes move from me to Jeff, who is now standing beside me.

"Wow, is that Dead Awakening two? I haven't picked my copy up yet. The graphics are killer." Jeff moves forward and extends his right hand. "I'm Dora's friend, Jeff, and you're Liam Chandler, if the magazines are correct."

Jeff is so natural at meeting new people. I've always envied his way of making people feel at ease. I've never met anyone who doesn't like him.

"Yeah, mate, that would be me." Liam stands and takes Jeff's hand.

I immediately realize why Liam is the way he is, stand offish, brooding and aloof. But his eyes light up when they rest on Jeff. I know his secret. My empath skills have kicked in. Liam is gay! And the world doesn't know it. Oh, how I wish I was alone with him to talk about this. I wonder if Drew and Colin know. They would have to, right? They're his best friends. I just want to hug Liam and tell him it will be okay.

"Dora? I swear, she goes off in her own little world all the time. Dora … hello, Dora?"

"Oh, shush, Jeff. I'm here. Just admiring how realistic the gore looks in this game … gross."

"Uh-huh," Jeff quips.

He and Liam start laughing and I have to join in. Maybe I could play matchmaker here.

"So, Liam, the reason we're interrupting your magnificent game-playing is that Drew, Jeff, and myself are going to Papa's for pizza, and we want you to come with," I say, hoping he won't say no.

"Sounds like a plan to me. I was going to spend the evening playing my game, but pizza, beer, and good company trumps that. Give me a few minutes and I'll be ready."

Back in my room, Jeff plops down on the couch and is silent, which is a definite first for him.

"Are you ready to go?"

"Yeah," he says, and again, silence.

"What's wrong?" I say, wanting to know what causing him to be so pensive.

"I like your roommates. I really think I'm going to enjoy my time here," he replies with a half-smile.

"Oh, no, sweetie. You're going to behave, because we need to study. If you don't, you'll be high-tailing it back to that cell you call a dorm room."

"Aww, Dora, I'll behave. I hate my dorm room. I tell my dad all the time how unbearable it is. It makes him happy that I'm living what he calls *normal* living conditions."

I adore Jeff's parents. They are truly wonderful people and my family enjoys their company. No, we haven't had them over for any of our dreaded Sunday dinners with everyone, thank goodness. So, they still live under the impression that I have a somewhat average family. When his parents are in town, we all meet up at a restaurant and hang out. They know that Jeff is gay, but it makes no difference to them. They just want him to be happy.

"Don't worry Jeff, the next few weeks will be anything but normal."

He grins, oh how I love his grin.

Ten

The ride to Papa's is kind of awkward. Drew is driving, since his car is the only four-seater of the house, and Liam sits up front with him. Jeff and I sit in the back. From my position, I see Drew glancing back continuously. I guess his gaydar is off and he thinks Jeff and I are an item. I can't believe Drew might be interested in me. I know, I need to quit putting myself down, but let's be honest.

"Have you heard from Colin lately?" Liam asks, and I immediately sit up and take notice.

"Yeah, everything's cool now. He should be back in a few days. Life throws some wicked curve balls," Drew replies.

Great, so much for getting the deets on what's going on. "Life throws wicked curves balls." What the hell is up with that? That doesn't tell me crap I could have said *shit*, but Henry would probably tell on me, and I'd be in big trouble. Per my mom, I have to be a role model for my younger siblings, and apparently real women don't cuss, except for Julie, who my mom gives a pass to. Really, I don't know why she gives Julie a pass. Not fair in my book. Not that I would cuss much, but it might be nice in certain circumstances.

As always, Papa's smells heavenly. With me leading the way inside, we're spotted immediately by Mama, who rushes forward and engulfs me in one of her famous bear hugs. It takes seconds for Papa to notice us, and I'm swallowed up by both of their round bodies at once.

"My bella, Dora, it is witha much delight that I welcome you home. I see you havea brought a stranger. Jeffrey, we have missed you, you handsome boy." Mama reaches out and drags Jeff into the hugfest.

"Ah, Mama, look, she broughta old friends. Liam and Drew, welcome. We're so honored to have you back in our small establishment."

Liam's smile is friendly and sincere, but Drew's seems to lack the warmth it normally has. What is up with that? Could he be jealous, like Jeff said? I hope not, because I don't get the warm fuzzies with him like I do with Colin. Warm fuzzies—yeah, right. More like rip-his-clothes-off fuzzies.

I end up sitting with Drew on one side and Jeff on the other. Liam sits opposite us with Mama and Papa. I hear a squeal and Julie and Kevin arrive at our table, causing another hugfest. I envy my friends, their faces glowing with happiness, something that seems so unobtainable to me. More chairs are added and questions fly about. Aromatic pizzas and ice-cold beers and wine soon appear on the table. My glum thoughts turn to happy ones as I'm surrounded by the warmth of my friends and food.

Okay, I've apparently drunk a little too much wine again, so sue me. I work hard and I need to let my hair down once in a while. So I can't walk. It's my shoes, I swear. I have three guys, each willing to help me, but there's only one of me and I'm giggling watching the testosterone-laden men, aka Drew and Jeff, fight over carrying me. Without a word, Liam pushes them aside and scoops me up into his arms while walking toward the elevator, leaving the other two speechless. The giggle monster won't let go of me as we ride the elevator to our floor. Drew opens the front door and steps aside to let Liam carry me over the threshold.

"I'm away for a few days and it looks like you guys have been having fun without me." The familiar British accent sends a shiver of fire throughout my nether regions. OMG, that is so funny and the giggling continues. "I see you didn't keep an eye on Dora. Too much wine?" I try to focus on his face, but it's not happening.

"Yep, the light weight had a few too many," Liam answers.

"Hi, I'm Jeff, and maybe I should take Dora and put her to bed. Come on, sweetie." Jeff's face comes into focus and he gently takes me from Liam's arms. I snuggle against his chest. "Say goodnight to your friends, Dora."

"Night, my awesomeness friends. Thanks for the night!" I close my eyes as Jeff moves to my room. The room is dark and I open my eyes until someone turns on a light. I'm not feeling too hot, and I welcome the motionless feeling of my bed. My boots are removed and a sheet is pulled over me, and I feel someone kiss my forehead.

"Good night, princess." I hear Jeff say, and then silence.

444

"Time to rise and shine, sweet Dora." Jeff's cheerful voice makes my ears hurt. No more drinking for me—nope, never ever. I force one eye open and see his grinning face. He's holding a steaming cup of sweet-smelling coffee.

"What time is it?" I croak. Damn, I sound like a frog.

"Time to get up and run. Nothing like a good run to get rid of the wine toxins. So get your butt up and get changed. Time is awastin'."

I feel a slap on my behind and I turn over quickly. He's gone, but the coffee is still there on the night stand. He's right. A run would do me good, and I don't have work for the next few days, since I took them off to study, so it would be a good time to start again.

An hour later, I'm dressed, stretched, and ready to go. I walk out into the living room and find not one or two, but all four warm bodies stretching. And you guessed it, dressed to exercise.

Please, if you can hear me, God, don't let them—I mean, Colin—come with me.

As if they sense me standing behind them, they all turn at once. How can my eyes stand looking at so much male perfection in one room?

"Hey, guys. Are you ready, Jeff?"

"Um, we're going to have some company. The guys want to tag along," he says, looking apologetic, as if he can sense my dismay.

"Well, I hope you can all keep up," I say, trying to act happy about the news.

I run for the front door, not waiting for a response. The elevator is standing open, and I dash forward and hit the button and gleefully watch as the doors shut before they can reach it.

"Morning, Dora. Nice day out for a jog." Brad's boyish grin is infectious.

"Yep, sure is. See you later." I move quickly, pushing open the doors, and dive into the bright sunshine. It's chilly but bearable, and I take off running for the nearby park, pacing myself, thankful I'm so far ahead of them.

The park is full of activity. During fall and winter, a sunny day is precious, so everyone takes advantage of it. Moms pushing strollers, dog walkers, bench sitters, and other runners fill my sight. It energizes me to push forward, upping my speed. I hear speedy footsteps behind me, and I notice the most females watching me.

I know it's not me, so it's got to be the fabulous four hotties on my heels. I feel sudden disgust for my female sisters. These men are just flesh and bones—okay, so fever-inspired hotness—but still, only guys with penises.

There I go with that word again. I'm going crazy. I've never been sex-crazed, but all of a sudden I'm thinking about penises. I need to find a nice guy and have nice sex. A guy my mom will approve of.

Quit it, Dora, just run.

Sex is overrated, even if it's with a hottie. Of course, I don't know for sure, but one of my mom's favorite sayings is: "It's all fluff with no substance." That's what Colin is. He has to be. I can't waste time pining after a dream.

Without any other thought, I pick up my speed, running so that the people I pass are just blurs.

I see a fountain up ahead. The water has been drained in preparation for the winter weather that will soon pounce on us. I make my way around it and travel back, following my steps back home. My breathing is steady. It amazes me that I'm still in such good shape after a few months of inactivity. The boys are just ahead, not wheezing or trying to catch their breath, as I'd evilly hoped. They're jogging as if they could go all day.

They smile at me and make a U-turn, ending up behind me again. I realize I'm giving them a view of my rear end. I haven't looked at it in forever. I hope it hasn't sagged since that time so long ago. Maybe I should get behind them. No, I'm not going to drool over perfection. Let them look. I don't care if it's as wide as a bus. At least I have one, not like those skinny anorexics they hang out with.

All I wanted was a nice jog in the park with Jeff. Is that too much to ask for? Yes, I guess it is. I bet everyone is wondering why four tall, amazingly attractive guys are following a short-legged, average-looking girl with fiery red curls. I don't blame them. I would be wondering the same thing.

I reach the building and quickly enter, waving at Brad. Thankfully, the elevator is open and I run in and press the button, giggling as I see the four fighting to get through the front door all at once.

444

Bath or shower? Such a dilemma, but I guess a shower will have to do because once I get into a bath, I won't want to leave. I spy Jeff's toiletry bag sitting on the counter and grab his shampoo. It's my fave, but it's not in the budget. Letting me have some is the least he can do since he sided with the others this morning.

"It's about time. I was going to call the Coast Guard to come and rescue you." Jeff is lying on my bed still wearing his sweaty exercise clothes when I exit the bathroom.

"Don't speak to me, you traitor," I hiss. I throw my dirty clothes at him and enter my closet wearing only a towel.

"Hey, I like your roommates. What's wrong with that?" he says, twirling my sports bra on his finger.

"Yeah, all you men stick together. I wanted just us to go for a run. You're here to study, and so far, we haven't."

"That's not my fault. You're the one who flaked out last night and couldn't get up this morning. I'm going to jump in the shower and maybe you'll be in a better mood when I get out."

I hear the bathroom door close as I throw on my clothes. Why am I so mad? Julie would say it's either that time of the month, which it's not, or it's sex deprivation/frustration.

Okay, so it's been six months, and I think I mentioned it wasn't that great anyway. But it must be good sometimes, if you have the right person. Maybe it's that mysterious climax that makes all the difference. As if I know how that feels.

God, I'm still a climax virgin. No, really … I've read about how awesome it feels, so I know I've never come close. Maybe I'm impotent. I know that describes men who can't get it up, but surely there's a similar female condition too. Maybe I need to go to that adult store a few blocks from the coffee shop and get one of those dildo thingies.

What am I thinking? Like I could walk into a sex shop. Knowing my luck, I'd know half the customers. Awkward much?

"Ready, Red?" Jeff's voice interrupts my X-rated thoughts. Okay, so not X-rated, but definitely not PG.

444

Jeff and I stop by the takeout restaurant across the street from our building and load up on Chinese food. I'm really sure if it's considered brain food, but it's so good. Brad is absent from his post when we re-enter the apartments, and we ride the empty elevator in silence, except for my stomach making loud noises at the yummy smell coming from our white plastic bags. Jeff stops at the front door, but I keep walking, not wanting to see the roommates right now. I open my door and Jeff jogs over and follows me in, shutting the door behind him.

Moving quickly to the coffee table in my sitting room, I start pulling out the little white containers. Luckily, I have plates and silverware in an armoire, so we don't have to leave the room for anything. I also have a medium-size fridge, so I grab a couple drinks—no, not alcohol. Remember, I've sworn off that evil stuff. There is no talking as we polish off all the food. Now pleasantly stuffed, we crack open our books and start studying.

"Sorry," I say later when a loud yawn escapes me.

"I guess it's time to call it a night," he says. "I'm so glad we have a few days off from work so we can sleep in. Oh, how

I miss sleeping in. Then we can run, and then off to school again. Do you ever think we'll have normal lives? You know, where we only work a sixty-hour week instead of the hundred we're doing now?"

"I know. It sucks, huh?"

"Well, at least your life has some spice in it now."

"I guess you could call it that. But really, Jeff, I wish I wasn't here. I'm so out of my league. It would be okay if I didn't have feelings for one of them. But damn my hormones! I just need to focus, exercise more, and think less about sex, penises, and dildos."

Jeff starts laughing, and then I start laughing and can't catch my breath. Suddenly, I'm trying not to pee my pants.

"Come in," I manage to say as I hear knocking at my door.

"Just had to come in and see what fun I might be missing." Drew pokes his head around the door, flashing a big smile when he sees us sitting on opposite sides of the room with piles of books around us. "Studying. That's a good way to spend an evening, and Chinese food for dinner, good choice."

"Come in, Drew, and join us. We've finished studying for the night," Jeff tells him.

"So, I won't be interrupting anything important?"

"Nope, like Jeff said, we're done. Where are Liam and Colin?" I ask, hoping he doesn't notice I stumbled over Colin's name. Damn me, talking about sex, dildos, and penises.

"They're watching a movie."

"Gosh, my idea of a model's life is way off. I thought it was work in the day and party all night," I say with a smirk.

"Yep, you're way off. There are some who do that, but they don't last long. Takes a toll on the body and looks," Drew says, stretching, which makes his shirt rise up.

I catch a glimpse of his washboard abs. Nope, they haven't changed since the day I came to answer the ad. Still nice and firm. Like an erect penis.

OMG, you are not even attracted to him. What's up with you?

As if Jeff can read my mind, he laughs, his eyes aimed at mine. I stick out my tongue and get up to get a bottle of water. The little devil just laughs harder and I pick up the nearest pillow and throw it at him. He easily bats it away. Drew sits in a chair close to the door, looking puzzled.

"Hello … can we come and join the party?"

I silently groan internally as I hear the one voice I've tried to avoid. My head is blocked by the open fridge, so I grab a bottle and put it to my forehead, trying to cool myself off. I swear the temp just went up a hundred degrees.

"Sure. The more, the merrier," Big Mouth Jeff replies.

Oooh, I could smack the shit out of him. See, he's making me swear. Pulling my head out of the freezer, I see Liam and Colin taking their seats, and the spacious room suddenly feels overcrowded.

"Would anyone like a drink?" I ask. My mom would be proud that she has brought me up right. All I really want to do is take a cold shower.

"Dora, are you okay?" Jeff's question has gotten what he wants: everyone's attention on me. Butthead.

"Just peachy," I repeat a phrase my mom says when she's mad at my dad. If Jeff grins, I will smack him right in front of everyone. But to my relief, he just looks concerned with a gleam in his eye.

I sit on an overstuffed ottoman, drinking my water, listening to the guys talking. I keep my eyes averted from the group, but I feel someone staring at me. I'm afraid to look up. Julie's ringtone saves me, and I stand, grabbing my cell and moving out of their earshot.

Hanging up, I say, "Hey, guys, that was Julie. She needs to see me. I'll be back in a few."

I don't give them time to answer, just grab my keys and quickly exit my door. In the elevator, I take a deep breath and try to calm my pounding heart.

444

Well, there goes my reason for being in here. Have I done something wrong? She seems so natural with this Jeff guy. Who is he to her? The others said he's her friend and study buddy. I wish he was ugly. Maybe she doesn't want a "shallow" model. That's how she sees me, I'm sure. Do I have a chance? Maybe I have to work harder to make her see the real me. She is so worth it.

Eleven

Four hours later, I sneak back into my room. Julie and Kevin had their first fight since being hitched. It lasted all of one hour, and then they made up. Unfortunately for them, I refused to leave until I felt it was safe to return to my room. Make-up sex probably started right after I left. I know it was mean of me to make them wait, but hey, how many sleepless nights did I endure because of them?

"So, the prodigal daughter returns." Jeff's voice startles me. "I'm irked at you for leaving me to entertain your guests."

I squint, trying to see where he's located, when a light suddenly comes on. He's lying on my bed in his pajama bottoms. How many times am I going to mention how terribly sad it is for the female population that he's gay?

"Oh, I'm sure it was such a chore hanging out with three models. Wait a minute while I play the world's smallest violin for you," I say in my snarkiest voice.

"You're right, it was fun. They aren't at all what I expected. Shallow, self-centered, or big on themselves is how I imagined them being, but instead they're just average guys."

"You do know that shallow, self-centered, or big on themselves is basically saying the same thing three times, right?" Again snarky. Love it when I'm right.

"I'll give you that one. So, what was the big emergency with Jules?"

"First post-marriage fight, lasted about an hour," I answer.

"You made them wait for make-up sex? That's an all-time low for you, Red."

"Yep. Payback for all those sleepless nights. So, spill."

"Spill what?"

"What did you guys talk about? Anything interesting?"

"Nope. They tried to pump me for info regarding a hot little redhead, but I'm not a telling kind of guy. All your secrets are safe with me. Two of them kept looking at their mega-expensive watches, like they were wondering where you had run off to."

"Was one of them Colin?"

"No. Liam and Drew," he says, his grin pure evil. I march over and smack him on his shoulder. "Ow, that hurt. I'll probably have a bruise in the morning."

"Quit being a wuss. So, Colin wasn't upset that I'd left?"

"I didn't say that. I only said that Liam and Drew checked their watches. They all stayed for about two hours and then bounced."

"Quit trying to be cool. You sound super lame," I say, plopping down on the bed next to him. "Jeff, I need a man."

"Sorry, my dear, not this man." Jeff's look of mock horror makes me giggle.

"Not you, moron. A nice, straight guy. He doesn't have to be uber attractive or anything, just nice," I say, biting my lip.

"What about Drew or Colin? They seem smitten with you."

"Smitten. How archaic. No, not them. I'm so out of their zip code. So who else?"

"Honey, you literally live in their zip code."

"You know what I mean," I say dryly.

"No, I don't. I've never seen you like this before. You're always so confident. You're so beautiful, and you have two men that know that."

"You don't understand. I don't want to be attracted to a pretty boy. I want regular. Relationships with stars never work out. I'm just a novelty, which will wear off quickly. They want a taste of something average, and they've picked me."

"So, have sex with Colin and scratch your itch." He pats me on the head like I'm a puppy.

"I don't want just casual sex, I want … oh, I don't know what I want. Just help me find me an average, nice guy so I can stop thinking about penises. Okay, one particular penis. Not that I've seen it or anything though."

Jeff pulls me into his arms and I begin to sob jokingly at my situation. Oh, hell. My mom will definitely call in the morning.

444

I wake up snuggled in Jeff's arms—him in only his pajama bottoms, and I'm still completely dressed. I don't want to wake him, but I have the sudden dire urge to pee.

I move carefully, and then I feel the stare. Jeff is awake and watching me. If I have to make a guess, he's trying to gauge my mood.

"Thanks for last night. Do I look as bad as I feel?" I ask, dreading the answer.

"You look beautiful. Now let's get up and go for a run. I think you need it."

"First, I have to use the little girls' room. Bladder is about to burst." I jump up and make it just in time. Sitting on the pot, I study my reflection in the mirror-laden walls and see Jeff is right. I don't look so bad. Beautiful? No, but at least my eyes aren't swollen slits.

Time to stop feeling sorry for my no-sex-for-a-long-time, frustrated self and get a move on.

Jeff and I quietly exit my door and take the stairs. I don't want company this morning, what with my nerve-endings still raw.

Brad is at his post, but to my dismay, he has company, and they look like they're waiting for us. How do I know? They look at us, smile and are dressed for running. At least they're wearing long pants and sweatshirts, like us. They must have checked the weather, as today is supposed to be thirty degrees colder than yesterday.

"Hey, Dora, did you take care of Julie's emergency? We missed you last night," Drew says, giving me one of his delicious smiles.

"Yep, took longer than I thought. You guys going out?" I ask innocently.

"We're just waiting for you. Jeff mentioned that once you start running again, you try not to miss a day. We need the exercise, and we know you don't mind us tagging along, right?"

What can I say? If I say yes, I look like a bitch, and if I say it's okay, I'll be near Colin, and that's not good right now with my emotions all over the place.

"We're happy to have you run with us, right, Dora?" Jeff prompts.

"Sure, try and keep up." Good thing I stretched in the apartment. I start running, hoping they need to stretch. But no, they take off with me, four tall trees and me, the little sapling.

Jeff stays with me and the others are close behind. I need to forget they're there. Of course, that's not going to happen without a little extra effort. I start thinking about my upcoming exams, and then I engage Jeff in some problems I've been having while studying. Before I know it, I've completely occupied my mind enough to forget the three models are behind us .... Yeah, right.

We get to a stretch of park where there is more room and Liam moves up beside me. He makes eye contact with me while smiling and I smile back. My mom's statement that I needed to help him and Drew makes me focus on that. I think I know what Liam's secret is, but Drew ... maybe it's his family. I know money doesn't always buy love, and maybe that's what Drew's problem is—a lack of love. Anyway, I need to take care of this soon.

The park is full of people again. As we near the fountain, I spot a crowd of young women. One of them looks our way and screams. They all look at where she's pointing and then rush forward, blocking our path and circling like vultures. They're carrying notepads and pens.

"Can I have your autograph, Drew?"

"Liam, I need your autograph."

"Colin, I want to have your baby," a tall curvy blonde yells, pushing me aside and making her way to her target.

What the hell? How dare that little skank push me! I grab her arm and pull her away from Colin. She goes to hit me with her bag and Jeff saves me from being clobbered with it by pulling her not so gently away from me. Jeff then grabs my hand and pushes his way through the crowd until we have a moment to catch our breath.

"Come on. They can take care of themselves, and here comes the cavalry." He points to a group of policemen making their way to the crowd.

"What the hell was all that?" I say as we jog back to the loft.

“I guess we were spotted yesterday and someone told someone, and then someone else, and thus, the mob formed.” Jeff shrugs his shoulders. “I’m so glad I’m not famous,” he says, slowing down as he realizes I’m not keeping up with him.

“See? How can I compete with that? It’s a lost cause. That woman who wanted Colin’s baby was beautiful—crazy as hell, yes—but beautiful.”

“But—” Jeff starts.

“Don’t you dare say I’m beautiful on the inside and any guy worth anything would see that.”

“I’m so happy you put words into my mouth. I was going to say, before I was rudely interrupted by a petulant child, that woman doesn’t hold a candle to you,” he comments.

I groan. “Jeff, why don’t you like girls? It would be so much easier for me.”

“Even if I did, you wouldn’t be my type. I’d go for the average ones.” He gives me a devilish grin and a side hug. “Let’s go finish our run in the gym. First one there gets the deluxe treadmill.”

He takes off, leaving me behind. I look back at the crowd and the police trying to control them and then follow Jeff, not caring for once if I win.

444

I'm dripping wet. My hair, clothes, socks, shoes and underwear are drenched with sweat. A shower is desperately needed, and I leave the gym hoping I don't bump into anyone. Jeff went up about half an hour ago, but I needed to work off my excess frustration. I hit the elevator button and hear the doors opening behind me. Please don't let it be them. Let it be Brad, Julie, or even Kevin, who will tease me, I can handle that. I don't turn around but hear footsteps behind me. They sound like sneakers.

"Dora, what happened? You look like you've been caught in a downpour," Drew asks.

"Nope, just good old-fashioned sweat. I had an awesome workout in your fabulous gym. Did you guys get to finish your run?" I ask as I enter the elevator and turn around, seeing the three looking me up and down. "Haven't you ever seen a person sweat before? Are you going to stand there all day, or are you going to get on? I need to take a shower. Some people have stuff to do today."

They all grin at me and then move forward before the doors shut. I have a great view as they stand in front of me, and my eyes focus on Colin's physique, which is still visible, even with his sweats on.

Standing in the cold shower—yes, cold—which I have to take since I'm so overheated from daydreaming for the few seconds it took the elevator to reach our floor. In my imagination, Colin had stripped naked in front of me before wrapping me up in his arms and pinning up against the wall of the elevator. We were a hot mess together, and I couldn't tell where his mouth stopped and mine began. After the ding of the elevator snapped my from my dirty thoughts, I suddenly realized how wet I was between the thighs and had to rush into the shower immediately in an attempt to quell my urges.

I know I've said it many times before, but I have to find a sensible guy to hook up with. Not just for sex, but for a real relationship. Someone who could totally rock my world and make me forget the dream guy down the hall.

Jeff is lying on my bed when I open the bathroom door after my shower. I toss the towel I've been drying my hair with at his head.

"What was that for?" he asks.

"The smug look on your face."

"Tell him how you feel, then."

"I don't feel anything." He grins and I stick my tongue out at him. "Okay, I have feelings. Like the feeling of drool running down my chin when I see him, or the feeling of a totally dry mouth when I think of him naked. But that's all. I need a nice guy though."

Jeff stretches, his body again only clad in his pajama bottoms, a visual delight for both males and females. "Nice guys are boring. You want me to ask him if he has feelings for you? I know Drew does."

"Don't you dare. As far as Drew is concerned, he's flighty, and not serious at all. Enough of this talk. We need to do what you're here for."

"To lie on your bed and look hot," he says with a smexy smile.

"No, to study, silly. Now get your butt up and get dressed.

His breath is hot on my neck. His tongue runs from my ear down my neck, leaving a trail of fire in its wake. A hand cradles my face as his tongue moves slowly back up my neck, and his lips meet mine. His tongue probes and gently forces my mouth open and then—oh my sweet heaven—our tongues meet, and I swear my blood starts to boil. His hand skims down my arm and then moves inward, caressing my sensitive stomach, drawing lazy circles as his lips dance with mine. His hand moves upward, and I feel my stomach plunge as he stops just beneath my right breast. I hold my breath, waiting for his touch, silently begging for the torture to stop. I want him to run his hands all over me.

His naked body pushes against me and I feel his hardness. Oh my, his hardness. I reach for the pulsating flesh as his hand finds its target, and my senses go on overload. I moan in his mouth and his kiss intensifies, filled with a passion I have only dreamed of.

"What the hell are you doing in that bed? Are you in pain?"

A voice pierces the haze, making me feel as if I've been doused with freezing cold water. It was a dream, just a dream. I'm all hot and bothered and drenched in sweat and filled with frustration.

"Cat got your tongue?" Jeff asks. "I swear, you wake me up from an awesome dream where I'm eating a piece of the best cheesecake I've ever had, only to hear you moaning. Menstrual cramps?"

"Something like that. Go back to sleep."

I jump out of bed and close the bathroom door, resting my head on the cool wood. The dream was so real. I can still feel his hand on my breast and his tongue caressing mine. I move from the door and turn on the shower. I feel like a horny teenage boy.

Twelve

"Dora? Dora?"

Jeff's chipper voice snaps me out of my daydream. Not really a daydream, more of a recap of my night dream.

"It's time to go to our institute of higher learning, and you don't want to be late for your art final."

"Don't remind me," I moan.

I thought art would be a safe class to take. I draw pretty well and I love the teacher, but he can be a little out there at times. Last week we did pottery. Not ordinary pottery, but abstract. Easy, right? No, it had to have depth. So I made a deep pot. Not what the teacher wanted though, and I ended up with a C. So my final, which is half my grade, needs to be outstanding. I wish I knew what he had planned, but when asked, all he did was smile. Darn professor.

A ringtone from my phone heralds a call from my all-knowing mom. She must have heard me think that cuss word last night, or should I say early this morning?

"Hi, Mom. I can't talk long. I'm off to take my art final."

"Are you sick, Dora? I sensed last night you were feverish. Darn Henry wouldn't tell me why. I hate this no-family clause."

"No, Mom, I'm fine. Everything's fine. You have nothing to worry about. How's Dad?" I ask, changing the subject.

"Don't change the subject. Something is brewing and I know I'm right. Tell me if I'm interfering, okay?"

"Mom, you're interfering."

"I only care about you and want what's best for you. Maybe I need a trip to the city," she rambles. As usual, she hasn't heard me. "I'm so stressed right now. Your grandma is reading that new adult book, something about graphic sex. I've heard it's not for the faint of heart. Of course, she's read racy stuff before, but you know she'll talk about it at Sunday dinner, even though I've told her it wouldn't be appropriate."

Yeah, that's an understatement. Grandmother would be all high and mighty and call her—well, I don't know what she'd call her—but it wouldn't be nice.

"I'll come, and set out a place for Jeff. He's staying with me so we can study for finals. We won't be able to stay long though."

"Oh, Dora. Thanks, sweetie. I don't know what I would do without you. Henry says to tell Liam to go for it, whatever that means, and you need to help Drew. Henry has never been this vague before. Maybe it's on purpose. Have you fallen for them? Maybe that's it."

I really don't think she's talking to me, but I'm used to that. "No, Mom, I haven't fallen for anyone. Besides, I'm not really into threesomes, but now that you brought it up, I might rethink the whole idea."

"What did you say? Your dad's calling on the other line and I don't know how to put this new smartphone on hold. I need a manual for dummies. Anyway, see you and Jeff on Sunday. Love you."

I breathe a sigh of relief. Thank God. The last thing I need right now is my mom getting my lust signals. Because that's what it is. Just a case of a plain girl lusting after a totally hot guy. I have to stop thinking about him or I'll need another shower and I don't have time.

Yikes, Jeff has already left. I grab my bag and keys and hightail it out the door.

I'm so late—thanks, Mom—my heart is pounding in my chest as I run through the empty corridors. I pull open the door to the art room and…

What the fuck?

Yes, I said it. Sitting on a stool at the front of the classroom is Drew STARK NAKED. Yep, everything is hanging out, or should I say *down*? He turns and sees me standing in the doorway and grins.

"Hey, Dora. Overslept, did ya?" Drew's voice sounds so loud, and of course everyone turns to look at me.

"Dora, come on in and take a seat. I was just telling the class that we have been blessed with a live male model to draw for your final exam. You can imagine my shock when he called me up and offered his services for free. Drew makes a great deal of money modeling, and yet he's gracing our school to further the study of art. Let's give Drew a hand, everyone, shall we?"

Mortified, and, yes, blushing from my toes to the top of my head, I hurry to my seat, avoiding the looks from my fellow classmates. I put up my sketchpad to block my view of a grinning Drew and the questioning eyes in front of me.

"Sweet Mother of the Universe," Karen, a New Ager I consider a friend, whispers to me. "You really do know the models, and you moved in with them. I'm right? Right?"

I shake my head and lean toward her. "Shush. I'll talk to you later," I say, avoiding looking to the front. Sweet unripe bananas and rotten tomatoes, what am I going to do? I can't possibly look at him, never mind draw him for two hours.

Karen smiles knowingly and picks up her charcoal. "He's staring at you. Are you sleeping with him? I'd do him in an instant. How could you have kept this from me? I heard the rumors that three famous hotties came looking for you at the beginning of school and wanted your body, but I thought it wasn't real. You definitely have a lot of explaining to do."

Maybe I can copy off of her without actually looking at Drew at all. I hear whispering all around me, but I'm trying to ignore it. I peek around my canvas and Drew waves at me, making me duck back behind my shield. Fuck—yes, I said it again—fuck, fuck, fuck! Oh, it feels so good to yell it in my mind. How am I going to draw him with his one-eyed Willy watching me?

Did I just think that? I mean his penis, of course, and it's a nice big one from what I saw while peeking around the corner of my blank canvas. He's definitely a shower.

Karen has started, and her sketch is good, like, really good. Of course she's started with the penis and is definitely doing it justice. She has a wide grin stretched across her mouth, and I wouldn't be surprised if she starts drooling soon.

"Ms. Phillips, is there a problem?" my professor asks over my shoulder, making my head swivel. I'm utterly embarrassed I've been caught staring at Drew's penis on Karen's canvas.

"Um no," I mumble and pick up my charcoal from the little shelf on the easel in front of me.

Damn Drew and his grinning penis. I peek again and see Drew has a serious face on and is all business. Maybe without his mischievous grin this might actually be doable.

Time flies, and I'm drawing like a madwoman wanting this torture to end. It's not as doable as I thought, because Drew has a habit of turning his head and winking at me from time to time.

"Hey, Dora, you better hurry. Not much time left to draw that piece you're still missing." Karen giggles as she points to the spot where Drew's penis should be hanging. I quickly fix the problem and will probably get a bad grade for drawing a loincloth over that area. But as much as I've tried, I can't do it.

"Time's up. Let's give Drew a hand for coming in and posing for us." Everyone claps vigorously, even the guys, which surprises me as I'm sure more than half are not as well-endowed as him. "Leave your canvases on your easels. Everyone, I hope you enjoy your holidays."

I grab my messenger bag and quickly move toward the exit, glad that the professor has Drew's attention. The last thing I need is to have Drew walk out with me through the campus. I'm humiliated enough by all the stares and whispers I'm already getting. Thank goodness I have only a few more days of exams, and then maybe by January everyone will have forgotten about this.

Yeah right, and hell will freeze over. I see Jeff ahead and quickly run up and slide my arm around his.

"Hey, what's up?" he says as I drag him toward our next class."

"Just keep moving and I'll explain later." He moves faster to keep up with me, which is a first since my short legs are usually trying to keep up with his long ones.

Have I told you math is not my best subject, and Jeff has done all he can to help me? I only hope all his hard work will pay off. Nobody looks happy as we file into Calculus, and when we see the thick test packet sitting on our desks, we let out a groan. Our professor is a sadist. Jeff squeezes my hand reassuringly and moves to the other side of the room to take his seat. I know you're wondering why we don't sit together. Mr. Cramer feels that seat assignment is a necessity in college. He should teach high school. We're adults, aren't we?

444

"So, how do you think you did?" Jeff asks when we're back out in the stark courtyard. The temperature has dropped at least twenty degrees since we started the test. I shiver, not from the cold but from what my grade will probably be.

"I don't know. I had problems with the second half, but I think I aced the first. I can't believe that SOB gave us a freaking booklet to finish in under an hour, not to mention we still have to take the second part of the final that he says most of our grade will be based on. Who has their students take a two-part final … in math? Sadist much?"

"I'm sure you did great. Let's go get some lunch. My treat." Jeff puts his arm around me and pulls me close, kissing the top of my head. I love Jeff, and even if I bombed the test, it won't be because of his tutoring.

444

"Is he as hot as what I imagine?" Jeff's grin is contagious as we wait for our lunch.

"I swear he has a twelve pack, and there isn't an ounce of fat on that body. It's sickening. Nobody should be that perfect."

"Twelve pack, huh? So let's get down to the real grit of the subject: his dick. Well?"

"Nothing special," I say with a straight face, and I love Jeff's shocked expression.

"No way. The boy has to be hung. I would bet my daddy's fortune on that," Jeff argues.

"I've seen worms bigger." I love that he's torn between believing me and not.

"Worms? Are you guys going fishing?" A familiar voice makes me freeze, hoping he hasn't heard more.

"Hey, Drew," Jeff says. "Take a seat. I was just reminiscing about the last time I went fishing. Dora just told me she hates worms. Despises them, in fact. It's a girl thing."

I kick Jeff under the table, hoping he won't say more. Drew moves in next to me in our booth, his thigh nestled next to mine.

“So, Dora told me about your little volunteer session this morning.” Jeff smiles. “She thoroughly enjoyed having a live model to draw instead of that boring old bowl of fruit.”

I grit my teeth, wanting so badly to smack him upside his goofy grinning head.

“Yeah, it was really fun. When I approached Tim with the idea, he was so excited. I guess this is the first time he’s had a real model come to his class, especially with all the university’s budget cuts.” While gesturing as he talks, Drew brushes his arm up against mine which cause him to grin at me.

So, it probably seems odd that I’m not reacting to him in a positive way. Mostly it’s because I know he’s not really into me, but I also don’t get those funny feelings in my stomach that I get around Colin.

“What’s it like, being naked in front of a class of artists?” Jeff’s question makes me want strangle him. Yes, my blushing mechanism is going full blast, and I quickly grab my cold drink, hoping it helps some.

“It’s something I’m used to, I guess. If you’re shy about nudity in the modeling biz, you don’t last too long. We constantly change in front of a crowd of photographers, makeup artists, directors, agents, and other models. So, modesty is quickly forgotten."

That wouldn't work for me. I've been naked in front of a select few, but a crowd? No way.

"Dora, how would you feel being naked in front of a group?" Jeff asks, raising one eyebrow, looking all innocent.

"I wouldn't do it. I'm not a prude, but I like my privacy," I say in a no-nonsense voice, with thoughts of how I will strangle him running through my mind.

"I wouldn't want you naked in front of a group, Dora." Drew nudges my arm, which makes me look up at him. I can tell he's serious. "There'd be broken jaws and black eyes, and several guys would end up hospitalized."

"Well, we won't have to worry about that, now will we?" Why would he be so upset with me naked in front of a group? "Where's that waitress? I'm starving," I say, changing the subject as the vision of Drew sitting naked in class revisits my mind.

Thirteen

Christmas shopping should only be done online.

There, I said it. Whoever doesn't like that statement can, well, deal with it. Julie and I are stuck in department store hell checkout lines with a thousand other grumpy people while cheery Christmas music continuously plays from hidden speakers.

Yes, I'm peeved. I haven't seen Colin for days, and tomorrow is the dreaded 'graphic sex of Sunday' dinner. It was supposed to happen last Sunday, but the flu bug hit my family, so I was given a reprieve. No, I'm not happy they had the flu, but I'm hoping and praying that Grandma Alice will have forgotten about the sex book she apparently raved about to all of her friends at bingo.

"Fuck, Dora," Julie gripes. "This line is fucking taking forever. My feet hurt and I'm thirsty."

I know she doesn't say the F word at work, so why can't she restrain herself out in public? The F word and Christmas music just don't mesh.

"Calm down, Jules. At least we're not at the back of the line. In fact, I can't even see the back of the line."

"Yeah, that really helps. Oh, look … they've opened another register. Hey, what the fuck? That lady was behind us and now she's being waited on."

I cover Jules' mouth, as any minute now she'll start a riot, and I don't want to be on the Channel Six news at eleven. Jules nips at one of my fingers and I gently tap her on the head. The people behind us are getting upset. Part of me wants to dump the stuff we have, but I persevere and we finally escape without inciting a riot.

Shivering, we enter the warm confines of the loft's lobby. Brad is sitting at his post, his hands wrapped around a huge mug of something that is steaming.

"Ooooooh, that looks yummy," Julie stutters with quivering lips.

"Would you like a cup? It's a special hot chocolate blend. I have a pot of it in the back." His grin is so adorable.

"We'll love you forever, won't we, Dora?" Julie replies.

Brad jumps off his stool and enters a door behind him. Seconds later, he's back with two mugs.

"You're such a lifesaver. Not only did we fight the cold today, we also did our dreaded holiday shopping. You're awesome." Julie takes a sip and her eyes close. "Mmmmmm, this is the best."

I take a drink of mine and have to agree—it's a chocolate orgasmic experience in my mouth. The ding of the elevator has all of us turning at the same time. My knees go weak as I see Colin standing there with Liam. Colin grins and Liam is, well, it looks kinda like smiling.

"Tis the season," Colin says.

"Yep. Long lines and evil people, but Brad has fucking saved the day." Oh, so full of Christmas cheer is Julie.

Liam and Colin look at my face and start laughing.

"You guys, stop that. It's not funny. You try keeping Ms. Potty Mouth under control. I'll gladly give you the job." I glare at them as they continue to laugh. Brad has his hand over his mouth. I'm sure he's laughing too.

"My mouth is not a toilet. They're only words, after all." Julie pretends she's in a huff, but she loves the attention. "Where are you two hot bods off to?" she continues, and I groan as the two "hot bods" stop laughing, smile, and stand up a little straighter.

With that, I take off toward the stairs, ignoring the foursome. What has me so mad? Julie is just being Julie, after all, and … I don't know. I haven't been this confused in my life.

I reach the fourth floor, realizing through rambling thoughts that I'm not out of breath. Pulling open the exit door, I run into a hard object—a really hard object. Raising my eyes, I meet Drew's smiling ones.

"Whoa, Dora, where's the fire?" His dimple deepens as his gorgeous grin widens.

"No fire. I felt like climbing the stairs."

"Lucky stairs," he replies, staring at my lips as if he wants to devour them.

What the hell? Where did that come from?

Bad boy. Remember, notches on bedposts and all that? I'm so not going to be the millionth and one girl on his list.

"Ha ha, very funny," I say.

"Ah, Dora, you wound me. Me, who adores you."

Oh, brother. Time to run—I mean, *walk*—away right now.

"Love to stand here and chat, Drew, but I think your cohorts are downstairs waiting for you, and I have presents to wrap," I say, lifting my packages to show him proof.

"I don't get it. I feel you're always trying to get rid of me, and it hurts my heart."

Gently pushing him away with my packages, I start off down the hall. "I'm so sure, Drew," I reply without even turning to look at him, instead banging on my door. I'm relieved when Jeff immediately opens it.

"Hey, Dora, what did this door ever do to you? Oh, hey, Drew," he says, looking down the hall as I push past him. "Rude much?" Jeff shuts the door and I can feel him staring at me.

I fling the packages on my bed before storming over to the refrigerator. "Why do you always side with them?" Anger fills my voice.

"Hey, I was just being neighborly. You really need to get laid, and I think I found you someone. You've been hard to live with lately, so I set you up on a blind date tonight. Whether you like it or not."

"You did? Without asking me first?"

"You tell me all the time to find someone for you, and I've done it. Don't make me regret this."

"You did? Oh, Jeff, I'm so sorry. I so love you!" He grins as I fling my arms around him and hug him tightly.

"Now go get ready. The little black number will do. In fact, if you let go of me, I'll even get your clothes ready for you."

444

I decide to take a bath, taking care to shave my legs, and then after a long soak, jump into the shower to rinse off. A date finally, one that Jeff approves of. What can go wrong? I mean, everything will be good. I feel it.

Jeff is missing from the room when I exit the bathroom, but my dress and shoes are laid out for me. I hear muffled voices coming from the door leading to the dining room of the loft. Creeping to the door, I turn the lock, as I don't want any unwanted company finding me in a towel. I quickly dress, apply minimal makeup, slip into my three-inch heels, and wait for Jeff to knock on the door to be let back in. Minutes pass and the voices continue. Sighing, I grab my clutch, move to the door, and open it to see my three roomies and Jeff lounging on the three couches.

"Beautiful," Jeff says with a shit-eating grin.

"Agreed," Colin and Drew reply almost in unison. Liam just nods his head.

"Your date is coming up the elevator. Brad just buzzed." Jeff grins and walks me to the door so I can't see Colin's reaction.

Jeff opens the door and the elevator dings at the same time. It opens and I see Ronald Caudwell, a math class buddy of ours, standing there with a bunch of flowers in his hand. He looks nervous, his smile a little wobbly when he sees Jeff and me. Jeff taps me on the shoulder and he magically has my coat in his hand. He helps me into it as Ron walks slowly toward us. I watch his eyes widen as he glances at my dress. He swallows hard. It takes a second for me to realize he's never seen me in anything but sweats, jeans, T-shirts, and shorts.

"Hi, Dora. Hope you're not disappointed," he says quietly.

"Disappointed? Definitely not," I reply with a wide smile.

I like Ron. His hair is a rich, chestnut brown, neither short nor long. He's just a few inches taller than me, even with my heels on. He has two adorable dimples that appear in each cheek when he smiles. He has a good build and definitely cleans up nicely. He hands me the flowers and I wonder where he found such beautiful ones this time of year.

"You look amazing, Dora." His voice interrupts my brain's musings.

"I was just thinking the same about you, Ron."

"Well, kids, you have fun. Don't keep her out too late, Ron." Jeff sounds like a stern father. I elbow him gently in the side as I take Ron's hand and lead him to the elevator.

"Oh … Jeff, be a dear and put these in water for me, and don't forget to put a penny in the bottom of the vase." I walk back and hand them to a grinning Jeff. "Also, don't wait up," I say before returning to Ron, who's holding the elevator door for me.

444

Ron's nervous, but his silence is killing me. We've been in the car for ten minutes and he hasn't said a word. Great.

"So where are we going?' I ask, trying to sound casual.

"A restaurant Jeff told me you love." He clears his throat. "I hope that's okay."

He keeps his eyes on the road, but he swallows hard, waiting for my answer. He's different in class. In fact, he loves telling jokes and making people laugh, so why is he so uptight right now?

"Has to be Papa's then, because that's my favorite."

"Yeah, that's it. We should be there soon," he replies woodenly.

Really? Like I don't know.

I want to ask him if something's wrong, but I don't think he'll tell me the truth. The warm bright lights of Papa's penetrate my deep thought, and luckily, we snag a parking spot a few feet from the front door.

The place is packed, full of happy, laughing people. Papa is playing host. His eyes widen and he belts out, "Dora, my beautiful, redheaded angel. My worlda has just become brighter." He holds out his arms and I move in for the hug. He smells of pizza sauce and Old Spice. "And who is this younga man?" he asks, staring hard at Ron, who looks like he wants to leave.

"Papa, this is my friend, Ron."

As the words leave my lips, I realize they're true. He is, and will stay, just a friend. There's no chemistry. I feel a little depressed.

"Aww. He looksa like a nice young man. I havea your table ready for you."

He leads us to the back, and Mama waves and blows a kiss to us from across the room. Several of the waiters say hello as we pass by. It's a big table that Papa takes us to, and I wonder why there are so many seats. Before I can mention it, I hear a commotion behind us. I inwardly groan as I realize we'll be joined by others. Not just any others, but my roomies and one of my so-called best friends, a grinning Jeff.

"Dora, what are you doing here?" Jeff asks, all innocent.

"Surprised? I think not. You told Ron this is my favorite place."

"I mentioned it, but he never said he was going to bring you here. Hey, Papa, these two are on a date, and it wouldn't be right to join them."

"Ah, Jeffrey, we are fulla. No more tables." Papa looks upset and I feel guilty.

"It's okay, they can join us. Right, Ron?"

Ron nods his answer and everyone grabs a seat. At least the models look to be chagrined. Not Jeff though, he still has the smug grin on his face.

"We had no idea you were going to be here. Honest." Colin's English accent sends a warm sensation down my spine. I don't look up from my menu. My tongue is a little too tied at the moment.

Jeff is sitting to my left, and I reach under the table and pinch his thigh as hard as I can, wondering what he's up to.

"Oww." He slightly jumps and then turns to me and glares.

"You deserve it," I whisper, leaning over and blocking the others' view with my menu.

"Wait until you get home. That's going to leave a bruise," he replies through clenched teeth.

"Okay, who's ready to order?" Sal, a part-time waiter and a new dad, pulls my attention away from Jeff.

After everyone orders, the mood at the table begins to resemble a funeral service. No one is talking and everyone is avoiding everyone's eyes. The only thing we're missing is bouts of crying. What a fun date. If I'm being honest, I'm kind of glad Ron and I aren't here alone. The friend thing is really beginning to sink in. I guess it's time to get this funeral—I mean *party*—started.

"So guys, any photo shoots coming up soon?" I ask and watch as all eyes zoom in on mine. I swear I hear sighs of relief from the whole table.

"No, it's pretty quiet this time of year. I have one Christmas gig on Monday, but then it's free time until January," Drew replies.

Mr. Aussie speaks up next. "I'm traveling home in two weeks where it's, like, ninety degrees. So, I booked a few shoots while I'm there."

"A couple of shoots in freezing cold London. What was I thinking?" Colin's voice makes me want to go with him just to keep him warm.

Stop it, Dora. Get a grip. Out of your league.

"Shoots?" Ron asks.

"Oh, Ron, I'm sorry. How rude of me. These are my roommates." I make the introductions and watch as poor Ron seems to sink into his chair. He's intimidated and I need to correct the situation. "Surely you've heard how I ended up with these nerds." I watch three sets of eyebrows shoot up, but I ignore them. "Liam has a superstition that the number four is lucky for him. Their old roommate left and they were so desperate they bullied me to move in."

"I had heard a rumor around campus about this, but thought it was just gossip."

The food arrives, saving me from having to talk anymore. Hopefully a few glasses of wine will relax Ron. My stomach growls and laughter erupts, breaking the tension, thank heavens. I would have been embarrassed, but for once I'm glad my stomach loves to talk.

After a couple of glasses of wine myself, I'm feeling like this evening has been salvaged. Ron seems like he's finally enjoying himself, and my roomies have made him feel like an old friend. They really are a cool bunch of guys. Pushy, yes, but they have hearts. Even Jeff is having fun, although that will end quickly when I ream him for his antics when we get home.

Papa and Mama stop by our table whenever they can. All in all, it's a great evening. Sal has been amazing, refilling empty glasses and making sure we're kept satisfied. I catch Ron looking at his watch. I check mine and see that it's almost one in the morning. I grab Sal and ask for our checks.

"Checks are taken care of," he replies and I shake my head.

"Who?"

Sal points across the table to Drew, who smiles at us. What a beautiful—I mean, handsome—smile.

Okay, so it's a freaking *hot* smile.

"It's the least I could do after crashing your date."

I watch his luscious lips as he talks, wondering what they would feel like against mine. *Damn, Dora, time to go home.*

"Hey, Ron, you live close by, right? Why don't we take Dora home? I know you have that thing in the morning," Jeff casually says.

"Well …" Ron starts, and then everyone reassures him that they'd be happy to take me home.

"Is that okay, Dora? You won't be upset?" Ron looks at me anxiously.

"No, Ron, it's fine. After all, they know where I live." I smile and then kick Jeff's leg, which goes unnoticed since it's hidden by the red-and-white checkered tablecloth. He grimaces, glaring in my direction. I stand and pull Ron up with me.

"I'll walk him to his car and meet up with you guys in a bit." I don't wait for an answer as we maneuver through the still-crowded restaurant.

"I had a really good time, Dora. Your roommates seem cool. Sorry I'm not taking you home."

"No worries, Ron." I kiss his cheek and then watch as he gets into his car.

Well, that went well. So happy there wasn't too much awkwardness. I'm also glad he didn't ask me out again since I hate letting people down.

I walk back into the warm restaurant and find our hosts and kiss them goodbye. My escorts wait patiently for me by the front door. I also kiss Sal on the cheek on my way over to meet up with Jeff and my roommates. Yes, I'm a little unsteady. I lost track of how many glasses of delicious wine I had. I don't say a word as they move aside. Jeff pushes open the door letting in the cold, frigid air. I don't remember it being cold when I said goodbye to Ron. The car is silent on the way home. I wish I could read minds.

This time, I stay awake until we reach the loft. Jeff takes his key and puts it onto the lock of my private entrance. I wave to the three as they go through the main entrance.

I hit the bed to stop the room from spinning and proceed to pass out.

I swear, that will be the last time I ever drink. Alcohol will never touch these lips again. My head feels like it's ready to explode, and my mouth feels like it's full of cotton, wool, or enough sand to fill the Sahara Desert. I'm so thirsty, but no water for me. That's not what I need. I spy a hand holding a glass with red liquid in it, and I know it's Jeff's special "you drank too much wine last night" drink concoction.

"Here, Ms. Lush."

I take the glass, giving him my evil, stink eye.

"How come you can drink as much as I do, but then you're fine the next day?"

"Good genes," The jackass says. Wait, that's not his name. It's already taken by the other jackass, my ex.

"I feel awful. I'm so glad I don't have to work today." I gulp down about half of the mysterious creation, and to be honest, it doesn't taste half as bad as it looks.

"Yep, but we are expected at your parents today, remember? It's Sunday."

"Did you have to remind me? Call them and tell them I'm sick." I end my sentence with a moan and put my pillow over my head.

"Nope. I'll tell your mom the truth. That her sweet little daughter has a vino hangover."

"You're so evil sometimes, Jeff, you know that? Oh, and what was with that stunt you pulled last night? Bringing everyone to Papa's?"

I feel him sit on the bed. "Well, it's like this: I like your roommates. And in my opinion, either Drew or Colin would be good enough for you."

He's smiling, I can hear it in his voice.

"So you set me up on a date just to sabotage it. Great, that makes sense." I open one eye and glare at him. Yep, he's smiling.

"No, Ron was an experiment. Yes, he's nice looking, but boring, and you need excitement in your life. Shake it up a little."

Now would be the time to tell him he's right, but I'm not going to give him the satisfaction. No, not going to happen.

"Now, it's time for little Dora to get up and get ready. We have a fun day ahead of us."

"Where did you ever get the impression I need more excitement? Spending time with my fam is plenty." I groan as I sit up, putting my feet in the plush carpet.

"See, that wasn't so hard. Now march your cute little butt into the shower, and I'll get some decent clothes for our outing."

I carefully close the bathroom door. I want to slam it, but I don't think my head could take the agony it will produce. Lukewarm water streams over my head and down my body, making me feel a little better. Minutes later, with my body wrapped up in a towel, I open the door and see Jeff lounging on the bed he apparently just made. Next to him are the clothes he picked out for me. Frankly, I could care less if they match. In fact, the bed looks so inviting I'm tempted to push him off and steal under the covers. But the determined look on my torturer's face makes me reach for my clothes and start to get dress.

"For the holy socks of mother earth, please turn down that screeching." The pounding music from Jeff's elaborate speaker setup in his car doesn't make me feel any better.

"Hey, you like this group. Don't be a grouch. You know I like listening to music when I drive."

Sliding down into the plush leather seat, I pull my sunglasses out of my purse to shield my eyes from the unforgiving onslaught from the sun, and try to relax.

What feels like only seconds later, I hear Jeff's joyful voice say, "We're here," and it pulls me out of my semi-sleep state.

"Just leave me in the car and—"

Before I can finish, he's out of the car, pulling open my door, and I'm standing on my parents' driveway. He tucks my hand in the crook of his arm, and I'm half walking, half being pulled to the front door.

Jeff opens the door and yells, "We're here," which shoots pain through my head like an electric shock. Seriously, no more wine for me, ever.

"Sweetie, you don't look too well," my mom says, always being the observant one. "You should have called and told us."

Yeah, and if I had, she would have driven into the city. She'd probably run over several people doing so and get a ticket for some reason just to see what was plaguing her baby girl.

"I'm fine, Mom, really." I wait for it, and yes, she puts her hand to my forehead and frowns.

"Not really warm, but maybe I should have your dad get the thermometer."

"Really, Mom, I'm fine."

"She's hung over," my awesome grandma says from behind her daughter.

"What? Are you?" My mom looks at me like I'm two and not twenty-two.

"Okay, so we went to Papa's last night and I may have had a glass too much," I admit, because I know I'm busted and it's time to own up.

"See, I knew I was right," Grandma says smugly, her arms crossed. I hate when she's right.

"When was anybody going to let me know Dora and Jeff arrived?" The regal voice of Grandmother makes me want to crawl into my bed in my old room. I will get the regal glare when she finds out about my night of drunkenness, and receive the lecture that if I had attended finishing school, this wouldn't have happened.

Yeah, right.

“They just arrived, Mother,” my dad speaks up, and I realize I didn’t even know he was here.

“I should have been informed. Hello, Dora and Jeffrey,” she says, reaching over and giving us air kisses on our cheeks.

“Time to eat.” My mom breaks up the awkward moment and we file like good little boys and girls into the dining room.

Minutes later, we’re joined by Taylor and Bridget, the latter looking disappointed by the absence of certain trio.

“Sorry, Bridg, the guys aren’t coming.”

“Oh nuts,” she quips as she plops down in her seat.

Thank goodness dinner is a quiet affair, as everyone seems preoccupied. I eat a little, but mainly just end up pushing my food around the plate since I still feel a little nauseous. Jeff’s thigh nudges mine every once in a while, and I completely ignore him. Yep, I’m still annoyed.

“We need a head count for Christmas Day,” Mom announces after she serves up a chocolate mousse pie for desert, which is my favorite, but not right now. No worries, though. I know I’ll be going home with a doggie bag.

“Can I be excused?” Bridget and Taylor chorus.

My mom nods her head, and they scramble to leave the room to escape the adults. Damn, I feel so old. I want to scramble off too.

"For Christmas it should be the eight of us, and Jeffrey, will you be joining us this year?" Grandmother asks in her proper tone.

"I would love to, if it's okay. My dad and mom are off to visit my sister in New Zealand to see the new baby." Jeffrey's family is spread out all over the world, but he rarely travels. He is always welcome at our family functions.

"Well, that makes nine so far then." My mom looks at me. "How about your roommates, Dora?"

"I don't think they'll be here for the holidays."

"It would be nice if you would ask them," my Grandmother states.

"Okay. Julie and Kevin will be here for most of the day, so I guess that makes eleven."

"Good, then we'll open gifts during the day." My mom is the greatest gift giver. She always buys stuff no one would re-gift, hide in a closet, or re-sell online. Each gift is thoughtfully bought and something we need or want.

I so want to leave now. My head is pounding again, and I've lost track of the conversation. I wonder what Colin is doing? He's probably spending the afternoon with some hot, long-legged beauty who completely complements him. I need to put him out of my mind.

"I don't think that's acceptable for a Christmas table." My Grandmother's stern voice penetrates my musings.

"There's that stick again. You need to lighten up and enjoy life."

Yep, that's Grandma. I must be missing a fight.

"I've never heard of a 'turducken,' and I have no desire to see it on the table. It sounds hideous," Grandmother fires back.

Turducken, what the heck is that?

Grandma shakes a finger at her adversary. "It's delicious, and I say we put it to a vote. I'm tired of roast beef every year."

I look around and notice that my mom, dad and granddad have fled the room. Only Jeff and I are left with the two warriors. This could get very bloody, and I don't want to get in the middle. I grab Jeff's hand and we slowly make our way out of the room and into the kitchen, where I know the rest are hiding. Neither woman notices us leaving as they do the famous Bannister-Phillips stare down.

The three previous escapees are standing in the kitchen. My mom is drinking something amber in a glass. My dad is patting my granddad on the back, probably because he knows if Grandma loses, it won't be a happy place when they get home.

"I say we're going to have a turducken, and if you don't like it, well, then just stay home and eat your roast beef."

"Next you'll want us to eat alligator or something equally bizarre." Grandmother's voice is now an octave higher.

"I've heard it tastes just like chicken!"

I watch Granddad grab Mom's glass and take a big gulp. It causes him to cough violently while my dad thumps his back. Oh, lord … just what my headache needs.

"I'm going in," my mom pipes up. She stands, taking another long drink from the glass.

Dad shakes his head. "Honey, do you think that's wise?"

"Wise or not, I'm so tired of this bullshit. Yes, I said it. *Bullshit.* We deal with this almost every Sunday and somebody has to take the bull by the balls and stop them."

Holy fried fish with bones removed, my mom is serious. She pulls her head up and her shoulders back before slowly leaving the room. We cowards follow her. Did she just say take the bull by the balls?

"I love your family. We really should videotape this. Just think of all the millions of hits we would get online." Jeff's voice is full of laughter. I elbow him in the stomach and go through the doorway that my mom went through.

"You two. Cease and desist." Her voice is loud, louder than I've heard in a long time. In fact, the last time it was this loud was when—oh, look … they're listening to her.

"I'm tired of you two always at odds with each other. It happens every Sunday. We're going to solve this. We'll have turducken and roast beef and that's that. Not another word."

Mom marches out of the room and up the stairs, with everyone—even Taylor and Bridget from over the balcony—watching her.

"See what you did?" Grandma whispers across the table.

"It wasn't my fault. You're the one who started this whole mess."

"I can hear you both from up here. Not another word," Mom shouts from the top of the stairs and then she disappears as we hear a door slam shut.

"Hope you're both proud of yourselves," Granddad says. "I'm sick of this little feud you two have too, and I think if you can't play nice, both of you should stay home. Dora, make sure your grandma gets home safely. I'm leaving." He kisses my cheek and then grabs his coat from the hallway closet before exiting the house.

Wow. Both grandmothers are speechless, as are all of us. Granddad has never spoken like that—ever. Good for you, Granddad.

After going upstairs and giving Mom a kiss goodbye and assuring her that everything was fine downstairs and nobody hated her, Jeff and I say bye to my dad and the speechless grand matriarchs before heading out ourselves.

No, we didn't forget Grandma. Shockingly, Grandmother said she would take her home. Things in this house never fail to surprise me.

Fifteen

"It's freezing. I can't feel my feet," I moan as we enter the warm, cozy lobby of my building.

"They're still there. I can see them."

"Well, I can't feel them. I wonder where Brad is. I haven't seen him since last week."

The lobby is dimly lit and quiet.

"Want me to knock on his door and see if he's okay?" Jeff nudges me with his elbow as he presses the elevator button.

"No, I don't want to be one of those nosey people. I just wonder, is all." The doors open, and Jeff gives me a gentle push inside the elevator.

The hallway upstairs is quiet too. I bypass the main door and put my key into my private entrance. I'm really not up to seeing the gorgeous trio when I know I look like hell frozen over. How do I know this? The bathroom mirror in my parents' house showed me. I feel as bad as I look and start stripping off my clothes as I make my way to the bathroom, desperately needing a hot bath.

"Hey, are you going to pick up your mess?" Jeff asks as he locks the door behind him.

"No, I thought you could do it for me," I say before I shut the door behind me, missing what I know would be a withering look. I shiver while standing in my underwear waiting for the massive tub to fill. A delicious smell fills the air as I pour in my favorite lavender-scented bubble bath. I pull my hair up into a half ponytail and toss my underwear across the room. I slide down into the soothing warmth. My bones seem to melt as the water swirls around me. It's a whirlpool bath, with the jets sending pulsating water all over my achy parts.

The bathroom door opens, as do my eyes in surprise. I'm temporarily shocked at the sight of Colin standing in the doorframe, dressed only in his boxers. He's as perfect as his images on the billboards and magazines—definitely no airbrushing there. His eyes are focused on mine, and I feel my body reacting from the top of my head to the bottom of my toes. I have never felt this aroused.

His eyes move downward and I notice my hardened nipples are peeking through the bubbles. In fact, my whole body is pretty much exposed as my bubble coverage has dissipated. I pull my eyes up and watch as he licks his lips and runs his right hand through his silky hair. The water has cooled, but my body temp has risen by a hundred degrees. He moves closer, and I see he his boxers are becoming tighter by the second as his arousal pushes to escape. He slowly puts his hands to his waist and in one move, his penis is free, and lord, it's just like I remembered it when I saw it in art class.

Wait.

I look up again to his face, and it's not Colin. It's Drew standing there with his penis pointing at me. How the fuc…

"Have you drowned in there?"

Jeff's voice shocks me to my senses. I realize I fell asleep and it was all a dream. More like a nightmare, with Colin turning into Drew.

I really need to get a life, I think as I look down and see my nipples still standing at attention. I pull the plug and watch the water swirl out of the tub. Shivering, I grab an oversized towel and wrap my totally aroused body, replaying my dream.

Drew? Who in their right mind would dream about Mr. Playboy? Okay, so maybe the majority of women in the world.

When I leave the bathroom, I see Jeff spread out on the recliner adjacent to my bed. "Still feeling like shit?" he inquires.

"No more wine for me. If you see me going for a glass, remind me of this horrible day."

"Okay, but last time you drank wine you said the same thing. I don't think it'll work. Now, to change the subject, are you up for some studying?" He pulls out our math book and raises an eyebrow at me.

"Like I have a choice. I need to nail this exam. Otherwise, I'll be a senior forever."

444

"Sounds like your roomies are home." Jeff stretches and rubs his eyes.

We hear laughing from the next room, male and female voices. Of course women would be included. Two of them are hot-blooded males, and the other one pretends to be. I really need to talk to Liam alone. My mom pulled me aside earlier this afternoon to reiterate Henry's requests to help Liam and Drew. I really don't know what I need to help Drew with. Yeah, he has a screwed up family, mom ran off, dad's been married several times, but who doesn't have family issues? He has all the attention anyone could want or need. Why would he need my help?

"Dora, I just turned straight, and I want to have kinky hot sex with you," Jeff's blurts out in an attempt to make me focus.

It's laughable, but I play along. "Okay, well then take off all your clothes so I can jump your bones."

Did I really just yell that? Yep, the voices have ceased. Good lord, Dora. Now they all probably think I'm about to hook up with someone in here. Well, that could work. If they think I'm involved with someone, maybe they'll leave me alone and let me return to my normal—okay, so semi-normal—life.

"What the…?"

I quickly place my hand over Jeff's mouth. "Play along," I whisper. Then, in a louder voice, I say, "Ted, what is that in your pants? I think it wants to come out and say hello. Oh, sweet caramel apple on a stick, your stick is more like a log. It needs to be freed. See, it's taunting me." I put my finger to my lips and nod my head at the door. Jeff looks at me, confused, then it's like a light bulb comes on and he gives me a shit-eating grin.

"Yeah, babe, it's all for you." I almost giggle at his fake deep voice.

"Wow, it's really hard. Oh, you want to put it where?"

I motion for Jeff to move with me to the door. We hear nothing—nada—coming from beyond the door. I mouth *on the count of three* and motion to the door. *One, two, three*, and we both grab the handle and pull the door open. Just as I figure, three heads attached to three bodies fall flat on the carpet. They look up at our grinning faces, and at least Colin has the grace to look embarrassed. Liam and Drew pick themselves up and try to act cool.

"Like what you heard?" I ask, watching Colin avert his eyes while the other two smirk and start to laugh.

"We were looking out for you," Drew responds, shrugging his shoulders.

"Yeah, you're like a little sis to us," Liam chuckles.

"So, you weren't being nosey, huh, Colin?" Colin looks uncomfortable. It's time to let him off the hook. "It's nice to know you guys have my back, but I do like my privacy. And if I was actually hooking up with someone in here, this little spy session you all had going on wouldn't have been cool."

"Hey, it was at least better than what we had to look forward to this evening." Liam has stopped chuckling and is back to his frowny self.

I gently push them aside and look into the living room to find it's empty. "Where are the ladies we heard earlier?" I ask, turning back to look at them. Jeff is grinning with his arms crossed, leaning against the open door.

Liam looks lazily at me. "Oh, they just came up for a drink, nothing else. At least, nothing on our part. I'm sure they would've loved to spend the night, but we just weren't feeling it."

"How about cards?" Drew blurts out.

"Yeah, sounds great." Liam glances at Jeff and me. "How about you two? Want to play a friendly game of poker?"

"Poker? I don't know how to play," I reply innocently, and they all fall for it.

Ten minutes later, we're sitting at the round kitchen table and cards are being dealt. In front of me are orange-colored chips. I wanted red, but Jeff grabbed them first.

Liam has blue, Colin purple, and Drew yellow, and each of us has the same amount … for now.

"So Dora, do you understand what I've just told you?" Drew asks like he's talking to a child.

"I think so. If I mess up, don't hate me." There I go with my Miss Innocent act again.

Half an hour later, I'm winning big. In fact, they each have a small hill of chips compared to my mountain.

Drew rolls his eyes as I win another hand. "Gentlemen, we've been had."

Yes. I have a great actual poker face, and one that my dad is so proud of since he taught it to me.

"What? Are you talking about my beginner's luck?" I'm trying so hard not to smile.

"Beginner my ass," Liam quips while leaning back in his chair and sending me a playful glare.

"And I must say, it's a nice ass too," I reply, keeping my face stoic.

"Very funny, little girl. You shouldn't try to pull one over on us big boys," he replies, liking my comeback.

Jeff, Drew, and Colin sit back and watch Liam and me sparring. It's fun.

"Are you guys conceding? Are we finished with the game?" All four walking testosterone machines shake their heads, and I start dealing the next hand.

"Dora, have you asked them yet?" Jeff asks, hiding his face behind his cards.

"Asked us what?" Drew looks at me with one sexy eyebrow raised.

"My mom asked me to invite you over for Christmas, but I told her you were all going home. Right?"

"I'm going home next week," Colin says. "My mum would never forgive me if I miss this Christmas. Our whole family will be together, which due to the size, is quite incredible." His dreamy accent makes me want to drool.

"I'm off to my homeland too." Liam interrupts my musings of the mind-blowing kiss Colin and I shared at Halloween. I've wondered why he hasn't tried again, not that I would allow it. Okay, I'm lying. I'd be all over him like a fat kid on cake.

"She always zones out like she's in another realm or something. Dora?" Jeff's voice floats into my consciousness and I raise my eyes to see that I'm the center of attention.

"Sorry, thinking about my last exam in two days. I really should be studying," I lie, and Jeff just grins. It's like he's a mind reader.

"Did you hear that Drew is free for Christmas, and he'd be delighted to join us? Isn't that right, Drew?"

"I would love to spend time with your family. Mine are … well, Christmas is just another day for them. I kind of miss having family time." The look on Drew's face is heart breaking. He's usually the happy-go-lucky guy who acts like he doesn't have a care in the world.

"Well, if you get a headache, it's not my fault" I say. "My family is different, so you've been warned. I will not be held responsible for what they do, or say."

I'm relieved when a smile appears on his beautiful lips. Hey, lips can be beautiful, right? Oh, great. I've missed something else.

Concentrate, Dora.

"Drew said he'll take his chances," Jeff explains. "I think it's time for me to put little Dora to bed. Her brain needs a rest."

Everyone laughs when I stick my tongue out at him. "Little Dora can put herself to bed, thank you. But I am tired. Good night. Come on, Jeff, I'll tuck you in."

Jeff flops on my bed after changing into some comfy sleeping clothes. "Well, that was fun."

"Yeah. It was like spending the evening with ordinary guys, not Greek gods." I pull on my pajama pants and look over at him.

"I told you they're normal and they just want to fit in," he replies, causing me to roll my eyes.

"They're not normal. *Normal* is only a few hundred people might know your name, not the whole world."

"Dora, that's an overstatement. I bet there's a tribe in Africa or some poor slob in Siberia who doesn't know of them."

"Okay, so maybe a hundred haven't seen their pics, but you have to admit it's a little daunting being around them sometimes."

"Only Liam causes me to be daunted."

"Yeah, if you like the gorgeous, tall, and solemn type that won't come out of the closet."

"Your mom told you Henry says you need to help him and Drew. So maybe your job is to help him come out. I get first shot when you do, okay?" Jeff is so good at pleading.

"Maybe you're too ugly for him. You are on the homely side." I giggle as Jeff sends a pillow flying through the air and it hits the top of my head as I bend over to miss it.

"I'm not ugly. I'll have you know I could've been a model, but I didn't want people attacking me, wanting a piece of this awesomeness." He laughs as I roll my eyes again, and I move his legs so I can lie beside him.

"Okay, stud, but I don't want to be mending your heart back together if he doesn't respond like you want him to. I have to get him by himself before he goes home. It must be horrible living a lie every day. No wonder he doesn't smile much."

"Yeah, I'm a lucky one. My family didn't even blink an eye when I came out to them."

I turn my head to look at Jeff, who is staring at the ceiling. I scoot over and put my arm across his taut stomach and he places his arm around me. The last thing I remember thinking is that I hope Liam doesn't break Jeff's heart.

444

Playing cards tonight was hard for me. All I wanted to do was stare at her. She has no idea what she's doing to me. I wish I was the one she's tucking into bed. I know Jeff's gay, but I still feel the green-eyed monster raising its dark, ugly head. I wish I knew what she thought about the kiss on Halloween. If I declare my feelings for her, would she laugh in my face? Would she even believe me? I'm so tied up in knots, which is something I've never encountered before. I have to bide my time until she trusts me and sees me for who I really am.

“I’m so glad it’s over. I never want to see another math book again for as long as I’m alive.” I grab Jeff’s arm and loop mine through his. It’s freezing. Winter has come early and I’m thankful I bundled up this morning. “I think I nailed it though. Thanks, Jeff. I couldn’t have done it without you.”

“Anytime, my friend. To pay me back, you can buy me lunch.”

“Okay, I guess that’s fair.”

The ringing of my cell has me pulling off one of my gloves and pulling the phone out of my coat pocket. “Hi, Mom. Yes, it’s finally over. I think I did well. Sorry I haven’t called. We’ve been hitting the books hard. Yeah, I asked them and Drew accepted. The other two are going home. Okay, he’s right here. I will. Love you too." I quickly end the call and throw my phone back into my pocket, pulling on my glove before my fingers drop off from frostbite. "Mom sends her love, and she's so happy Drew is going to be able to make it. Now she's stressed about what to buy him."

"She has a point. What do you buy a zillionaire?" Jeff responds, pulling my hand through his arm again.

We pick up the pace and finally arrive at his car without my frozen nose falling off. The blast of hot air from the vents is almost painful for a few seconds, and then it feels wonderful. I love Jeff's little sports car. I don't know what make or model it is though. Cars aren't really my thing.

"So, where are we going for lunch?"

"Somewhere cheap. Remember, I haven't worked for a few weeks, and Christmas shopping just about wiped me out."

"Well, I guess I'll pay, because I'm not going to eat cheap when I received my Christmas money from my parents today. I went from dirt poor to—let's just say I have money now."

"Then we'll go all out for lunch." I smile at Jeff's cute smirk and settle back in the plush leather seats, letting the warm air wash over me.

"I'm stuffed. I shouldn't have had that dessert, but it was oh-so-good." I feel like a bloated pig. My three-course meal was amazingly scrumptious, and I finished it off like I hadn't eaten for months. Now I'm searching through my messenger bag looking for something to calm my tummy.

"If you're looking for antacids, I could use a few as well. I don't think the lobster is sitting very well with me at the moment."

"I thought I had them in here, but they must be in my medicine cabinet. Damn."

"We'll be home in a few minutes," Jeff says as he swerves to miss an idiot who pulls out in front of us.

"I'm glad I'm in the car with you and not my mom. She would've chewed that driver out just then, even though he wouldn't have heard her. I hate when she drives. It's a wonder she hasn't been arrested yet."

"It doesn't do any good yelling at them. It just makes your own blood pressure go up. Most terrible drivers couldn't care less."

We pull into the parking garage entrance and Jeff swipes his card across the machine's sensor. Within seconds the security gate slides to the side, allowing us to enter. There aren't any other cars on the basement parking floor, and I'm relieved. All I want to do is to go upstairs, take my tummy meds and lie down.

The lobby is warm and Brad is MIA, which allows for Jeff and me to enter the elevator unseen. Okay, so there are security cameras all over the hallways, but no human has seen us, unless someone is looking at the monitors.

"Jeff, do you know where the monitors are that those cameras feed into?"

"Never thought about it. Maybe they're in that locked room behind the front desk?"

"I just realized how creepy it is being videotaped and not knowing who's watching." I shiver as the elevator doors close and we start to ascend.

"It's not like there are cameras everywhere, Dora. Just in the stairwells, hallways, and lobby. Or maybe I'm mistaken and there's one in your bathroom."

I hit him on the shoulder and he laughs. I storm out of the elevator as soon as the doors open.

"You're a butt, you know that? Now I'm going to be paranoid about going to the bathroom and showering now, thanks." I unlock my door and try to shut it before he comes in.

"Dora, I'm only kidding. Look, I'll show you there's no camera in the bathroom, and then you can rest easy." Jeff takes me by the hand and we go into the humongous bathroom to begin our search.

I'm still not convinced ten minutes later. Jeff laughs after I tell him so and he leaves the bathroom. I hear knock at my door and then hear Jeff talking to someone. I open the medicine cabinet and pull out my bottle of antacids and pop a few in my mouth, hoping it helps, but also hoping that whoever Jeff is talking to will be gone when I come out. No such luck. I walk out and there's Liam, Drew and Colin lounging in my sitting room, making themselves at home.

"Hey, Dora." Drew's grin holds me spellbound for a second, and then Colin draws my attention by patting the empty seat next to him on the couch. I plop down, gracefully, of course, and listen to them banter. Apparently, tomorrow is the last day Liam and Colin will be here before departing for home, and they want to go out tonight and celebrate Christmas early.

"What do you two think? Are you up for an evening with us poor unfortunate souls?" Drew glances at me then Jeff.

"We just ate and are stuffed. Frankly, we were going to take some antacids and have a nap. Our last exam was today, and it was brutal."

"Well, that's okay. You guys rest, and we'll leave about seven. We'll make it a 'last exam and farewell until New Year's' celebration." I start to shake my head, but Drew raises his hand and shakes his head first. "Not going to take no for an answer. We'll go to my club so it won't be crowded, and we'll just hang out and have a few drinks." He smiles at my grimace at the word "drinks." "Or not, and dance, so be ready by around six-thirty, okay? We'll take my car."

He stands up and so does his silent partners as they leave without another word.

"Well, I guess we're going out tonight," Jeff says as he makes his way to the bathroom.

I lie down on the bed and close my eyes. I feel the bed dip as Jeff joins me. I snuggle up to him and sigh. "I guess we have to go."

"Yep, we do."

444

Drew's club is exactly the same as it was the last time we were here. The same girl is checking coats and her bright, white smile greets him and then encompasses all of us in her cheerful hello. Its cozy feel is still there, and the music isn't blaring.

Drew leads us to the farthest booth in the back, where we can actually talk without having to yell at each other. The booth is a semicircle, and somehow I end up between Drew and Jeff, with Liam and Colin opposite us. Can I say I'm disappointed? Well, I am. Colin keeps looking at his phone and Liam is brooding. Yeah, I can feel it. Remember, empath.

A waiter arrives at our table and takes our orders. I move a little in my seat and I feel a thigh pressing against mine. Drew is a little too close for comfort. In fact, I feel a little claustrophobic, or maybe it's something else. I look over at Colin and catch his eye, and his smile should make me forget the thigh, but no dice. My leg is warm and so are other regions of my body, really warm, in fact. I must be coming down with the flu, that's it. It is flu season, and I didn't have the shot. Drew shifts his body so that his whole side presses against mine.

Damn flu.

"Jeff, I need to go to the ladies' room," I whisper to him.

He quickly gets up and I scoot over and out, nearly colliding with our waiter, who is bringing our drinks. I find the bathroom and make a beeline for the sink, grabbing a paper towel along the way. I wet it with ice-cold water and pat my neck and forehead. My eyes don't look feverish, and I don't look pale, or feel clammy, so maybe it's not the flu. Maybe it's early menopause hot flashes, or maybe I'm starting my period several days before it's due.

Or maybe it's being too close to a hot guy? I'm going out there to see if it happens when I sit next to Colin. I did have butterflies before.

Arriving back at the table, I lean over and whisper in Liam's ear and I move back as he gets up and lets me slide in next to Colin. Jeff raises an eyebrow and Drew looks puzzled.

"I want to look at your handsome faces."

Jeff looks skeptical and Drew flashes an Earth-shattering smile. What the heck … Earth-shattering? What am I thinking?

"I'm too ugly for you to look at?" Liam asks with a straight face.

"Well, you aren't all that handsome when you frown all the time, so yes, it's hard to look at you," I quip and then giggle when he turns to gives me the most beautiful smile.

Me? Giggle? Go figure. Wonders never cease. These three have really done a number on me.

"So I'm ugly too?" Colin's proper English accent makes the butterflies flutter in the old stomach, or maybe it's gas, but I'll go with butterflies.

"No, you're too handsome for me to stare at for any length of time."

Before I can finish, he reaches for my left hand that is resting on the table and kisses the back of it. I can feel my face turning beet red, and I hope none of them can see it in this light? I have to act normal and not like some awkward teenager.

"Why, thank you, kind sir. You're definitely the only gentleman of this group." Yep, the laughter stops and I feel so smug. "Jeff, would you be a love and pass me my drink?"

He does, and Colin reaches over to grab it in order to place it in front of me. His arm and thigh are glued to mine, and I begin to feel overheated. Hot guys do funny things to me. Maybe I should call it lust. I just need a normal guy to give me WOW, that's all.

"Care for a dance, sweet thing?"

What the F? Oh, lord, I almost said it, but it's Liam who's asking for a dance. I nod my head and he pulls me out of the booth and out onto the dance floor. It's a slow song, so we move close together and even though my heels are high, he still towers over me.

He bends down and whispers in my ear. "Is something wrong?"

"Well, first of all I feel like dwarf compared to you, even in my heels. And second, I'm kind of trying to figure out how I'm supposed help you."

"Help me?" He pulls back, looking at me intently.

"Yeah. My mom says I'm supposed to help you. Well, really Henry told her and then she told me," I ramble, not wanting to start this conversation, but when I talked to my mom this morning, she told me Liam needed my help sooner than later.

"Maybe we should go outside for a minute."

I nod my head. He grabs my arm and we head out the nearest exit. The cold stings me in the face like a dozen icicles, and I start to shiver. Liam guides me to a little alcove, which keeps most of the frigid wind away from us. He stands in front of me, blocking the rest.

"So, what exactly do I need help with?" he asks.

I look up at his face. It's semi-illuminated by a weak yellow light attached the building above us. "I know about your secret, and I know it must be so hard for you to conceal it from everybody you love."

He runs his right hand through his hair and sighs. "How did you find out?"

"I'm what they call an empath, which means I feel people's emotions. You don't give off the signals, but I felt your sadness, which most people view as being aloof. There were other signs too, like for instance the way you always look at Jeff."

He looks at me with a sad smile, which makes me want to hug him, but I need to wait for him to reply.

"Yes, it's hard," he admits. "I think Drew and Colin know, but they just don't know what to say. It's not easy being me. I know that sounds trite, but it's true. I'm from a small town, and being gay isn't an accepted lifestyle there, no matter who you are. God that sounded good to finally say it out loud." Gone is his sad smile. He actually looks part happy and part amazed.

"Henry wants me to help you, and my gut feeling tells me that you're supposed to tell your family when you go home tomorrow. No, wait …" I take his hands in mine when he starts to object, and then look deep into his eyes. "I don't say this lightly. I feel it will turn out that some of them already know.

They're just waiting for you to say something. Trust me, Liam. Everything will be good. Now, we better get back inside before we catch pneumonia. My family will kill me if I'm sick over Christmas."

"Thank you, Dora. I'm so glad you're our lucky number four. Thank your mom and Henry too." He leans down and wraps his arms around me, pulling me in close for a hug.

"One thing you definitely have to do is to call me after you talk to them, and let me know how it goes."

He beams at me again and puts his arm around my shoulder before pulling out a key card and sliding it into a slot near the door.

Entering the warmth of the club feels like a million bucks, and I realize I had suddenly forgotten how cold I was outside. We bypass the dance floor and make a beeline for the booth, with me holding Liam's hand the whole way. Now I only have to help Drew. But with what? I need to pump Henry for more info.

"Where have you two been? We looked for you on the dance floor, but guess what? You weren't out there." Jeff looks at us with eyes that say he has many questions. It's kind of cool to be so in tune with someone.

"Wouldn't you like to know? Sorry, it's our little secret. Right, Liam?" He looks at me, and yes, I feel so much joy as he gives me the most stunning smile. I know Liam will be just fine.

444

"Okay, spill it," Jeff spits out as soon as he closes the door to my room.

"Spill what?" I ask innocently.

"The two of you go missing for a few? And?"

"Okay, Mr. I Need to Know Everything, we were talking about him coming out to his family over the holidays."

He looks at me with worry in his eyes. "Wow, that's really deep. Are you sure they're going to be accepting?"

"I think someone has a crush."

"Maybe, but I'm concerned. It's a big step." Jeff takes off his coat and sits on the edge of the bed to pull off his boots.

"Henry is always right, and I think—no, I *know* everything will be fine for Liam." I kiss the top of Jeff's head and enter my closet, stripping down as I go.

444

Tonight was different. Dora was different. How long do I have to wait until she notices how much I want her in my life? What will I do if she doesn't want me? Do I wait longer? Will it make a difference? Oh, what the hell? I have to be patient. Yeah, patient. I can't lose her.

Seventeen

Christmas is easily one of my favorite times of the year, especially when my mom tells me she has threatened the senior women to behave again. Way to go, Mom! Jeff and I have all of our presents wrapped and placed in huge bags that I found for a buck each at a nearby dollar store.

"Jeff, go tell Drew we're ready to head out. You're going to drive my car, right?" He nods as he opens the door.

"Hey, Drew, you ready?" he yells.

"No need to yell. I'm right here," I hear Drew's deep voice answer.

"Wow, what's all this?" Jeff asks, causing me to turn and watch Drew walk into the room with several bags.

"Presents. It is Christmas, right? The time for giving." He laughs after looking at both Jeff and me. We're stunned. The bags are barely able hold the plethora of brightly wrapped items.

"Yes, but you didn't have to buy anything," I say. "My family invited you to dinner. They don't expect presents."

"Well, I guess that's too bad, because here they are." He shrugs his wide shoulders and takes a seat on the bed.

"I don't know how we'll fit everything in my car." I shake my head at the idea of trying to.

"No worries. We'll take the sedan. It'll all fit in the trunk. I love big trunks." He beams before leaving the room, and returns seconds later with his coat in one hand and a Santa hat in the other. "Have I mentioned to you two that I love Christmas? Well, if I haven't, I do. Hurry, get your coats on so we can get on the road."

Drew takes his bags, and we grab ours before following him to the elevator. I'm rush to catch up with Jeff and Drew after making sure the door is locked. Drew holds the elevator open for me with a grin on his face, and I just can't help but grin back at him. He looks so adorable in his Santa hat.

Jeff helps Drew put the bags in the trunk, and I scramble into backseat, loving the feel of the soft leather. My car has more than a hundred thousand miles and crappy cloth seats. I'm not into cars, but I know luxury when I feel it. The few times I've ridden in Drew's car, I failed to notice how decadent it is, and I immediately have a vision of Drew and some girl utilizing the backseat. The girl is blocked by Drew's head and I feel a little jealous of whoever she is.

Damn, where the hell did the word "jealous" come from? I'm sure this backseat and his bedroom have seen some action. The tabloids have field days with his love life, or should I say sex life? A different woman every night. Okay, so maybe it's more like once a week.

Nope, not jealous. In fact, I pity them, falling for someone they can't hold on to. I feel that Colin would be different. According to all the info I've found on him, he likes long-term relationships, and isn't into one-night stands.

Dora, wake up. You don't need any more drama in your life, so forget about Colin and never in a million years think about Drew in this way again … even though he bought presents for your whole family and can be so sweet when he wants to.

"Are you asleep?" Jeff asks, and I open my eyes to see him and Drew looking at me.

"Nope, just enjoying the fact I have this awesome, leathery backseat all to myself. Drew, drive on. God forbid we're late. I'll never hear the end of it."

Both guys turn back around, and I hear the engine purr to life before we roll smoothly out of our garage.

"Dora, we're here."

Jeff opens my door, startling me. I can't believe I fell asleep. Did I snore? I feel my face. At least I didn't drool. Drew is hidden by the trunk as I let Jeff help me out of the car.

"It snowed." I look around in wonder at the light layer of white stuff covering everything.

"You were out cold. I thought your snoring would shake the car, but thank goodness it has good shocks."

"I didn't snore," I stammer. "Did I?" I smack Jeff's shoulder as he gives me a wicked grin.

"Ow. You're so gullible."

"What did I miss?" Drew chimes in, his hands full of bags. I relieve Drew of a couple of the bags while sending him a smile, but then turn back to glare at Jeff.

"Nothing. Here, Jeff, you get the rest." I start up the driveway, careful to avoid the black ice, with Drew following closely behind. Before I can knock, the door swings open and my dad's beaming face greets us.

"Merry Christmas, all. Drew, I love your hat." My dad points to his own identical Santa hat.

"Seems we have good taste, sir." Drew attempts to shake hands with my dad, but it's awkward with his hands full.

"What did I tell you about calling me sir? It's Alex, and here, let me help you with those." He grabs some of the bags and moves out of the way so we can move inside. Behind us we hear a "whoa," and Jeff slides on the slick driveway, somehow managing to stay on his feet.

"Wow, that was smooth, Jeff." Bridget peeks her head around us and gives him a thumbs up. Is it bad that I'm secretly happy his grin is a little wobbly?

"Hey, Bridget, it's good to see you again," Drew says.

She blushes bright red as he leans down to give her a hug. "Yeah, you too. Have to go and help Mom," she mumbles, and I see her grab her phone from her pocket. I'd bet a million dollars that she's conference calling her posse as she runs into the house.

"Did I hear my name?" My beautiful mom looks amazing in her red Christmas sweater and long black skirt, and even her fuzzy bunny slippers don't seem to ruin the outfit.

"Yeah, Bridget said she was coming to help you, but unless that means going upstairs and making a phone call, she forgot," I say dryly.

"For gosh sakes, Alex, let everyone in. Are you trying to heat the outdoors?" Mom pulls us in and Jeff follows right behind us.

Dad shakes his head, and the white bobble thing on the top of his hat jumps around. "FYI, I was admiring Drew's car and the snow."

"Oh my goodness, look at all of these presents." Mom says. "Let's get them under the tree. I have to hurry back into the kitchen. Your grandmothers are in there by themselves. Dora, you come with me. I need to have you there just in case we need a referee. Alex, take Jeff and Drew into the living room, and make sure you wake up Dad. He's had a long enough nap. Dinner is going to be a little late. It seems the turducken needs more time than the roast. Oh, I forgot hugs."

She motions for Jeff to lean down and gives him a big hug and then motions for Drew and gives him the same. My heart jumps a little at the look on Drew's face when my mom hugs him. He even closes his eyes.

"Now, off you men go and leave the cooking to us. That doesn't mean you won't get out of doing dishes though." She pivots and I follow her into the oddly quiet kitchen.

Grandma stands at the stove stirring something, and Grandmother is sitting at the kitchen table peeling potatoes. The kitchen smells lovely and my stomach growls, letting me know it didn't have breakfast this morning.

Grandmother looks at me sternly. "I heard that, young lady. Breakfast is the most important meal of the day."

"I was too busy wrapping presents, but I usually do eat breakfast." A lecture on Christmas Day is just what I need.

"A body is a machine that will not work if not properly maintained," she continues. Oh brother. How many times have I heard this in my life? A times million at least. "When I was your age, I ate a nutritional meal three times a day. Not like you youngsters who drink those power drinks and eat doughnuts. I swear, our country is in trouble with the shape of the youth today."

It's best to not say anything and just let her rant. I hope when I'm her age—okay, if I make it to her age—I will not act anything like the woman peeling potatoes in front of me.

"Merry Christmas, sweetheart." Grandma grabs me in a hug and smacks a kiss on my cheek. Then she turns to her adversary. "Take the stick out. It's Christmas for Pete's sake." And with that, she goes back to the stove with a wide smile on her face. I look at my mom, who's trying to keep a straight face, but fails to as she opens the refrigerator pretending to look for something.

Yes, it's a typical start to Christmas. Love, family, and comments about my grandmother's stick…what more could I ask for?

"So, Dora, only Drew could make it? Where's his family at this time of year? Are they Jewish? Do they know he's queer?"

Grandma doesn't even take a breath, and I'm left wondering if I should answer or let her grill him herself. In light of the holiday I decide to answer her questions. "His parents are divorced and are off with their new families, and his sister is visiting her boyfriend's family in Spain. Yes, the country Spain. No, they're not Jewish, and finally, he's not gay."

"As usual, your insensitivity is spot on," Grandmother says. "Wait, what? He's not gay? I only allowed you to live there under the assumption they were all gay. I think we need to discuss this."

Allow me to live with them? For all that is holy, I don't need her permission. But I keep my mouth shut and look to my mom, who has finally come out of the fridge empty-handed but in control of her emotions.

"Beatrice, Dora is an adult, and she has her own little apartment within their loft. I think she's sensible and levelheaded." Good ol' Mom always comes through for me.

"Yeah, Beatrice, butt out. Our Dora is not looking for some eye candy, who may or may not be gay," Grandma adds.

"If she had gone to finishing school, this wouldn't have happened. She would have graduated by now, and we'd be planning a society wedding. She would most definitely not be living in sin with three men. I can assure you of that."

Should I keep my mouth shut, or should I blast away? It's a family holiday, so I bite my tongue. I'm getting tired of her attitude toward me though. I guess I'll be a wimp and let it slide like I always do.

"Beatrice," my mom says in a shocked voice. "She is not living in sin. That would mean she's sleeping with one of them, and …" My mom's face is full of anger.

"Mother, you apologize to Dora." Dad snuck by us and is now standing in front of Grandmother. His face is flushed and as he puts an arm around my mom.

"I just meant that we would have never thought of—"

"I know what you meant, and I don't like it. So apologize right now." His tone is stern and Grandmother's eyes widen as she realizes her mistake.

"Dora, sweetheart, you know what I meant. I have only your best interests at heart. I'm sorry if what I said was inappropriate." She sniffles at the end, and I swear I see tears glistening in her eyes.

"You're forgiven, Grandmother." I lean down, side hug her and place a kiss on her cheek. Deep down, I know she means well.

"Turducken's done!" Grandma says, opening the oven and pulling out the roasting dish.

"Dora, you go out and entertain Jeff and Drew. We'll handle this." My mom shoos me out of the kitchen before I can say another word.

The door shuts behind me, and I spy Drew standing in the foyer with a huge grin on his face.

"Tell me you didn't hear all that."

"I'm afraid I did. Jeff got a phone call, so I stepped out to give him some privacy. I couldn't help but hear how sinful you are. I can't believe you didn't tell me before we let you move in with us."

He laughs and I join in. I move closer and he startles me when he takes hold of my arm and pulls me toward him. My heart misses a beat, and then it starts racing, thumping so loudly he must hear it. With his other hand, he points up to the ceiling and I see not one, but several pieces of mistletoe hanging above us.

"I'm afraid I'm going to have to kiss you. Those are the rules." I'm almost drooling at the sexy look he's giving me. It's also making my palms sweat.

"Would that be considered sinful? I'm already branded, so what the heck?" I giggle as I see his eyes widen at my statement, and I pull down his head and plant a loud kiss on his cheek. He pulls back and smiles wickedly.

"You call that a sinful kiss? Let me show you sin." He grasps my arms, holding them firmly while pulling me close.

"Oh my." A voice sounds behind me just as his lips are planted on mine. We break apart quickly and I turn to see both matriarchs standing there, one with a grin plastered on her face and the other one a deep frown.

"I see you two have found the mistletoe. I made your granddad put that up when we got here this morning. So glad you two are making good use of it," Grandma says, dragging my grandmother into the dining room behind her.

The doorbell rings. I move to the door and shiver as a blast of cold air greets me when I open it. Julie and Kevin are standing on the step, their hands full of presents.

"Hey, Dora, are we late?" Julie asks, pushing past me, dumping her presents into my arms. Kevin follows, kissing my cheek, and Taylor suddenly appears, grabbing the presents from me before leading Kevin into the living room toward the highly festive Christmas tree.

"I'm starved, and it looks like people are being seated. Hurry up, Kevin." Julie fails to wait for him and makes a beeline to the dining room. "Holy shit, it smells delish in here."

Drew is still standing under the mistletoe, looking bemused at the tornado that has just blown through the house. He raises one eyebrow at me and looks up at the mistletoe. "Mmm, I guess we better follow them," I say.

What a geek I am, and a chicken too. Drew sighs as I walk past him. I wonder what his kiss would have tasted like. Just once I'd like a kiss from a "bad boy." Blushing, I remember his naked body in art class.

Great. Just what I need … sinful, X-rated thoughts on Christmas Day. I'm going to get a seat in hell for sure.

"Are you okay, Dora? You look a little flushed." Jeff's voice brings me back to the present, and I feel myself getting redder as he smiles like he knows what I was just thinking about. I elbow him on my way past him to the table and laugh when I hear his "oof."

"No, I don't want any of that mess," Grandmother sniffs as the plate of turducken is passed to her.

"Oh, for heaven's sake, Beatrice. It's just turkey, duck, and chicken, not arsenic." Grandma is so eloquent.

"Mrs. Phillips, it's quite good," Jeff says from the left side of me.

"I'm a traditionalist—roast beef for me, none of this newfangled food."

Can she sound any snootier? Drew sends me a quick half-smile from across the table and my stomach jumps. I really have to get control of myself. If I want to take a plunge on the wild side, Drew isn't my choice. Colin, yes. I mean, maybe.

"Well, I like it," Julie interjects, stuffing more food into her mouth.

"I'm with Grandmother. It's weird." Bridget, the traitor, speaks up and then looks down again when she notices Drew peering over at her.

No female is immune to him. When we go out, it's not normal, especially when all three of them are together. But Drew is the center, the eye of the storm, so to speak. But damn, he is adorable, smexy, and delicious all in one. And well-endowed too. Okay, so I'm not an expert. I've seen only a few in my whole life—four in real life, and, no, I'm not giving names, and some in magazines—but Drew's most definitely measures up.

"Dora, please pass the potatoes." My mom's voice penetrates my musings, and when I look up, Drew is staring at me like I'm the only person in the room. Or maybe I've got something on my face.

"Jeff," I whisper, turning my head to him. "Do I have something on my face?"

"No. Why?" he whispers back.

"Drew is staring at me like I do."

"I think he wants to take a bite of you, Red."

"Some help you are. And you have gravy on your chin, by the way."

Is he right? What would Drew want with me? Why do I care? I think I may need to start seeing a therapist. I beginning to think I talk way too much with myself.

Eighteen

"I'm so full," Dad says while leaned back in his chair, rubbing his stomach.

"I agree. I'll be hitting up the gym next week for sure … or maybe after New Year's." Julie pats her stomach and I realize she's gained weight. How could I have missed that? She sees me looking at her and winks. Oh, sweet fertile mother, she's pregnant. I want to say something, but it's not my place to blab the news.

"Me too. Hey, Julie, why don't you help me put some of this away?" I raise my hand as Drew and Jeff get up and start grabbing plates from the table. "No, Julie and I will do that. Everyone else go into the living room. It won't take us long, since there's not much left." I grab a few dishes and so does Julie before we move into the kitchen.

"Okay, explain the belly." I grab Julie and turn her to face me.

"I'm fucking pregnant. Oh shit, I've really got to stop cussing. They say the baby can hear everything." Julie's eyes are shining with unshed tears, and I pull her in for a hug.

"I don't think the baby hears yet, so you're safe. When did you find out? I'm so happy! You and Kevin are happy, right? How could you not be? A baby. How far along are you? How many others know?" Julie pulls back from me as I continue to ramble and wipes the tears trickling down her face.

"I'm about two months in. I go to the doctor on January fifth. We're so happy, Dora. At first, I thought Kevin wouldn't be. We hadn't really talked about kids, but he's so excited. We told our parents last night, and they're beyond happy for us. At first I thought I had the stomach flu, like everyone in my office, but after I threw up, I felt good and the sick feeling didn't linger. I still can't believe it." Julie's face glows with glee.

"Are you going to tell my family today?"

"Hell yeah we are, but I wanted you to know first. I don't know the first thing about being a mother. What if I'm a terrible at it?" The tears return and begin to travel slowly down her cheeks.

"You'll be an awesome mom." I hug her again and feel relief as she laughs.

"Hey, you two, we're waiting to open presents." We turn to see Taylor standing there with his hands on his hips. "And the grannies are at it again. We need you out there ASAP."

I put my arm around Julie and we make our way to the living room, hearing a heated discussion between the grandmothers.

"I'm just saying the money is wasted on that ratty old museum. We need new bingo balls and a new paint job on the community center."

"Ratty old museum? How dare you talk like that about such a place? It is a wealth of information for the population of our town. Bingo balls are a frivolous waste of money, and I will definitely veto it."

"And I will vote for it, and so will my friends. The money will be ours."

"Ah, thank goodness. Here they are. Julie, Dora, we're ready to open presents, so take a seat," Mom says, looking frazzled.

"First, Julie and Kevin have some exciting news."

Everyone's attention focuses on Julie and me, and Julie motions for Kevin to join us. "As our second family, we want to tell you all some great news we recently found out." Julie swallows hard and the good old tears are back.

"What Julie is trying to say," Kevin takes her hand and gently squeezes it, "is that we're going to have a baby."

A little lump forms in my throat as I see the joy and love in Kevin's eyes as he looks at his wife. Little niggles of jealousy momentarily blind me, or it might just be these tears, but then I push them away as the room erupts with congratulations followed by a massive hugging session. Blinking away the tears, I find Drew's eyes glued to mine, and for a brief moment I wonder what kind of father he'd be.

"Well, that was fun." Jeff turns to look at me in the backseat.

"It's always fun at the Phillips' house. Never normal, but always fun." I'm so drowsy, and the comfy leather seat makes me want to take a nap.

"I love your family. I can't thank them enough for allowing me to join all of you. I think this is the best Christmas I've ever had."

Drew's sexy deep voice makes me sit up straighter. Wait. Why am I thinking about his sexy voice when this poor guy just admitted he's never had a good Christmas? How utterly sad. I wish I could hug him right now, but I don't think that would be wise since he's driving.

"Really? The best? Man, I'm sorry. Well, I don't know what to say." Jeff, Mr. Always Knows What to Say, is at a loss for words. I so wish Julie was here to witness this.

"I'm glad you enjoyed yourself. I'd apologize for the grandmothers, but you knew what you were in for. And, Drew, I love my present. It's beautiful." I do love the silver necklace he gave me. It's an intricate silver design wrapped around a turquoise ball that chimes when I move. "Does it have a meaning?"

Drew laughs, which is a wonderful sound to my ears. What kind of childhood did this guy have when spending a Christmas with people he met only a few months ago is the best he's ever had? I really need to find out how I'm supposed to help him. I'm most definitely calling Mom tomorrow. We need to pump Henry for more info. Every gift Drew gave out today brought joy to each and every one of us. I'm so confused. He's projects this image of being a big player, and yet he's so incredibly sweet and thoughtful at the same time.

"No, it's just something I saw and I thought of you," he replies, but I have a sneaking suspicion that he's not being completely honest with me.

I don't want to get out of the warm car when we get home. I know it's only a few steps to the elevator, but the parking garage is freezing and I'm already shivering when Drew opens my door and to let me out. With teeth chattering, I practically run to the elevator, leaving Jeff and Drew following, carrying our Christmas haul in their arms.

"I need to move to a tropical island," I grumble through pursed lips. "I'm so over cold weather. I love the other three seasons, but winter needs to take a hike."

"You just need to grow a thicker skin. You're such a wimp." Jeff nudges me and Drew dazzles me with a smile. Yep, I said dazzle—see what the cold does to me? I might also be thinking I'd love for him to warm me up too.

Oh lord, I'm losing it majorly. One minute I want to comfort him, and the next I want to make out with him furiously.

"Since we have our arms full, do you think you could open the door for us, or are your hands numb from the cold?" Sarcasm so suits Jeff. He can see I have my gloves on. I pull out the old-fashioned key and open my door, leading Santa's little helpers into the room beyond.

"Do you want a beer, Drew?" Jeff asks, opening the fridge.

He pulls two out as Drew nods. I loathe beer. It tastes nasty. I don't care what brand it is, it all tastes like shit. No, I haven't tasted shit, but it's what I think it might taste like. Give me wine or a fruity mixed drink and I'm there. Or at least I was until my last bout with wine where I lost miserably.

"I'm going to take a shower," Jeff says after taking a gulp from the bottle. "Try not to gossip about me while I'm away, okay?"

"Aww, you take all the fun out of it," I reply. "But really, we have more enjoyable and entertaining topics to discuss. It's not all about you."

He chuckles and closes the bathroom door. The silence is deafening. All of a sudden, I don't know what to say to Drew. Awkward? Check. We've never been alone before, and I think I finally know the meaning of "cat got your tongue?" because mine is MIA.

"Would you like some hot chocolate?" Drew's voice startles me, and I turn around to see him leaning up against the fridge, looking solemn. Does he feel as awkward as I do right now? No, how could he, he has women eating out of his hands all the time. Yet for some reason I get the feeling he is as nervous as I am.

"I'd love some, but I don't have any."

"I have a stash of gourmet mixes that I received in a basket from my agent, and I'd be willing to share." He pushes away from the fridge and opens the door into the main loft.

I follow behind him. I can think of several other ways we could warm up, but my face just warmed up enough for the both of us. Damn my red hair and fair complexion. I feel my skin grow even warmer as I watch Drew's tight derriere making its way into the kitchen.

For the love of baloney and cheese, Dora, pull yourself together and quit thinking about naked butts. Oh heavens, his butt isn't naked. It's encased in a tight pair of butt-loving jeans.

My temperature soars to a new high, and I stop following Drew's butt and plop down on the nearest sofa. What I wouldn't give for a handful of snow right about now.

"Almost ready. I picked French vanilla and double milk chocolate with tiny marshmallows. Is that okay?"

"Perfect," I croak out.

My current state has affected my vocal cords. I'm a mess, a total mess. I haven't whined this much in years. I used to be a person who was grounded and boring. Boring boyfriends, boring sex, and a boring life, and now all I can think about are penises and butts. What's next? Hot kinky sex? Sadism? Masochism? Bondage? Nope. I have a low tolerance for pain, and I'd be too chicken to dish it out. Okay, so I may punch Kevin and Jeff occasionally when they act like morons, but no, kinky sex will definitely not make it on my bucket list.

I hear Drew clear his throat and look up to find him standing beside me holding a mug that reads, "Models do it model perfect."

"Corny, huh? Our agent put it in the gift basket. He may be a good agent, but he's a total dork."

"He probably means well," I say, taking the cup from him. I expect him to sit opposite me, but he settles down right beside me on the couch. There are a dozen more seats he could have picked, and next to me is a little too close for comfort.

"It's going to get cold, so drink up," he says in his husky voice. It causes me to quiver. I sure hope he thinks I'm still a little cold. "Would you like a blanket?"

I shake my head. I can't speak because a vision of him and me naked under a blanket comes to mind. My mind has turned into a guy's these last few months. I've never thought this much about sex in my whole life.

"If you change your mind, let me know." His thigh is so close to mine, I start to sweat, or "glow" as grandmother says. Nope, it's sweat.

I take a long drink from my mug. OMG, it's like nirvana. The flavor pops in my mouth, and I moan at the mouthwatering flavor that travels past my taste buds and down my throat.

"It's an orgasmic experience. I knew you'd love it."

I turn to look at Drew, who has a satisfied smile on his face as he takes a long drink. Orgasmic? I wouldn't know about that. Finding someone to actually give me an orgasm is the hard part. The closest I've come is the encounter with Colin, but he seems to have lost interest, or maybe he just wanted to see if I was worth the effort. I guess I wasn't.

See? I'm right about pretty boys. It's all about them.

"You seem preoccupied. Is something up?" Drew's voice interrupts me.

"Mmm, I was thinking that this is the best cup of hot chocolate I've ever had, and I want to know where your agent found it." There you go, Dora. That sounded normal, not like you've been thinking about hot orgasms.

"Did I hear 'hot chocolate'?"

Relief flows through me at Jeff's voice. I jump up and move away from the hot package beside me, handing Jeff my mug.

"Take a drink and tell me what you think."

"No need to share, Dora. I'm off to make him one." Drew rises from his seat and brushes past me on his way to the kitchen. Yep, there go those hot flashes again.

"Here take mine. I need a shower stat." I practically throw the mug at Jeff.

"Cold shower?"

"Shut up, and wipe that silly grin off your face. Some days I almost hate men, gay or straight." I stomp off—yes, juvenile, but I feel like throwing a fit. Damn sonofabitch hormones.

444

All the good work the hot chocolate did is wiped out by the cool shower. I say "cool" because I don't want Jeff to be right about the cold shower.

Jeff walks into the room an hour later, looking like a cat that just swallowed a canary.

"Can't believe you bailed on me. It's so dangerous leaving such a delicious morsel alone with me." He makes himself comfortable on my bed, propping himself up on one of my overstuffed pillows.

"Oh, don't flatter yourself. He's so not into you. He's so straight it's sickening. Have you seen the thousands of women he's scored with? He's been in so many magazine tabloids and on all those sleazy celebrity news shows. I bet he's even lost count of how many women he's had."

Why am I so angry?

"I think you're wrong. I think it's the women who have scored. Being seen with the great Drew would boost anyone's status. I find it hard to believe he's slept with every woman he's been seen with. He's just doesn't seem like that kind of guy."

"How would you know? Have you interviewed all of them?"

"Why so much interest? Could he possibly be on your radar? Could he be the one who cures your lack of penis problem? Your one-night stand perhaps?" I want to wipe the smirk off his face, but he moves quickly and pulls me down onto the bed with him.

"You love me, I know you do. Why would it be so hard for you to give him a chance?"

"Because I want a one-night stand with a stranger or a long-term relationship with someone who will give me great sex, love, and not cheat on me. And Drew is definitely not either of those people to me. I don't want a pretty man. I want a normal-looking man who won't cause women to trip over their own feet when they see him. I'm such a failure." I bury my head in my hands, shaking my head.

"I believe he has a thing for you, and you know I'm usually right about this stuff."

"Oh, please. Me? Short, little, red-haired, plain old me? Give me a break. According to Henry, I'm supposed to help Drew, not hump him. I help, that's what I do. That's why I'm becoming a therapist, isn't it?"

"There are plenty of ways to help someone, and dating him could be what he needs help with."

"Sometimes I think you're on drugs with the words that come out of your mouth. Why don't you go put in *Bridget Jones's Diary* so I can see someone having problems like me, even if she's only a fictional character?"

"Okay, but in the end, she gets her man. You know that always pisses you off." He pulls my hair back from my face and smacks a kiss on my cheek.

"I hate being so predictable." I throw a pillow at his retreating back and then snuggle up with another one, waiting for the movie to start.

"I love you, Dora. Please love me back."

Colin's pleading eyes break me down and I throw my arms around him. I can't believe he loves me. He moves down on the bed with my body wrapped up in his as our lips meet in a passionate embrace. His tongue slowly pries open my lips and moves in to mate with mine. I caress his shoulders, and I'm frustrated because I long to feel his naked skin. I move my hands in between us, unbuttoning his shirt until my fingertips graze his solid, smooth chest. His kiss deepens, and I move so he's flush against me and I can feel every delicious inch of him. It's hard, all of it.

He moves ever-so-slightly, and without breaking our kiss, he removes his shirt. I watch as his muscles flex when he pushes himself up, and I suddenly feel abandoned by the lack of his warm lips upon mine. I soon forget the loss as he moves to the side and reciprocates by unbuttoning me while our mouths lock once more. He slides down my zipper, exposing the hot pink panties underneath. I lift my hips so he can peel my pants down my legs, touching every inch of my exposed flesh as he goes. I bite my lip as he circles my navel, and then he leans down to replace his finger with his tongue. I rise off the bed as tendrils of fiery heat shoot throughout me. I move my restless legs as his fingers inch their way to the top of my hips and skim over my silky underwear, missing the spot I want him to touch, caress, or anything else he can think of. He moves to the end of the bed and stands up, keeping his smoldering eyes glued to mine. He unbuttons his jeans and pushes them down along with his underwear. I close my eyes as I feel the heat building up in me. I open them as he climbs back onto the bed, and I look up.

It's not Colin, it's Drew. I would recognize that penis anywhere.

My eyes meet his, and my heart begins to pound so hard I feel like my chest won't be able to contain it. The last thing I see is his wicked smile as he moves up the bed to hover over me.

"Dora. Honey, wakey, wakey."

"What? Oh, Jeff, it's you."

"Who else would it be? So, what you were dreaming about? You did a lot of moving and moaning. It's like the other time—"

"Shush, shut it, quiet, and don't speak."

I throw off the cover and enter the bathroom, shutting the door behind me. The mirror shows a flushed face, one that looks like she's been thoroughly caught up in a sex dream. Except there wasn't any sex. At least I could have dreamed that. And what the hell? Again it starts out with Colin and when the deed is about to happen, it turns to Drew and his winking penis.

I'm losing my mind. Jeff will not let me live this down. He'll tease me mercilessly at least for the next twenty-four hours.

"Dora, I need to pee. Like, really need to," Jeff whines through the door.

I pull it open and avoid eye contact, moving into my closet and shutting the door. Juvenile, but I need more time to analyze my dream. It's all Jeff's fault, putting the idea into my head. Yes, that's it. It's not what I subconsciously want, it's because he planted the seed and I allowed it to grow. It's time I forget about anything sexual and just concentrate on graduating school and getting on with my life. I will only stay in the loft until I graduate, and then I'll find another place.

Of course, I could always become a nun, and that would take care of a place to live and make it easier to forget about sex. Oh hell, I'm going to hell for that thought, and I'm sure Henry won't be able to help me.

"Is there a reason you're hiding in your closet?" Jeff asks through the door, "or is this some new thing you're trying out? I want to go and hit the after Christmas sales, so hurry your cute little butt up and let's go fight the hordes. We have money to spend."

I quickly get dressed, and we're out the door in roughly fifteen minutes. We have money to spend, and I'm good at that. Heck, I could use the distraction anyway.

Nineteen

New Year's Eve is usually both a sad and happy time for me. Saying goodbye to the old year and starting out with a clean slate. New resolutions—okay, so technically not new … but the old ones I didn't follow through on, redirected to the New Year. This year, I will stick with them until completion.

The first one is to lose the ten frickin' pounds I gained this year. Okay, so it was the year before, but it's a new resolution this year. Next, get grow a backbone and start telling people no. No to overtime, no to Sunday dinner when I don't want to go, and no to boyfriends who cheat. Okay, so that's a new one because last year I was still with The Jackass, and was completely oblivious to the fact he was cheating on me.

Another new resolution is to get financially sound so I can live by myself. So save, save, and save some more for me because I don't want roommates. I want to live by myself just in case I find the perfect man, with a job, and who's completely devoted to me, that I can have sex in every room without having to worry about being interrupted.

Colin and Liam are returning today, and except for the text Drew received on Christmas from Liam saying his family was relieved that he finally revealed his secret, we hadn't heard much from either of them. As for Liam's "secret," it wasn't a secret. Apparently, the whole town knew. They were waiting for him to tell them. I can't wait to talk to him. He told Drew to tell me that he couldn't wait to hug me when he gets back. Yeah, hug. For me, from Liam. Life is good.

Jeff is also waiting patiently—not—to see him again. I so hope there's a connection on Liam's part because I think Jeff really wants this to happen. Then, three of my best friends will be in committed relationships and I'll be poor Dora who gets invited to things as an awkward third, fifth, or even seventh wheel. I can't believe I'm a spinster at twenty-two. I guess there's no hope for me. All I have to look forward to in the future romance department are probably a few one-night stands, but nothing more.

Great, now I've totally bummed myself out on a day that's supposed to herald new beginnings. Out with the old and in with the new. Yeah, right. Whoever started this brilliant idea?

"What are you wearing to the party tonight?" Jeff asks, looking over his shoulder at me.

"I don't want to go."

"You can't avoid it. After all, it's going to be right here, so you kind of have to attend." Jeff's head swivels back to the football game he's been watching.

"I still don't have to go. I can just lock my door and no one will miss me."

"Julie, Kevin, Drew, Colin, Liam, and me, we'll miss you. So, get in that closet and find something hot and sexy," he says, not bothering to turn around.

"Hot and sexy? The place will be filled with hot and sexy. I'll just come as plain and boring. No one will notice."

"Quit fishing for compliments. You know you're beautiful, so quit feeling sorry for yourself. You can hang with those skinny sticks any old day."

He won't give up, so I guess I'd better find something to wear. There's the little black dress, but I've worn that so many times. Nothing else seems New Yearish in my wardrobe.

"Check out the bag hanging up in the back," Jeff yells at me like I'm across town, even though we're only a few feet from each other.

There's a black bag hanging up with his clothes, so I grab it and lay it on the bed. I pull down the zipper slowly, revealing a dress that is way out of my price range, like maybe two years' worth of my meager income. It's in one word: indescribably beautiful. Okay, so that's two words. Sue me.

"So, do you like it?" Jeff somehow snuck up behind me, and he lays his head on my shoulder, watching me feel the fabric. It's so soft and is a lovely turquoise color.

"Jeff, it's beautiful, but how can you afford this? Your parents have you on a strict budget of nothing but what you earn. We spent your Christmas money, didn't we?"

"No, we didn't. I'm not that foolish. I kept enough so I don't have to work like crazy my last semester, and to buy you this. I saw it the other day and I thought, 'That would look amazing on Dora with her gorgeous curly red hair,' so I bought it. Look at the bottom of the bag. I found shoes to match. Yep, they're 'fuck me' pumps—I mean 'fuck you' pumps. You know what I mean."

I shake my head. Tears cloud my eyesight as I grab the amazing platform heels that match the dress perfectly. I turn quickly and hug him, at a loss for words. He stands back, holding me at an arm's length away, giving me a goofy smile.

"Happy tears, I hope."

I nod my head and drag him in for another hug.

"Now go and try it on. I know it'll fit, but I want to see it on you, and I promised your mom I would take a picture and send it to her."

"Yeah, like she'll be able to open it on her phone. Jeff I…I love you, and I don't think I tell you that enough."

"And I love you too, so move your cute little butt and do some modeling for me. You're going to leave them breathless tonight."

I release a squeal and then laugh when Jeff covers his ears. I make a beeline for the bathroom to take a quick shower. I'm not trying on that amazing creation with dirty skin—okay, so unwashed-since-yesterday skin.

"Dora, I thought you were going to take a quick shower, but it's been more than an hour," Jeff says through the closed door.

"Come in. I'm just putting lotion on my legs. I want to look perfect for my perfect outfit. At least I don't have to paint my toenails, not that anyone will see them in my shoes. How should I wear my hair, up or down? And makeup? Subtle but still sexy? Don't stand there, help me." Yeah, I know I'm whining a bit. I really want to make everyone notice me.

"Slow down there, fireball. We have a few hours before the event, and I ordered pizza. Before you say anything, I made it half vegetable for me and half sausage for you."

"Have I told you lately how much I love you?"

"Yes, about an hour ago, but I'll never tire of it. Just remember this moment when you get angry next time, and remind yourself how wonderful of a friend I am to you," he laughs.

"You're more than a friend. You're my soul mate," I say and watch his eyebrow rise at my statement.

"But I'm gay. We can't be soul mates."

"Yes, we can. My mom says so. Everyone thinks that when you marry or are in love with someone that they're your soul mate, but it can be anyone. We hit it off immediately, and I feel like I've known you forever and can trust you with anything. So, we're soul mates."

"I need to buy you clothes more often. I didn't know you felt like this. I felt that instant connection too, but always shrugged it off as something new for me to explore. But you just nailed it. Your mom is right, as usual. Of course, she has Henry, so is that really fair?" he says, putting his hands on his hips and cocking his head to one side with a cheeky smile on his face. He laughs. “We definitely have our work cut out for us, don’t we? It’s going to take hours to get you just right.”

I giggle with a playful glare as he squeezes my waist. Why can’t Jeff be my soul mate and my real mate forever? Life isn’t fair.

444

Two hours later—I had to paint my fingernails, and it took me forever to pick out a color from my stash—I can’t believe what I’m seeing in the mirror. I know it’s me, but frickin’ hell, it sure doesn’t look like me. I truly look like I just stepped out of a fashion magazine. I’m not bragging. Jeff said the same thing when we were done.

“Smile for the camera. No, a smile, not a grimace. I want to see those pearly whites of yours”

I stick out my tongue and then I pose like I’m really on a photo shoot. Or what I think of when I think photo shoot.

“That’s it. Work it…work it…turn to your left…now your right. And pout.”

It’s like he’s reading my mind, and I can’t wait to see the photos. I’ll have to choose the most respectable one to send to my mom, but like I said, hopefully she’ll be able to open it on her phone. She wanted a smartphone for her birthday this year because her best girlfriend got one. The only problem is that she's extremely knowledgeable about the spirit world, but is so challenged with modern technology. Even her computer doesn't like her. That's what she says anyways. At least she can work the computer to some extent, but her phone is a different story. She's the mistress of butt dialing, forgetting to charge the phone, and complaining about how much social media takes up her time. I'm on her friend's list. She threatened me as she did Taylor and Bridget, so we're careful what we post because Big Mother is watching.

"Is that really me?" I can't believe it's really me in the pics he's taken. I'm not vain, but I think I kind of love this look and can't wait for the others to see me. "Is it time yet?" I look anxiously at the clock and realize we have an hour to go until reveal time.

"For the hundredth time, it's you, and no, you have to be patient. I want you to make an entrance after everyone has arrived. I want to make the male population drool and the females turn green with envy. I predict they will, and every man but the gay people and Kevin will want to get in your pants. I mean, your red bra and panties. Just think if you made an entrance in only those and your shoes. A riot would ensue."

"Yeah, I'd be arrested for exposing fat in a room full of skinnies."

"For the last effing time, you're not fat, you're just right."

I'm feeling a little nervous. What if I look like a joke to these beautiful people? "Promise me you'll stick to me like glue in there. Please don't leave me alone."

"Darlin'," Jeff drapes his arm around my shoulders and pulls me to him. We stare at each other in my full-length mirror. "You won't be alone tonight, but if it's glue you want, glue you will get until you tell me to get lost."

Twenty

The minutes seem to drag on and Jeff is lounging on the couch watching some apocalyptic movie, all calm as people are screaming and dying all over place.

"Grab that bottle of wine out of the fridge. I think you need a pre-party drink to calm those nerves."

I grab the bottle and two glasses and plop down beside him. He takes the bottle from me. My hands are shaking a little and I know the bottle cost a bomb, so I don't want to spill a drop.

"It'll be fine. While you were in the bathroom looking for antacids, I called Julie and told her to come to your door a little early. They should be here any minute. See? You'll be surrounded by family, so nerves be gone."

I take a sip and it's smooth, sweet, and perfect. A knock—more like a bang—sounds at my front door before it swings opens and Julie and Kevin make their entrance.

"Are we ready to fucking party or what? Shit, sorry, little one. Mommy's trying really hard. More money for the swear jar. Damn." Julie stomps her foot and looks up from her stomach. "Oh … my … freaking … God, you look incredible, Dora. Seeing that dress on the hanger, I thought it was delish, but you make it look like Jeff paid a million dollars for it. I would hug you, but I don't want to mess up anything. Kevin, wipe the drool off your face. You married the right friend," Julie jokes. He's not drooling, but he is staring at me like he's seeing me for the first time.

"Damn, girl, you clean up well," he says in a gangster voice, and everyone laughs because he sounds so corny since it doesn't fit the way he looks. Which, by the way, he's incredibly handsome in jet-black jeans and a white button-down shirt complete with a purple tie. Julie looks just as wonderful in her long white skirt and purple silky maternity blouse.

"You don't look too bad yourself," I say. "Of course, it was probably all Julie who put you two together."

Julie confirms by nodding and smiling smugly.

"Hey, that wine looks expensive. Are you guys going to share?" Kevin eyes the bottle, and yes, now he's drooling. The boy loves fine wine.

Seconds later, Kevin's glass is full, Julie's nursing a bottle of water, and for the first time today I begin to relax. I lay my head on the back of the couch, not worried about my hair since it's up in a high ponytail. The leather feels cool on my neck, relaxing me even more. In fact, I think the two glasses of wine were just the medicine I needed, even though I did made a pack with myself to never drink the stuff again. I only hope when I get off the couch I can still walk straight in these shoes.

The other three all make small talk, and I close my eyes, wondering how I'll act when I see the boys. I can't wait to hug Liam. I hope he's ready to live his life the way he wants to. The other two, well, I'm not interested. Okay, so I am a little, but not stupid enough to go for it.

"Time to go, ladies and gent." I open my eyes and Jeff's hand is eye level, waiting for me to grab it so he can haul my butt up from the couch. "Kevin, get the door and you and Julie go first. I want Dora to make a grand entrance."

Jeff squeezes my arm, which is now linked with his, and Kevin and Julie open the door. The place is packed. People are everywhere. I don't know if we four will even be able to find a place to stand, never mind move about.

"So much for an entrance," Jeff complains as we push our way through the noisy throng.

"Attention, everyone. We're opening up the patio. I know it's cold outside, but we have the heaters going, so it should be pleasant. No, you won't need your coats."

I look toward the direction of the voice, but can't see over the tall heads in front of me. If you're a woman and are tall, why in the freaking hell do you wear high heels?

Amazingly, the crowd thins. I guess everyone wants to be on the patio. At least we can breathe now. I'm letting Jeff lead me to wherever we're going. I lost track of Julie and Kevin. I guess that's the price I pay for being short. Jeff stops abruptly, and I almost stumble, which would've been just great. I peek around him to see what has him standing still. Liam is in front of him, and he's smiling wide. I move to stand at Jeff's side, and Liam's eyes go from Jeff's to mine, and he picks me up and swings me around like I'm a toy doll.

"Darlin', you look amazing, and I love you. 'Thank you' doesn't begin to cover what you've done for me."

My smile is wobbly. I hope he's not drunk and won't drop me. I also hope my underwear isn't showing to the crowd of people.

"I didn't do anything, Liam. It was all you. Now, as much as I love this, could you please put me down? Two glasses of wine and pizza, plus spinning, are not mixing very well together. Oh, and I love you too."

"Sorry, love, but I'm so excited to start the New Year free from secrets," he says as he puts me down gently and kisses my cheek.

"I'm so happy for you." I feel Jeff watching and pull him close to us. I guess he backed up when Liam started his twirling act.

"Hey, Jeff, how were your holidays?" Liam looks uncomfortable all of a sudden, and even though he's tan, I see a hint of blush on his cheeks.

"Pretty awesome. Spent it with Dora and her family, or as I think of them, my second family." Jeff beams. I'm sure he noticed the blush too. If I could, I would cross my fingers, toes, legs, arms, and wish on a shooting star that these two gel.

"Beer?" Liam asks, but I shake my head. "Oh, right. Fireball doesn't like beer."

I can't believe the change, and he's calling me fireball.

"I'll have one," Jeff announces, and Liam makes his way to the kitchen with Jeff trailing behind. The crowd closes in, and I lose sight of both of them. Wait until I get a hold of Jeff. He promised he'd stick to me like glue. I feel eyes on me. I seem to be the center of attention of the group in front of me.

"Who's your agent?" a tall, dark, long-legged male with shaggy hair addresses me.

"Me? I don't have one," I reply, watching his eyes widen in surprise.

"Everyone does. It's unheard of not to have one in this town."

Is that disdain on his face?

"I don't do what everyone else does. It's so common." I can't believe those words just came out of my mouth.

"Hey, Chilton, are you harassing our roomie?" Thank the stars that are absent in the sky. It's delectable Colin to the rescue.

"Oh, so she's not one of us?" Chilton's tone is starting to grate on my nerves, and yes, I'm getting fired up. I think Colin thinks so too, as he takes my arm and guides me to the other side of the room.

"You didn't have to rescue me. Okay, maybe you did. He's quite the pompous ass. Remind me to not buy any magazines with him in it."

Colin laughs and it sounds so good. But no butterflies. What is up with that? Are they drunk on the wine and don't have the energy to flutter?

"I know you can hold your own. I was worried for Chilton. He's never met a Pandora before, and I don't know if he's up for it. How were your holidays?" He's looking into my eyes, and yep, no butterflies. Oh, well. It never had a chance anyway.

But what about that kiss? Surely he hasn't forgotten about that.

"Oh, just abnormal, as usual. Poor Drew had to put up with us, but he's still hanging around, so we haven't scared him off yet. And yours?" I ask as he looks me up and down.

"Dora, has anyone told you how amazing you look in that dress? It totally matches your hair. No wonder Chilton was talking to you. My holidays were brilliant. I found out I'm going to be an uncle again. My family loves to procreate. My mum always drops hints to me. I'm the baby and everyone else is settled."

"Mothers have a way of doing that. I'm glad you like the dress. Jeff picked it out for me." I brazenly turn around, letting him get the full effect." He responds with a soft whistle, causing people in our immediate area to stare.

"Well, he has good taste. Speaking of which, thanks for what you did for Liam. Drew and I have known he was gay for years, but he wouldn't even break his silence for us. He called me from his home on Boxing Day, which is the day after Christmas, and told me the news. Also, between us, I think he's got his eye on someone we both know."

"Jeff. Tell me it's Jeff." Stupid, Dora, stupid. Of course it's Jeff.

"Are you all right with that?" He looks warily at me.

"Are you kidding? I would flippin' love it. Jeff is a wonderful guy, and the two of them would be perfect together." I reach up and hug Colin, who returns it with gusto. My feet are barely touching the floor.

"Hey, what's this? What am I missing?" Drew's deep, smexy voice washes over me and the butterflies stir. I mean they're *jumping*. Maybe it's the pizza or the wine mixing together.

"I was thanking our Dora for helping Liam."

"Yeah, I've been meaning to drop by, but I've been tied up since Christmas on a project I'm working on." Drew's eyes meet mine, and the psychotic butterflies, pizza, and wine are having a wild party. I can't believe these two can't hear them. I can't be attracted to Drew. It was Colin, always Colin. Drew wouldn't have bowed and kissed my hand before he ravished me. For the love of chocolate…I used the word ravished.

"Dora?"

Oh, great. Now I've missed something.

"Sorry, what did you say?"

"Colin just said you're okay with Liam and Jeff." Drew's voice is now sending shivers through me and goose bumps have popped up all over my arms and legs.

"Uh-huh, of course. I couldn't think of a better match, except for Kevin and Julie." Why does that depress me all of a sudden?

"Anyone taking your fancy?" Colin asks, and I realize he's asking if I'm into anyone.

"Too busy. School, work, and Sunday dinners leave little time for anything else."

I feel Drew's eyes on me, and then all over me as if he's just noticed how I look. I bite my lip. I can't remember the last time I bit my lip. I'm nervous. What does he think? Too slutty?

No, Jeff wouldn't let me look slutty, and I didn't appear slutty in my mirror, and hey, Drew hangs around with models who look slutty all the time.

What the hell is wrong with me? Bitchy much, Dora?

"She's talking to herself," Jeff's voice punches through my thoughts.

"Are you talking to me?"

"You're the only female standing with us."

I look around. He's right. Just Drew, Colin, Liam, Jeff and I are standing in this little intimate circle.

"Shouldn't you guys be circulating? You're the hosts," I say a little too quickly and maybe a little defensively.

"So are you," Drew replies with a little delicious smirk.

How the hell can a smirk be delicious? What was in that wine? I feel my arm being taken, and I look up to see Drew gazing at me.

"Come with me, Dora. We need to do some hosting."

I can't think of a damn response. My brain has gone on strike, but my stomach is full of activity.

The crowd parts as we move along, and I'm the object of many stares. Instead of being nervous, I stare back. How dare they look at me like I don't belong here. Chilton did, but who the heck is he? I hear whispering and I want to yell that my mom taught me it's rude to whisper. If you can't say it out loud, then drop dead.

Okay, my mom never said the last part, but it sounds better than what she says.

Drew doesn't stop as we make a sweep around the apartment, even though he's hailed by everyone. He just smiles and keeps moving.

"Shouldn't you stop and speak to your fans?" I finally ask.

"I see these people all the time. They're phony, Dora. They only like me because they think I can help their careers. They don't care a lick about me. They're shallow, and I'm tired of all this bullshit."

He sounds so sad. I want to take him in my arms and hold him, and then run my fingers through his hair. Okay, so maybe not that, but I'm supposed to help him. I wish I could strangle Henry for being so vague. I'm not good at guessing games. I'm a spell-everything-out-for-me type of girl.

"There are phony people everywhere," I say, "but I'm sure not everyone in this room is fake."

Yeah, Dora, that sounds good. Way to pick up his mood.

"Nope. Every single one of them, except for our little group, of course. Agents, models and makeup artists, they all want a huge piece of the pie and expect us to give it to them. I worked hard to get where I am, and I didn't step on people to get here. Sorry to be such a downer on New Year's. Maybe we should dance."

"But there's no music," I say as he takes me in his arms and moves flush against me and sways like he can hear music.

He leans down. "I love that you're wearing my present," he whispers.

I suddenly forget that we're surrounded by people. My focus is solely on the sound of his heartbeat and the chime of my necklace.

"Are you cold?" he whispers, his voice mesmerizing.

"No, why?"

"Because you're shivering."

He pulls me closer. My legs wobble. Jumping stomach and wobbly legs are nothing to laugh at, and I'm definitely not laughing right now. I'm burning up, hotter than Hades, but I don't want to leave his arms.

What am I saying? Here I am in the arms of the "bad boy" of modeling and I want to stay. The flu, that's it. I didn't have my shot this year. All the symptoms: shivering, upset stomach, wobbly legs, and fever. Yes, it's the flu. Whew, close one there.

"Ten, nine, eight, seven…"

Why is Drew counting? Oh, shit—it's almost New Year's, and what happens at the end of the countdown? People kiss, and I don't want him to catch my sickness. Trying to pull away, I hear "two" and I pull a little harder, but it's like I'm strapped into a straitjacket. I had to endure one of those in a psych class this year.

"Happy New Year, Dora." Drew leans down and gently lifts my chin, sealing his lips to mine.

And then it happens.

Fireworks.

Okay, so there are some going off outside, but I mean within me. His tongue pushes its way in, and my body goes wild, just like it did on Halloween. In fact, it's exactly the same feeling and the same lips. Sweet Jesus, it was Drew, not Colin.

A feeling of panic washes over me. I have to get out of here. I break contact, and before Drew can react, I lose myself in the horn-blowing, screaming crowd.

Where the hell is my door? Great, all the tallest people in the room have surrounded me. I look up and see Jeff. He makes his way to me, looking worried.

"Dora, what's wrong?" he yells.

"I have to get back to my room. Please help me." I grab his hand and let him lead me through the mayhem. Finally, I see my door and Jeff opens it, pushing me before closing it behind him.

"What's up? You look like you've seen a ghost." He reaches into the fridge, grabs a bottle of water, and then tosses it to me.

"Worse," I say while taking a deep swallow of the cold liquid. "I'm in a nightmare." I cap the bottle and lie on the bed.

"What nightmare?" Jeff lies beside me on his side, his face inches from mine. He gently pushes back a rogue hair that has come loose from my ponytail and runs his cool fingers down my heated cheeks.

"I thought it was the flu, but it's Drew."

"You're making about as much sense as trying to make peace with zombies. Great. I got you to smile. That zombie marathon the other night is still giving me the creeps. Let's start from when I lost you."

"Yeah, remind me I'm mad at you for subjecting me to all those movies after I tell you what happened," I joke. I still have the goofy smile on my face from his zombie remark. Love my zombie movies. "I lost you, and then I found Colin, and he didn't give me butterflies and Drew did, and it's because it's him, not Colin."

He lets out a soft chuckle. "That pretty much cleared up nothing."

"Oh, for the love of Sunday dinners with my family, it's Drew. Drew is the Modelteer who kissed me on Halloween. He's the one who almost gave me an orgasm right there in a dark hallway. Or what I think an almost orgasm feels like."

"Whoa, Drew? Bad boy, Drew?"

"Yes, him. I can't believe it. I'm going to have to move. This isn't going to work, me living here. Why is he doing this to me? I was happy with my boring, mundane life."

"Thanks for calling me boring. Or am I mundane?" Jeff remarks, still wearing that silly grin of his.

"Oh hush. You know what I meant. Sexless, dateless, and the only worries I had were passing math and enduring my crazy family. I passed math, and my family will always be crazy, so I have to deal. But having a fling with a famous—correction, *mega* famous—hottie isn't needed or wanted in my world. No, sir." A few tears slip down my face and Jeff gently wipes them away.

"Are you finished? I think you're overreacting. I've come to know Drew. Wait, it's my time to speak," he says, shushing me when I try to argue. “Liam says he’s a good guy. The fights in the tabloids were provoked, and the women? Each one of them only wanted to be photographed with him for their own gain. Yes, he’s slept with a few of them. He is a guy, after all. But Liam says that over the last few years, Drew’s changed and has become more distant with people. He also told Liam you’re like a breath of fresh air, and he’s happy you moved in.”

“When did Liam tell you this? How long have you known this and let me believe he was this love-’em-and-leave-’em type of guy?” I turn so I’m facing Jeff side by side and I watch the guilty look cover his face. “Fess up, buddy.”

“I’ve known for a short time. But wait—I saw the way he looked at you, and I guess I got a little possessive. I wanted to see if it was true before I told you. I think Liam is right. Forgive me for loving you so much.” He leans over and kisses my nose and I melt. How can I be angry after that?

“I forgive you, and I won’t hit you for losing track of me tonight. But, Jeff, in all honesty, I felt like I had the flu when Drew and I were dancing. I had all the symptoms, and now they’ve disappeared. That can only mean one thing: I’m attracted to him. I don’t want, or need this.”

I know I sound like I'm whining. I know a million women would love to have Drew in their sights, but it will make my life so complicated, and when it fizzles out on his end, when he's tired of this "breath of fresh air," how awkward will it be to be living in the same space? One of my resolutions is to move out, but that's only if I get a good job, and the unemployment stats scare me.

"Take a chance, Dora. What have you got to lose? You have so much to gain. I bet that man will give you countless orgasms and you'll think you've died and gone to the great beyond."

"Easy for you to say. And what if I don't like orgasms? That was a stupid question. Stop laughing at me. Forget about me for a minute, what about you and Liam? Is it a go?"

"You are so nosy, always in everyone's business," he says after getting his laughter under control.

"Oh, and you don't pry, huh? So now it's your turn to spill."

"Okay." He lies back on the bed, staring up at the ceiling. I wait patiently for him to continue. "We're talking, and we have a date for tomorrow night. Satisfied?" He rolls back and stares at me.

"Ohhhhhh, I'm so happy. You have no idea how happy I am for you. Are you excited? Of course you are. You and Liam are perfect for each other." I reach over and pull him in for a hug, which he reciprocates. I swear he's breaking a few of my ribs in the process.

"Now go back to the party and let me think. No shaking your head. I'm fine, and I want you to go back to Liam." I push him away from me and he slowly rises.

"Are you sure?"

"I'm positive. Now get your sexy ass out there before someone steals Liam away from you." He jumps off the bed and turns, blowing me a kiss. "I love you, Jeff."

"Ditto, but I love you more." He grins and slips through the door, shutting out the loud mayhem when he closes it. I get up and lock it. He has a key, so I'm not worried. Anyway, he might get lucky and not need to sleep here tonight.

My cell rings a few minutes later and I grab it off my dresser. It shows a picture of my mom and dad acting silly. "Happy New Year, Dora," they yell as soon as I answer.

"Happy New Year to you, my wonderful parentals."

"Have you made your resolution list yet?" Mom asks, and my dad says he loves me and I hear a click. "So, now that your dad is off the phone, I have to tell you that Henry has been bugging me to call you. He says you aren't helping Drew, and I told him he's wrong. Of course, Mr. Arrogant says he's never wrong. So tell me I'm right. You are helping Drew, aren't you, sweetie?"

What do I say? Henry will know I'm lying, and since he has an in with upstairs management, I don't know if pissing him off will be any good for me. But I don't want my mom to know the truth, so I do what I'm being trained to do: I compromise.

"Don't worry, Mom. I'm working on it. I just wish Henry would stop being so vague about how I'm supposed to be helping Drew." I roll my eyes and pray she doesn't hear the little white lie in my voice.

"Okay, I'll tell him. So, about this Sunday, are you and Jeff free for dinner? Please tell me you are. Taylor and Bridget are going skiing and won't be back until late, so I really need reinforcements."

"I'll check with Jeff and let you know. Love you, Mom. My battery is in the red zone," I say as another little white lie slips out.

"All right. Please try for Sunday. I don't ask for much. Talk to you soon. I'm off to tell Henry he's wrong. Love it. Night, sweetie, and Happy New Year again."

My phone clicks before I can respond. Happy frickin' New Year to me. All I have to look forward to in the next few days is a dysfunctional Sunday. Joy oh joy.

Twenty-One

"For Christ's sake, please stop that pounding." What time is it? I must've dozed off. What is that pounding noise, and where is Jeff?

Oh, yeah … now I remember. He's probably with Liam. The room is partially dark. The only light is a decorative flameless candle that I keep on at night so I don't break my neck if I need to get up. The pounding is coming from the door to the loft. I slide off the bed, still in my beautiful dress and my eff- me pumps.

"This better be important," I remark as I open the door.

It's Drew. My heart starts beating crazily as he moves past me. I shut the door since the party noise is still deafening and my head isn't really up to it.

"Dora, we need to talk." I find Drew standing behind me, not close, but too close for comfort.

"Can't it wait until tomorrow? I'm a little tired." Please let him just go. I can't deal with this right now. My emotions are all over the place, and the monsters in my stomach are awakening, as is my fever and wobbly legs. Great, I'm having another case of Drew flu.

"I've been waiting for months now, and I know it sounds corny, but it's a new year and I want—God, Dora, I want to talk." He sounds so forlorn and lost, and now he's tugging at my heart with his words, which by the way just skipped a beat. His voice is enough to make me melt into a puddle of hot goo.

"Okay, but let me go splash some water on my face first."

I don't wait for an answer as I move past him to the bathroom. I need to pee, but I didn't want to discuss bodily functions when most of my body is not functioning right as it is. I turn on the faucet so it will mask the noise, and then I wash my hands, splashing a little cool water on my face. I don't want to mess up my makeup since I want to look halfway decent when we talk.

What is there to talk about? He kissed me on Halloween and tonight, big deal. I guess I need to go find out.

Calm down, Dora. It's just Drew.

"Sorry, it took me so long. Wine is not my friend, and it makes me sleepy. I'm awake now, so what's up?" I hope I sound calm. I think I do. Nonchalant is what I'm really going for.

Shut up, Dora, and listen to him.

"It's okay." Drew is sitting on the couch, and I watch as he runs his hand through his hair. By the look of it, he's done it more than a few times since I left him in. "Come sit beside me, please." He pats the leather cushion next to him, and I wobble on my heels over to him.

"Wait, let me take these damn shoes off before I fall and break my neck." Stop rambling, Dora.

"Did I tell you how beautiful you look tonight?"

I stumble at the huskiness in his voice and look up to see him watching me remove my shoes. I kick them aside and sit on the edge of the cushion, not knowing what to do with my hands. I end up placing them in my lap as our eyes meet.

"First, I want to explain Halloween."

My eyes drop down to my lap when he bows his head. "You don't have to. You were drunk and I was there, and well, we kissed."

"I wasn't drunk. In fact, I hadn't had a sip of anything but water. I saw you as soon as I walked into the room, and I followed you. From the first time I met you, you have haunted my thoughts, and I needed to see if what I felt was real. It *was* real. I've never felt anything more real in my life. My question is: Do I have a chance with you?"

His head is still bowed, and I'm speechless. He wants to have a chance with me. Maybe I didn't hear him right. My heart is pounding loudly and the menacing butterflies are going hog wild. Maybe I'm dreaming.

Ow! Pinching myself proves I'm wide awake.

"Dora, did you hear me?" He lifts his head, and I see the confident Drew missing.

This is real. He wants me. What should I do? *Kiss him, fool*, inner Dora shouts. I move closer and take his head in my hands and pull him close so his lips are even with mine. Then I kiss him. This time it's my tongue that is the initiator, and I feel myself go from warm to burning hot in a matter of milliseconds.

I want this man. I really want him. Not just a kiss, but all of him. I want him in my bed with our bodies fused together. Even if it's only for a short while, I want him and he wants me.

I push any doubts aside and moan as he pulls me into his arms, deepening the kiss. I feel his hands burning a trail up and down my back, and he pulls me with him as he lays down on the couch. I'm on fire, everywhere. I want him naked, and I boldly reach between us and undo his jeans. He stills, and I wonder if I've done something wrong.

"Dora, are you sure?" he whispers as he breaks contact with my mouth.

"I'm so sure," I say.

He abruptly sits up and lifts me like I weigh ounces instead of pounds. He pulls back the covers on the bed and places me gently on the cool sheets. I panic as he stands up straight, and I think maybe he's changing his mind, but instead he yanks the polo he's wearing over his head, revealing the most beautiful twelve pack I remember from art class. With a ghost of a smile, he finishes the job I started and pulls down his jeans, removing his underwear and socks and kicking off his shoes in one fluid motion. The low light in the room shows the extent of his lean muscles, and I'm itching to touch every inch of him. He's hard and ready, and I stroke him, delighted when he closes his eyes and moans. I can't believe I made him do that.

He leans down and puts his hand on my thigh, slowly moving up, taking my dress as he goes. Impatiently, I sit up and turn my back to him so he can unzip my dress, which he does again slowly, caressing every inch of my naked skin as it's unveiled. I shimmy out of it, not sexy, but I'll make a better effort next time. I shiver as the cool air hits my skin, and I sit there dressed only in my barely-there underwear.

Scooting over, I make room for him to join me, which he does instantly. We're face to face, eyes to eyes, and I realize I've never had such an intense feeling like this. His gaze moves down to my bra, and before I realize it, it's gone the way of my dress, and my scrap of underwear meets the same fate. His hand strokes me. I watch as his tanned skin moves over my pale body. The ache and the need for him to be inside me intensifies. I take his hardness in my hand and gently tug him, hoping he understands what I want—no, what I desire.

"I won't last long if you keep that up, Dora. I want this to be special," he groans as I continue stroking him.

"We can do it again, right?"

I can't believe I just asked that. He reacts by moving down the bed to circle my left nipple with his tongue. My hips move upward, and I feel like I'm going to explode. Every nerve in my body is on edge. I tug on his hair, but he doesn't budge. Instead, he latches on and gently sucks until I feel like I will lose my mind. His hand starts drawing circles on my stomach, inching closer to the place I want him to be. My hips move involuntarily as his hand cups me, and then he places his palm flat against me. I swear I'm going to die from the agony and intense sensations he's causing to burst within me. I tug his hair again, and his tongue lets go of my nipple. I feel a loss, but then his fingers begin stroking me, and I want something different.

I scoot down until my lips meet his. His fingers are pulled away, and I reach down and grab him, guiding him inside me. He doesn't resist. Instead, he pushes farther until I feel I can't wait anymore. I want—God, I don't know what I want. But the pressure is so pleasurable that I wrap my legs around his waist, and then he's moving quickly and I'm matching him stroke for stroke, and—

What the hell?

I scream into his mouth as a feeling so incredible washes over me. I hold onto him, riding on the waves of unbelievable sensations shooting through me.

I'm exhausted, but so purely satisfied. Finally, I know what it feels like to have a big O, and it's so not a disappointment. I'm lying here with the most famous face in the world, my arms and legs wrapped around him, and I never want to move.

"Am I too heavy?" he asks, sounding like he's trying to catch his breath.

"No. Not at all. I don't want you to move."

"That was more than I could have ever dreamed of. Yes, I've dreamed about you. I wanted to touch you all the time. It was so hard to keep my hands off you."

"I can tell how hard." I giggle as I think about how hard he'd been.

"Wait a few minutes and I'll show you hard." He nuzzles my neck and gently nips me.

"A few minutes, really? Oh, you aren't kidding."

"See what you do to me? I spent many a night hard as hell and with no relief, so I'm going to make you suffer as I did." His hips move, and I feel the delicious pressure building again.

"You call this suffering? Bring it on." He kisses me soundly, and I can feel him grinning.

"What time is it?" I ask, too tired to lift my head and look at the clock.

"Who cares? I just care that I'm finally holding you in my arms. Time means nothing." He gently squeezes me, and my feelings are all over the place. I lost track of how many times I had the big O, but all I can say is that the hype is so real.

"Dora, go pack a bag. Not much. In fact, just clothes you'll be traveling in." He kisses the top of my head and jumps out of bed. Oh, lord, his butt is so tight, and his muscles, so many lean, hard muscles, I could look at him all day.

"What for? Come back to bed." I love this bolder Dora. I bet it's because of the O's—yep, I'll have to look it up on the Internet.

"Nope, you get up. We have somewhere to go, and I want to get there soon." He picks up his pants, pulls them on, grabs his other clothes and then kisses me thoroughly.

"I need a shower first, and you could join me."

"Tempting, but where we're going—well, let's say we'll have plenty of time for showers. Now hurry." He yanks open the door and closes it quietly behind him.

Stretching, I feel little aches in places that have been ache free for so long. I always thought running was better than the phantom orgasm, but I was so wrong. The door suddenly opens.

"You have fifteen minutes, so hurry." Drew looks stern, but winks at me before he turns around and exits again.

444

"Your father really owns this?" I can't believe my eyes. I'm standing in the most beautiful penthouse suite atop a world-famous hotel, and I've just been informed we aren't leaving for a week. I guess Sunday dinner won't be happening.

"Yes, but don't hold it against me. I'm not my father. I'm selfish. I want you all to myself. The only interruptions will be room service, which we won't see, as they've been instructed to leave the trolley in the foyer. Is that okay with you? I know school doesn't start for another two weeks, and work too, so I want you and only you with me—in here with me." He attempts a pitiful puppy-dog look, but it loses its effect when he adds a wicked smile.

"Hmmm, I'll have to think about this. Smexy guy with a hot body, or spending days with my roomies and friends, and let's not forget Sunday dinner with my family? Gosh, I just don't know."

I see him moving toward me with a grin. I try to dodge him playfully, but he grabs my waist before scooping me up to carry me over to the bed. "I guess I'll have to persuade you to see it my way. Oh, I'm going to love this week together."

444

I'm sad the week is over, and I feel like it's the end. No, nothing has really happened to make me feel this way. Being in paradise for seven days has been wonderful, but now the real world beckons me to come back to it.

Last time I talked to anyone other than Drew was when I called my mom and told her I had plans and couldn't make dinner. She told me I owed her big time, and then I called Jeff and he already knew about Drew's secret plan, as did Julie and Kevin. After that, I did something I thought would never happen. I turned it off. No, not the sex. My phone.

I lost count of the mind-blowing orgasms after the tenth, or was it twentieth? I've never felt so comfortable with someone of the opposite sex. Okay, there's Jeff … but he doesn't count.

Drew snores lightly and turns over, uncovering his body from under the sheet. I now know every inch of him. Yes, I know I saw him naked in class, but seeing him for seven days has spoiled me for any other body. I long to run my fingers over him now, but I must start detaching myself. Whatever this is won't last. It's time to be honest with myself. We move in different worlds, poles apart. I should be happy that we got to spend this time together, but I can't muster one ounce of happiness.

Hell, I think I've fallen for him. What would he say if I told him that? He wouldn't say anything because he'd move halfway across the world to avoid me.

"Morning." His deep voice pulls my eyes up to his smiling ones.

"Good Morning." I smile back and hope it looks genuine.

All I want to do is fling myself into his arms and declare my undying devotion—okay, it should be another word, but he would definitely die of heart failure if I said "love."

He begins tracing one of his fingers down my cheek and leans over, allowing his mouth to follow his finger as it makes its way all the way down. Desire washes through me as it has many times during this past week. We come together like it's been forever since we last touched one another instead of only a couple of hours.

444

Two hours later, we're showered, dressed and ready to leave. It's quiet as we ride down the private elevator and drive out of the empty, secluded parking garage. The one little thing that gives me hope is that since we entered the car, Drew has held my hand. His thumb rubs circles that make me want to make him pull over the car and rub his thumb somewhere else.

"Dora, we need to talk," he says as we pull into the parking space at our building.

Here it comes: "It's been great, wonderful, really, but you have your life and I've got mine and it just won't work." I say to myself as I stiffen, preparing for the inevitable conversation.

"I have a shoot I have to do in Florida, and I have to leave tonight. I was wondering, actually hoping, that you'd come with me. You still have another week until school and work start again, right?"

Oh, sweet Jesus. I've died and gone to heaven. A reprieve.

"You're not tired of me yet?" I ask, trying to sound light-hearted. Inside, I'm jumping up and down for joy, pushing all dread aside.

"Of course not. I've found I'm extremely partial to a certain special short, fiery redhead, and I don't want her out of my sight for a minute."

Don't cry, Dora, don't you dare. My eyes are filling up, and I turn my head to look out the window so he won't see.

"Yeah, I've still got a hankering for a tall, model type, and I too don't want him to be out of my sight. What a coincidence." Finally in control of my emotions, I turn and pull his head down so I can kiss him gently—except he has other plans, and I swear if a horn hadn't honked, we would've been naked in seconds.

444

I've never been on a private jet before, and sitting in the overstuffed leather reclining seats makes my fear of flying more bearable. Drew had brought my hand to his lips after he buckled me in and he hasn't let go. We've been up in the air for an hour. In front of me is a Coke I ordered, as I didn't trust drinking alcohol. I didn't want to take a chance of throwing up miles above ground. We're on our way to a private beach resort in south Florida, and should arrive in a few hours.

"Did you know there's a bed in the back?" Drew leans over and whispers to me, even though we're all alone.

"Don't you be getting any ideas. For one thing, I don't think I'm up to joining the mile-high club, especially since I'm not even sure I can move from my seat without throwing up. Second, I don't want an accidental audience. And three, I've lost track of how many times we've done the deed, and I think my lady bits need a breather." I giggle as he swoops down, silencing me with a hard kiss.

"Okay, but when we get there, you're mine all night. And it's been at least more than a forty times because we've gone through several boxes of Trojans."

I blush, and oh God, I love that I'll be his tonight.

I must have somehow dozed off. I feel the plane descending, and I see crystal blue water and sandy beaches outside my window.

"Hello, sleepyhead. Anyone would think you haven't had much sleep lately. Oh wait, you haven't." He kisses me swiftly as the wheels touch down on the runway, bouncing us a little.

It's beautiful. Sunny skies and a mild, balmy temperature greet us when we leave the plane. It's heavenly not to have inches of snow and shivering ice-cold winds tearing through my clothes. A limo is waiting for us at the bottom of the stairs. I feel like royalty as I sink into the backseat, absorbing the lavish luxury surrounding me. Let me tell you, kissing in the back of a tricked-out limo is amazing. Of course, we put up the privacy window thingy. There's so much groping and clothes rearranging that I feel when we stop and the door opens, everyone will know what we've been up too.

444

"Dinner out or dinner in?"

I'm standing at a window in a penthouse suite, in awe of the panoramic view of the gulf, complete with a setting sun.

"Whichever you'd like," I reply, still watching the sun as it continues to sink into the water.

Drew pulls me into his arms and we watch the dying rays together.

"Okay, let's eat in and then walk on the beach, and then…"

"Then?" I prompt as he pulls me closer and I feel what "then" is, but it seems like it will be "now" and "then."

A long hour later, we're seated at a cozy patio table on the veranda, eating an abundance of food. We're dressed in matching plush white robes and the cool sea breeze is gently caressing our exposed skin.

"I think I just gained about ten pounds," I say as I pull away from the table, amazed at the amount of food I just ingested.

"We'll just have to find a way to work those off then, now won't we?" Drew scoots his chair over and pulls me onto his lap, his hand working at the knot in my robe.

"Wait, we have to wait an hour after eating," I state firmly and giggle at his awkward attempt at undoing my robe.

"That applies to swimming, and that's not what I have in mind. What the hell have you done to this knot?"

"It's called a 'keep your hands off me' knot, and that means you." I slap playfully at his hands and he pulls up the bottom of my robe. The devilish strokes of his hand on my exposed skin cause me to shiver. He stands up, and I moan at the loss of his hand. He holds me tightly as he takes me to the massive California King-sized bed, throws me in the middle and joins me, shedding his own robe in one fluid motion.

444

Several hours later, I'm exhausted, so spent that I haven't even the energy to walk on the moonlit beach like we talked about earlier. Drew is sound asleep, and I curl up next to him. I feel his arm drape around me before pulling me closer. I feel my eyes growing heavy. I sigh as Drew plants a kiss on my head.

I wish we could stay this way forever.

Twenty-Two

"But I want you to come with me. I don't want us separated for a minute," Drew says sweetly.

"Okay, I'll hang out with you today, but tomorrow I'm going to the beach. I need to get a tan."

"No way are you sunbathing on the beach. I'll have to beat all the guys to a pulp who get a glimpse of you. Anyway, I bet you don't tan." He puts his hands on his hips, looking me up and down.

"No, but they have umbrellas I can hide under, and if I take it slow, I'll get some color."

"But I love your skin just the way it is. I don't want it burned." He's running a finger down my arm now.

"You're just looking out for you. If I get burned, it will be no more fun. I'm a big girl and I'll make the decision. Don't worry, I won't burn." I lift his finger from my arm and slide my mouth up and down it, watching his eyes go dark with desire.

"Not fair. We have to leave, and I can't do a shoot all hard and horny. I don't have time for a cold shower. I'll make you pay for this later."

I giggle and move quickly away from him, grabbing my bag and heading for the door. Let's just say the elevator ride down didn't cure either of his problems.

444

The shoot is a beehive of activity, and I'm suddenly really nervous being here with Drew. Moving down the sand, I walk a few feet behind him. A guy with a clipboard has been by his side since we left the limo. The sun is bright, even with my sunglasses, and the sand is loose, so it's really hard to walk on. I'm praying I don't fall flat on my face. That would be a total fail and would probably embarrass both Drew and me.

I tug on the short shorts I'm wearing, feeling self-conscious as a few people start staring at me. I left my hair down and the wind is blowing the curls in my eyes. I dig in my bag for a headband to keep it out of my face.

When I look up, Drew is far ahead of me and clipboard boy trying to keep up with his long strides. The sight would probably have made me laugh if I wasn't feeling so self-conscious right now. More people join the original gawkers as I pass by them. I feel like there's a spotlight on me instead of the sun.

As if Drew can read my mind, he stops in mid-stride and pivots, ignoring Mr. Clipboard. He jogs back and puts his arm around me, making more people take notice.

"Sorry, Dora. I had to work out some problems with the shoot. I didn't forget about you, honest. Don't worry about our audience. They're just wondering where I found such a hot woman." He squeezes me close, and my confidence rises by at least ten percent.

"Drew, hurry. The lighting is perfect for a morning shot, and then I think we'll break until sunset to get the rest. Alex is waiting for you in the red tent, so get a move on," an older woman with a cigarette hanging out of her mouth belts out like she thinks he's hard of hearing. Her hair looks like a bird's nest, and pencils are stuck behind both ears. The best part is that she's as short as I am, so I immediately feel a kinship with her.

"Sandra, this is Dora Phillips, and those things are going to kill you." He points at her cigarette while shaking his head.

"Hi, nice to meet ya, Dora, and no, these won't kill me. Angela will. I can't believe Joe put her on this shoot. She's a fuckin' bitch, and I refuse to be nice to her. I'll probably be handed a pink slip, but I'm fuck-nuts fed up with that prima donna attitude of hers. She thinks that just because she's the hot thing right now, she can act like a complete twat." Sandra stops her tirade, takes a drag and then turns to shout at a man nearby.

"Sorry, have to run. Red tent, Drew, and Dora, hope you enjoy yourself." She doesn't wait for a reply as she rushes toward the poor man she just yelled at. He looks petrified.

"Don't let the cursing like a sailor and chain smoking fool you, she's actually a really sweet woman," Drew says. "She's been married three times, has four children, and six grandchildren. She's the director of this organized chaos, and she won't get fired because everyone is scared of her. We better get to the tent before I get yelled at too." He leads me to a row of huge tents, all different loud colors. "Yeah, the prop man loves color." Again, it's like he's reading my mind.

Inside the tent, the air is cooler, and two chairs that look like they belong in a beauty salon are sitting in the middle.

Surrounding the chairs are rolling carts full of drawers and bins. A multicolored-haired young woman popping her gum is standing by one of the chairs buffing her nails.

"Thank god you're here. I thought Sandra was going to have a heart attack. I know CPR, but everyone would hate me if I brought her back to life. Now get your ass in the chair. I have to make your ugly butt beautiful." Her New York accent is obvious, and I instantly like her feistiness.

"Alex, Sandra will outlive all of us, and I'm not late. I'm so sorry I'm ugly, but you'll make me handsome like you always do, right?" Drew grins at her and then winks. She ignores him and points to the chair.

"Drew, where are your manners? Aren't you going to introduce me?" Alex nods her head my way and smiles.

"Sorry. Dora, Alex. Alex, Dora." He laughs as we both roll our eyes.

"Hi, I'm Alex, short for Alexandria. I make the monsters look pretty, which isn't easy. It's good to meet you. Why are you are hanging around with this one? There really are no words to explain him, but I guess you know that."

"Nice to meet you, Alex. I'm Dora, short for Pandora, and I don't know why I am either, except for the fact he feeds me." We both laugh when Drew scoffs.

"Nice. I love the fact you're both ganging up on me. You better hurry, Alex. Sandra will be by soon to check up on me."

"Have a seat, Dora." Alex points to the empty chair beside Drew. "I have to go to work, but we must chat later." She grins wickedly as Drew groans while closing his eyes … but not before he winks at me.

It doesn't take Alex long to make Drew "handsome," and we move to the green tent, which is wardrobe. Rows of swimwear line one wall and then gauzy cover-ups line another. A willowy man is in charge and flips through the clothes like he's disgusted at what he sees.

"Ah, Drew, so glad you could join us," the man says. I look around, but there's no one else in the tent. "Here are the changes for this morning. Turquoise pair first. Chop, chop. Time is flying as we speak."

To my surprise, Drew undresses and pulls on the trunks, which fit him like they were custom fitted. Duh, of course they would totally fit, Dora. Can't have too tight or baggy drawers on one of the world's top models.

"And who is this little hottie?" I feel like I'm being undressed as the man scans me up and down.

"She's with me, Bernard, and don't get any ideas. She's not in the biz." Drew puts his arm around me as if to solidify his statement.

"She has a wild look about her—untamed hair and pure skin. Watch out, someone might snatch her up." I decide I'm not a fan of this guy, and I sense the feeling is mutual with Drew.

"We're out of here." Drew waits as I go first and then follows me.

"God, I loathe that man, and if he comes within ten feet of you, scream, seriously." Drew sounds serious and I wonder what Bernard has done to deserve his hatred.

444

We make our way down hand-in-hand toward the water, where the majority of people are hanging out.

"Here's Drew, Sandra," a voice calls, making the crowd turn their heads to watch us until we reach them. I feel like I'm under a microscope, and it's not a good feeling.

"Great, Drew. Get your ass over here and let's get started. Dora, have a seat beside me." Sandra points to an empty chair. I let go of Drew's hand and do as I'm told.

"Okay, ready. These are just Drew pics. I just got a call the bitch prima donna is running late so we'll get started without her."

The next few hours are full of excitement as I watch what at first appeared to be a chaotic mess completely transform into a well-oiled machine. Drew is a natural, and between shots he jokes with the crew. I can tell he likes all of them and the feeling seems to be mutual.

"Oh, shit. The twat-monster approaches," Sandra mumbles.

I turn to see a face and body that I've seen many times. Angela Paige is beautiful, and she knows it. She wears self-confidence like a coat. Her attire is the scantest of bikinis. I wonder why she's wearing anything at all. She's tall, long-legged and blonde, which she swears in every article I've read is her real color. She's looking straight ahead, and people move out of her way as she makes her way toward the shoot. I realize her gaze is fixed on one person, and it's Drew. Drew is talking to one of the other male models, and he turns when he hears all the murmurs.

When Angela makes eye-contact with the object of her attention, she breaks into a breathtaking smile and seductively saunters up to him and—I can't believe my eyes—she kisses him like they're all alone on this beach. The crowd swells around them, and I can't see Drew's reaction. I'm overcome with jealousy. The green-eyed monster is definitely bubbling up inside me. There have always been rumors in the tabloids that they secretly had a thing for each other. Of course, each one has vehemently denied them, but my mom always says where there's smoke, there's usually fire. I feel like running away, but I sit in the seat with what I hope is a neutral look on my face.

Sandra jumps to her feet and yells for everyone to take their marks, and they all scramble to do her bidding. I spy Drew talking to the cameraman. Angela is having a young girl put color on her lips. How thoughtful of her to wait until she kissed Drew so he wouldn't have to remove it from his lips.

The rest of the shoot is a blur. No longer is it exciting. I feel like I'm watching two people madly in love. My hands start to hurt, and I look down to see them pale white, clenching the sides of the chair. The umbrella that's attached to my chair is no longer keeping me shaded, and I decide I'm going back to the hotel, even if I have to walk back alone.

"Take five," Sandra yells, almost bursting my eardrums.

Drew walks away from Angela and makes his way to me with a worried expression on his face.

"Dora, are you okay? You're getting a little sun," he says, reaching up and angling the umbrella so I'm in the shade again.

"I'm fine, thank you." Great, I sound so stiff and formal that he looks at me strangely.

"You don't sound fine," he replies, stroking my cheek.

"I guess I'm just tired."

"I'm tired too," a sultry voice from behind Drew says. "Who is this little person? Did you finally get an assistant like I told you to?" Angela moves beside Drew and lays her head against his shoulder, looking at me like I'm insignificant. She proves it by moving between us and putting her hand up to his cheek. "Sweetie, I think we should go over to the tent and get some refreshments and talk about our next session. I'm not turning red, am I? I put maximum sunscreen on, and I wouldn't want this body to get burned." She's standing so close to him that I want to drag her by her bottle-colored hair and beat the crap out of her.

"You go and I'll be there in a minute." Drew moves around her and leans down to me.

"Okay, but don't be too long. I haven't seen you in days, and we need to catch up." She doesn't look back, but walks toward the tent as if she's walking down a runway.

"I'll bring you something back to drink, okay?" Drew kisses my cheek and then follows Angela like a little puppy dog.

That seals it. I'm leaving. I don't belong in this world. I watch as he catches up with her and the perfect-looking couple strolls into the tent together. I grab my bag and make my getaway. Luckily, when I reach the top of the sand dune, limos are lined up waiting to shuttle people back to the hotel. I snag the one we came in. I say, "Hotel, please," as I settle in and he takes me there without question. I ask him to wait for me, as I need to grab my things before heading to the airport. He doesn't bat an eye, just nods his head.

The maid has been busy. Our hotel room looks immaculate. I quickly stuff all of my things into the carry-on bag. With tear-filled eyes, I leave, taking a long ride to the airport.

444

Flying back is so different. No plush seats, just economy, but I'm lucky that a seat was available. Even though I have to change planes, it's worth it to get home.

Home. I don't want to go back to the loft, and I don't want to go back to my parents', and I'm not going to go to Julie and Kevin's, so I call Jeff when I land, hoping he's not at the loft with Liam.

Twenty-Three

"I can't believe you just up and left him without leaving a note or anything."

This isn't the first time Jeff has said that since he picked me up from the airport. All I can do is cry my heart out and let him rant. "It was a shoot. Drew had to look like it was real because that's what he gets paid to do." He hands me another tissue at a stoplight and turns to look at me. "Dora, quit bawling. Let's talk this out."

"I can't. My heart is breaking," I get out between sobs.

"What else did he do? Did he say he and Angela are an item? Did you even ask?"

"I don't belong in his world. It was just a fling, but now my heart is broken … again." I finally catch my breath, and though my heart is aching, my tears begin to subside.

"You need to call him. Don't leave him hanging like this," he continues, giving me advice until we pull into the parking lot of the student apartments on campus.

About an hour later, sitting on the plush blue couch in his apartment, he hands me my cell and tells me to call Drew or he'll call my mom and tell her I've had a breakdown. I glare at him and his devious blackmail attempt.

I look at my phone and see twenty missed calls—all from Drew. Shit, my ringer has been off. I hit the call button and hear it ring. The butterflies are back and they're going crazy. I know my blood sugar is out of whack because the last time I had anything to eat was, like, twelve hours ago. I'm starting to shake and feel drained of all emotion.

"Hello," a familiar female voice answers.

"Um, yes, can I speak to Drew?" The shaking is getting worse. What is Angela doing answering his cell?

"He's in the shower. Can I take a message?" she purrs. I swear she is.

"Tell him Dora called." I should've just hung up, but I don't.

"Does he have your number?"

"Yes," I reply, thinking how dumb she must be since my number will be saved in Drew's call log.

"Okay, I'll tell him, but we'll be out until late tonight, so he probably won't call you until tomorrow sometime." And before I can say anything, she hangs up. More tears stream down my face, and Jeff holds me as I sob my heart out again.

444

"Dora you're going to be late for class." Jeff's voice seems so far away, but when I open my eyes, he's right in front of me.

"Go away," I say, pulling a pillow over my swollen eyes.

"Nope, not doing it. It's okay to miss the first day of class, and maybe the second, but not the third. So, get your lazy butt out of bed and hit the shower." He pulls the pillow away from my face, and I stick out my tongue. "Really mature. Clean that body while I make breakfast. You're so lucky to have a friend like me."

"I know," I mumble, and I hear his laugh as I enter the bathroom.

"You look better. Except for the dark circles and puffy eyes." Jeff puts a plate of eggs, bacon and toast in front of me.

I resist a snappy comeback because I don't have one. It's been more than a week since I left Drew in Florida. After I talked to Angela, I decided to block all of Drew's calls. I didn't want to hear any of his lame excuses. Of course, that didn't stop him from harassing Julie, Kevin, and Jeff. Thank God he didn't contact my parents. It's been about three weeks since I've seen them, and I'm running out of reasons for why I can't make the trip. I know as soon as my mom sees my face, she'll be trying to find out what's wrong. She can't use her psychic powers on me, but her motherly instincts work just fine in that department.

"Eat up before it gets cold."

"Yes, Mom. Okay, Mom. Anything you say, Mom," I say sarcastically, but it just rolls off Jeff's back.

"Speaking of Mom, I said we'll be there on Sunday for dinner." Jeff smirks at me, and yeah, my tongue automatically sticks out. Great. Only five days to get my eyes back to normal.

"Such a good friend you are."

"I know," he replies, seeming proud of himself.

Classes move at a snail's pace all week. My nerves are stretched thin, as I'm constantly on the lookout for Drew to surprise me and show up at school. Of course, Jeff waits until Friday afternoon to let me know Drew is halfway around the world on another shoot. I have to punch him, since he also said Liam had told him Monday morning. I resist the urge to ask when Drew's coming back, as I don't want to hear Jeff lecturing me again.

Sunday, I wake up to a beautiful sunny morning, and if it wasn't for the foot of snow covering the ground, you'd think it was spring or summer and not frigid winter. All bundled up in layers of clothing, I wait on the couch for Jeff to finish getting ready. I'm proud of myself for being up and ready before him. Maybe it means my heart is beginning to mend. Oh, who in the heck am I kidding?

"Boy, aren't we anxious for dinner with the fam?"

"Yeah, right. Don't mention anything about the whole Drew thing, okay?" I ask. Yes, I'm anxious. I'd give anything to avoid them finding out about my wild week of pre-marital sexual activity followed by a sudden breakup. They're from a different generation and wouldn't understand.

"Of course I won't. I think Julie, Kevin, and I are doing a great job of telling you that you screwed up, so we don't need any help."

"Oh hush, and let's just get this over with."

An hour and a half later, we arrive at my parents' house. The roads were a little busy for a Sunday, and several people decided they needed more excitement in their lives and got themselves into a few car accidents. Everyone is at the house, and luckily, there's no time for small talk, as dinner is on the table and Mom tells us to take our seats as soon as we walk through the door.

"So, Dora, I tried to call you yesterday, it went straight to your voice mail, and you didn't return my calls.

Great. Trust Grandma to bring this up the moment dinner starts.

"I was getting weird calls, so I turned it off during the day."

"Weird calls? Did you call the police?"

Awesome. Now everyone at the table, even Bridget, who likes to eat and then excuse herself because she's too cool for us, is staring at me.

"Not police-calling weird, just wrong numbers, telemarketers, and such. No big deal, but it wastes my minutes when I answer them." They don't need to know I have an unlimited minute plan, do they?

My dad, the sweet man that he is, changes the subject. "So, how does it feel to be graduating in less than five months?"

I let Jeff answer first, and then I say something appropriate. To my relief, everyone seems to be concentrating on their plates.

Right after dinner, Jeff, Granddad, and my dad disappear into the den. Bridget and Taylor sneak away as usual, and I'm on kitchen duty with the women.

"Dora, how are your queer—I mean—*gay* roommates doing?"

Oh, Grandma. You just have to love her.

"They're fine. In fact, they're all out of the country right now. I hardly see them between work and school." My back is to them, thank goodness, because even though they're out of the country, Jeff's my roomie now, so that would be a lie.

"They're nice young men. I just don't understand why they wouldn't want to settle down with a woman and have a family." Now Grandmother has to put in her two cents.

"Maybe because they haven't found the right women, and I told you, two of them aren't gay."

There, I said it. Now they either deal or decide to live in their "our granddaughter is living with gays, so she's safe" world.

Total silence. Not a creature is stirring, not even a mouse. Don't ask me why that popped into my head.

"Well, let's get these dishes washed. They won't clean themselves," my mom says briskly, and we do as she says without another word.

Just before we're about to escape, my mom asks to speak with me alone. I follow her with a sense of dread building up in my stomach. Maybe Henry has told her something about me, which he isn't supposed to, as it breaks the family code.

"Have a seat. This won't take long." She points to the kitchen chair opposite the one she takes for herself. "Henry told me this morning that Drew still needs your help. Dora, part of who we are is to help others, and I'm tired of Henry's bitching—yes, I said bitching—about you not holding up your part."

"Tell Henry to help Drew himself then, if he thinks I'm not doing a good enough job."

"I told him to shut up and let you be, and I haven't heard from him since. He will not let me forget this. I swear, sometimes I just want to be normal." My mom looks tired, and I feel guilty that I'm adding to her problems.

"I'll try harder, Mom, but it's difficult when the object I'm supposed to be helping is absent all the time. Don't worry, I'll fix this." I get up and put my arms around her and she leans back. I kiss the top of her head. "Love you, Mom. Jeff and I have to go. We've got an early class tomorrow." I kiss her cheek and we walk arm in arm back into the living room.

444

"So Henry didn't tell? What a relief for you now, but if it's your job to help Drew, then that's what needs to happen," Jeff says, driving back to his apartment.

"Did you see the tabloid when we went grocery shopping yesterday? Did Drew look like he needs help, or is pining for me? No. He looked happy posing with Angela. So no more talk about Drew. I'll handle my mom if it comes up again."

"Okay, I'll butt out. We need to concentrate on graduating anyway, and we have no time for love."

"Wait. What about Liam? You haven't done anything stupid, have you?" I turn to look at him and see him smiling in the light from the dash.

"No. We're taking it slow. It's a new world for him, and I understand that, so we talk on the phone most nights. He'll be gone for a month, so we'll see."

"I hope he sees what a catch you are. What am I saying? Your ego is big enough already. Scratch that from your memory." We burst out laughing, and it feels good. I haven't laughed it what seems like forever.

Twenty-Four

Valentine's Day. It's either a truly wonderful day or it sucks. And mine is at an epic level of suck.

Waking up this morning, I threw up violently, which means I either have the stomach flu or food poisoning. It doesn't even matter because I don't have a date or someone to share this "great" holiday with. Not like I could if I did, since I have this whole upchucking thing going on. Jeff brings me a cool washcloth and places it on my forehead, and it makes me feel at least fifty percent better.

"I'll stop by all your classes and get any work you need to finish. You just stay in bed and drink plenty of fluids. The last thing you need to do is get dehydrated."

"I will. Jeff, don't call my mom. I just want to just lay here and die in peace."

"You're not going to die. It's just the flu, and you're healthy, so you should get over it fast. Is there anything you need before I go, besides another stomach?"

Yep, Mr. Psychic knows what I was going to say.

"No. Just go to class and don't come home. You have a date tonight, so take your clothes with you and dress at the loft. If I die, I'll call and let you know." I give a halfhearted laugh and then shoot out of bed, making it to the porcelain God just in time.

"I don't think I should leave you," Jeff says as he holds my hair.

"Get me some Saltines and I'll nibble on those. I'm sure I'll feel better soon. Now, go and stop mothering me. Thanks for holding my hair, and I love you, so scoot."

I make it back to bed, barely, and Jeff brings me three bottles of water and a box of Saltines, blows me a kiss, and leaves after telling me to call him if I need anything.

I look at the clock. It's been three hours since Jeff left for school, and with the nap, some water, and Saltines, I'm feeling better. Okay, I feel better as long as I don't move.

I can't remember the last time I was sick. I just never had the time. Before I fell asleep, I did call work and tell them I was sick, and my boss was in awe that the mighty Pandora Phillips had allowed a bug to bring her down. I've never missed a day of work in more than four years. I should get a medal or something for that. She told me to get better and call her when I was up to it.

I turn on the television and the morning shows are full of helpful hints of what to get and do with your love on this special day. Great. I flip channels, and every movie station is showing romantic films, so I turn it off.

Since I've changed my number, I've had no more missed calls from Drew. I avoid the tabloids so I don't have to see that he's moved on. My heart hasn't healed like I had hoped it would. I type "how long does it take a broken heart to mend" into to Google, but don't get a definitive answer. I'll have to wait, I guess, and then one day it may fix itself.

My cell rings and I grab it off the bedside table. It's Jeff.

"How are you feeling?"

"Better," I reply.

"Are you lying to me?"

I roll my eyes as if he can see me.

"Rolling your eyes is not an answer."

"I'm better—ate a handful of Saltines, drank some water, and thankfully haven't vomited once since you left. So stop worrying and just enjoy your time with Liam."

"Okay, but if you need me, I'm only a phone call away. Get some sleep and I'll call you again in a few hours. Bye, love you."

"Yeah, love you too."

444

I'm drifting in and out of sleep when the phone rings. This time, it's my mom.

"Happy Valentine's Day, sweetie." I hear my dad yelling the same thing in the background. "What exciting plans do you have tonight?"

Should I tell the truth? Hell no. She'll get in the car and drive here, and that'd be terrible for everyone. I'll have to lie and hope she buys it.

"Jeff and I are ordering a pizza and then watching romantic comedies all night. What are you and Dad doing?"

"We have dinner reservations. Bridget is out with her friends, and Taylor is going out with—honey, what's her name again? Skye, that's it. We haven't met her yet, but he says she's nice. And we think Bridget has a crush on someone, but she's not telling. I wish you'd find a nice guy, not like that jerk you dated for three years. I never liked him. He had beady eyes. Well, you and Jeff have a nice time. While you're looking for a nice guy, find one for Jeff too. He needs to find happiness. Love you, sweetie."

That went well. Lie told and believed. So why do I feel dejected? Everyone has a life but me. I can't even go out looking for anyone with this bug, so I guess I'll have to wait it out.

What am I saying? I'm still into Drew, and who knows when I'll get over him.

Depressed now, I switch on the boob tube again and find a movie that isn't a freaking romance. It's about the end of the world. Yes, definitely a more fitting choice.

I wake up the next morning with the television is still on. Jeff must not have come home, or he would've turned it off.

I get up to go pee and my stomach instantly rebels. I make it to the bathroom with seconds to spare. I'm so over this. I can't afford to be sick any longer. I need to go back to school and work. I pull myself up from my sitting position on the floor and barely make it to the bed without falling. I cram a Saltine in my mouth and down a sip of water. I'll just have another nap.

444

"Are you sure she's okay?" I hear Julie's anxious voice.

"She's just sick. I checked on her all day yesterday and last night, but I didn't disturb her when I came home this morning since she was sleeping. She needs rest." Jeff sounds defensive, and I really don't have the energy to get involved with this discussion.

"You stayed out all night? What if she had fucking died?" Julie isn't happy. No, she's not.

"Jules, calm down. Jeff is taking good care of her." It's Kevin, the peacemaker.

"He should've called me yesterday. I could've taken care of her."

"Yeah, right. It was Valentine's Day." Jeff's getting offensive now.

"Okay, all three of you please talk quietly. I'm trying to get better here." I finally open my eyes.

"Aww, honey, how are you feeling?" Julie grabs my hand like I'm on my way out.

"Just peachy, especially for someone that has the stomach flu. Maybe you guys should sanitize yourselves and stay away from me. I don't want anyone else to suffer through this. What am I saying? Julie you're pregnant. Get out of here. Go wash your hands and leave. You can't get sick."

I begin to worry that I may have sat up quickly when a queasy feeling washes over me, and yep, you guessed it. I didn't make it to the toilet this time. Jeff is there, holding my hair and clucking like a mother hen.

"She's right. Don't worry, I won't leave her until she's better, so you two leave now."

I can't open my eyes. I'm so tired. Jeff helps me back into bed.

The room is dark when I wake up again. I guess Jeff was able to convince Julie and Kevin to leave, since I find myself here alone. My clock says it's nine, and I'm thirsty.

Turning on the lamp, I see my water supply is nil. I grab a cracker and slowly sit up in the bed, swing my legs to the side of it, and drop my feet to the floor. So far, so good. Stomach isn't rolling.

I stand up as Jeff walks in the door. My eyes meet his while I try to balance myself and I send him a weak smile. I suddenly feel dizzy and Jeff's image begins to blur. I hear his voice ring out when I feel myself stagger before collapsing to the floor, and then nothing.

"Ms. Phillips? Dora, can you hear me? Please open your eyes."

I don't know this male voice, and my eyes can't open because it's too bright.

"Dora, wake up. It's me, Jeff."

Duh, Jeff. My mouth is so dry and my head is throbbing. I wish they would turn off the lights.

"Jeff, turn off the lights." I'm croaking like a frog, wonderful.

"Ms. Phillips, I'm Dr. Banner. You gave your boyfriend and us quite a scare. You probably have a little headache from the bump on the head. Nurse, dim the lights so Ms. Phillips can focus on us."

Boyfriend? Does he mean Jeff?

"Okay, it's safe to open your eyes now." The doctor's voice is smooth and calming, and I do as he asks.

There's a crowd surrounding my hospital bed—yes, I've figured out that's where I am. Everyone is smiling but Jeff, who looks like he might pass out any moment. He moves closer, takes my hand and leans down to kiss my forehead which succeeds in bringing tears to my eyes.

"Dora, you had me so worried. I couldn't catch you before you fell. I'm so sorry." A tear trickles down his cheek and I let go of his hand to wipe it away with my finger.

"I'm okay, see? It's not your fault."

I hear a sigh and a young … I guess nurse, is looking at us with a dreamy smile.

"Doctor, I have Ms. Phillips' test results." Another older woman puts a piece of paper in his hand.

"Well, it's as I thought, Ms. Phillips. You don't have the stomach flu. You have morning sickness, or in your case, not just morning but a little more extensive. I'd say you're about six weeks along. I'll prescribe rest and a bland diet as tolerated. We've given you IV fluids to get you hydrated. I'm sure you and your boyfriend would like to be alone to digest this news."

With that, he and his staff disappear around a green curtain. Jeff and I are left looking at each other in stunned silence.

Pregnant? Me? I can't be. We used protection every time.

No, we didn't. Not on New Year's we didn't. I was too anxious.

It's all my fault. How could this happen?

"Dora, say something. You're scaring me." Jeff grabs my hand again and sits partially on my bed.

"Tell me this is a flu induced dream, and that I'll wake up soon. I can't be pregnant."

Jeff just shakes his head. "Tests don't lie, and it makes sense. You have no fever, Saltines calm your stomach, and you've been crying a lot more than usual lately. Yep, you're totally pregnant."

"What am I going to do? My mom is going to kill me. Never mind my grandmother, who will tell me if I had gone to finishing school, I'd have learned to keep my legs closed."

I cover my eyes with my arm. I feel the beginning of a panic attack, which I've never had, but I think I'm about to experience one.

"Your mom won't kill you, but you're right about your grandmother. She won't be happy, and you'll be banned from the family."

"Thanks for the pep talk. What am I going to do?"

Panic is starting to take over. My whole body starts to shake.

"Hey, now. Relax. Maybe it's time to talk to Drew," he says.

He lies down beside me, pulling me into his arms. I'm trembling uncontrollably, and he's making soothing sounds and rubbing my non-IVed arm. I'm relishing the heat from his body, and the warmth seems to help. My panic button has seemed to have reset itself.

"Hmmrph. Excuse me, is she okay?" A fresh-faced nurse is staring at us, and I bet she's wondering if it's her job to tell him that he should get out of the bed. But she doesn't say another word, just winks and leaves.

"Jeff, promise me something, and I mean really promise me, not just lip service."

"Anything for you, Dora."

He smiles, and I suddenly feel like I can do this. Other single women have babies and the children turn out all right. After all, I have seven and a half months to prepare. I'll have to find a job to support us. Of course I have to finish school.

But what about my family? What kind of role model am I for Bridget and Taylor? Oh, hell, I start to shake again as the enormity of the situation hits me. I'm going to be someone's mom.

"I'm waiting."

"For what?"

"You said I have to promise, so I'm waiting to see what I have to promise you."

"Oh, yes. Don't roll your eyes. I've just realized I'm going to be someone's mother. But I digress. Promise me you won't tell Drew or anyone else until I've thought this through. You'll have to cross your heart, pinky swear, and anything else you can think of."

I feel his body vibrate and realize he's laughing.

"Hey, it's not funny," I semi-yell at him.

"Pinky swear? Really?" He chuckles and I join in.

"You know what I mean. I'm serious. This is serious." My eyes fill up with tears. God, this hormone thing is real.

"Okay, don't cry. I'll do anything if you don't cry. I won't tell a soul, promise. Dora, I'm here for you and the baby. I won't desert you, but I think down the road, Drew needs to know. It's his baby too."

"But it's my fault. I was so careless and worked up that night, and didn't have him use a condom. We were so mindful after than night though. Who gets pregnant the first time?"

"How many first times are we talking about? How many times that night?" He looks at me in amazement.

"I lost track after the first, but it was quite a few," I say sheepishly, the law of averages was definitely against me.

"So it seems you played the odds and gained a bundle."

He did *not* just say that. Just wait until I get my strength back.

"Something tells me you're angry now. If the sparks shooting out of your eyes are any indication, then you are, but at least you're not crying." Jeff jumps off the bed and sits in a chair, a few safe feet away when I send him a playful glare.

The last few weeks have been a complete blur. I felt much better after the hospital visit, and Jeff has been the ultimate caretaker. He made me an appointment after doing tons of research on every obstetric doctor in the area. Thank heaven, it's a woman. She doesn't normally take my insurance, but miraculously, she made an exception. Jeff won't tell me why though. All he said was it must be his magnetic personality, which is a bunch of bull.

The doctor visit went okay. I got a clean bill of health and a prescription for horse-sized vitamin pills. She said the ER doctor was right, and she agrees I got pregnant on New Year's once I informed her that we had used protection every time after that. Jeff came in with me and used the same line that allowed him to be in the ER with me—that he was my boyfriend. Which technically isn't a lie since he is both my friend and a boy.

Every day after my first appointment, Jeff has made sure I follow the instructions of the doctor and eat three meals a day, all bland tasting of course. Luckily, my nausea has started to subside. In fact, it seems surreal that I have a "bun in the oven," as Jeff lovingly refers to the baby.

I still don't know how I'm going to tell everyone, so I've distracted myself by concentrating on my studies. My heart is still mending, and I lie in bed every night wondering where Drew is, and what he's doing. It really hurts. Jeff and I had a blowout or up, whatever, the other day, as he took it upon himself to tell my job I won't be coming back. I was mad for a whole day and told him I needed the money, and he said he would pay for all my stuff, which is ludicrous. His parents have always made him work to pay his bills. He says not to worry, and I wonder where he's getting the money since he quit his job as well just to take care of me.

I promise to pay him back one day, but I'm not sure how realistic of a promise that is. Every time I think of what it takes to raise a child, it makes me sick to my stomach. Termination or adoption are most definitely both out. I want to keep this baby, so I'll just have to make it work.

"Dora, how about Papa's tonight?" Jeff asks from the living room.

"We can't afford to eat out. I wish you would tell me where you're getting all this money." I come out of my bedroom and put my hands on my hips. I'm going to get him to spill or die trying. Okay, I'm not going to die … it's just a saying. "Anyway, my pants are getting tighter, and soon I'll have to wear bigger clothes. Everyone will know soon. But I'm giving you an out, so spill. Where's the money coming from?" I glare at him, hoping I'll scare his gorgeous face into fessing up.

"Okay, stop nagging at me. I have a trust fund. I swore to myself that I'd support myself with a job and never dip into it. My parents agreed that it'd do me good to have to work for things, but things have changed. This is what I want to spend my money on," he says. "I want to help you, Dora."

"How will I ever pay you back?" I moan, putting my face in my hands. My life is such a mess.

"We're family. You mean the world to me, and I can't wait to be Uncle Jeff to your little bump." He pulls my hands from my face and pulls me in for a hug. He gives the absolute best hugs, and yes, my eyes fill up with tears at his words. "Now, no crying. Grab your coat and let's go. I won't take *no* for an answer." He pushes me away and I go to my room to retrieve my coat.

444

Papa's is busy, but it's no surprise with it being Friday night. Jeff is leading me through the crowded place and every table is full. I wonder if we're going to sit at the special kitchen table. We make our way to the back, and when I move to the side to avoid a customer getting up from his seat, I see two people I truly want to avoid. They're waving to us, and Jeff pulls me with him to their table. Later, we'll have a heated discussion, but I put on a smile and both Liam and Colin take turns hugging me and telling me they're happy to see me.

I know Drew won't be joining us, as the Internet says he's in Australia on a job. Yes, I may have been stalking him recently. Jeff avoids my eyes and I think of ways I can get him back for his deception, making me believe this was a spur-of-the-moment decision.

"We've missed you two." Liam's eyes sweep both of us, but linger longer on Jeff.

"The loft isn't the same without you, Dora. When are you coming back? Jeff says you're temporarily with him because of the bad weather and he worries about you driving to school in it," Colin says, and I restrain from eye-rolling at such a lame explanation.

"I know it's more convenient, and now that Jeff has a two-bedroom, it's handy. You guys have been traveling a lot, so I would've been alone anyway." There's a huge elephant in the room. Nobody is talking about Drew and me, and maybe they don't know? But surely he would have told them. They've been best friends forever.

"Oh, it'sa my favorite people in the wholea wide world. How did you sneaka in here?" Papa's loud voice makes me jump a little.

Tears well up in my eyes as he leans down and kisses my cheek and hugs me. Then it's Mama's turn, and our table erupts in laughter as they tell us about the crazy customers they've had in lately. We order, and when the food arrives it smells delicious as always.

My mouth waters, but as soon as I take a bite of perfectly made lasagna, my stomach rolls and I reach for the bottle of antacids in my bag. I bend down like I've lost my napkin and throw two in my mouth. I chew them quickly and then sit up to find three sets of eyes fixed on me.

"Napkin fell," I say, and they continue eating.

It's hard to pretend to eat. I finally give up and ask for a doggie bag, which makes Papa's eyebrows rise. I've never needed a to-go bag in all the years I've been coming here. He looks at me suspiciously, but says nothing.

"So, how's Drew?" Trust Jeff to drop the bomb. Nobody has mentioned him, and we might have gone all evening without saying his name. Now I have two bones to pick with him, and it won't be pleasant. Just the mention of his name makes me tear up a little.

"He's been working hard, and he's really unhappy. We haven't ever seen him this unhappy." Liam states without looking in my direction.

"Yeah, he's really down, and he won't let us in. He's flying in from Milan tonight." Colin does look at me. In fact, his eyes are glued to mine.

"Sorry to hear that. Did he mention why?"

Jeff, I swear—shut your mouth. But secretly I'm waiting for the answer, my nerves strung tightly.

"We all know the reason. All he said was he has no idea what he did wrong. Everything was going well, and poof, you were gone." I wish Colin would look at someone else.

"Well, we should probably head out. Jeff and I have an early class tomorrow."

I get up quickly, and whoa, dizzy much? Jeff grabs my arm and steadies me so I don't fall over. I say my quick goodbyes, and then push my way out of the restaurant, not waiting to see if Jeff is following. I'll walk back to the apartment if I have to, but Jeff catches up with me at the front door and holds it open. We say nothing to each other as we make our way to the car. The silence between us continues until we're in his living room. Jeff pushes me gently onto the couch and then plops down beside me.

"Sounds like Drew isn't very happy." Jeff puts his arm around me so I can't flee.

"Maybe Angela dumped him," I quip, and my heart skips a beat thinking it might be true.

"Or maybe, like Liam and Colin suggested, it's you he's missing." Jeff's arm tightens around me. He's good. He knows that if he wasn't holding me, I'd flee to my room. "You're going to sit here, and we're going to discuss this. No excuses, not even if you throw up everywhere. It won't deter me. Drew is miserable, and it's because of you. Liam says he's been like a zombie, and they're worried about him. You need to talk to him and explain why you left like you did. You need to call him. He comes back tonight. You don't have to tell him about the baby, but I think you need to talk, and tell him the truth. Think about it. Think hard. I think you're wrong about him—hell, I know you are. He's suffered for more than four months, and it's time to tell him you love him and you want to be with him."

Jeff releases me, gets up and without another word, he goes into his room and shuts the door. That's it. He tells me I love Drew and that's it.

Do I love Drew? That would explain why my heart felt shattered when I left him. Not to mention all the buckets of tears I've shed. Am I too late? Drew comes home tonight. Do I have the courage to call him? What if he doesn't love me? What about our baby?

Oh hell, it's *our* baby. Not mine, but ours. Could we make it work? He's famous and jets all over the world, and I'm a nobody with a psychic mother and a crazy family. I wonder if he's home yet. I just have to call him to find out. But what do I say?

Well, here goes nothing.

I pluck my phone out of my back pocket and hit one on my phone. Yeah, I have him on speed dial under number one. Liam is number four. Yeah, I know I'm buying into his superstition.

My stomach clenches. I feel sick. What if he sees an unknown number calling and doesn't answer? It's still ringing, and then I hear him say, "Hello."

"Hi, it's me Dora. Drew, I need to talk to you…if you want to, that is."

He's silent and I almost hang up. I fear he'll say no and my heart will never, ever mend.

"Yes, I think we do." I feel relief. His deep husky voice makes me shiver.

"When are you free? Maybe we could do lunch on Saturday?" I hope he says sooner. It's only Tuesday, and I don't think I can wait that long.

"I'm coming over now," he says firmly, and I want to do a happy dance, but I know my legs won't support me. They're like watery Jell-O. "Dora, are you there? Is that all right?"

"Yes. Do you need directions?"

"No, I've known where you've been since … well, we'll discuss that once I get there."

"Be careful. See you soon." I don't know what else to say.

"I will."

And then click, he's gone. I stare at my phone. I can't believe that just happened. He wants to see me. I've got to go do my hair and freshen up and change clothes. I scramble as fast as my pregnant self will allow to my room to get ready.

Twenty-Five

It's been an hour, and I've worn a path in the carpet. It should have only taken Drew fifteen minutes to get here. I keep looking outside. A light snow is falling. It's April…it's not supposed to snow in April.

I let the curtain fall and take a seat on the couch for the millionth time—okay, not that many, but quite a few. My nerves are frayed. My mom says that all the time, but now I know what she means by it.

I feel like this night will be the turning point in my life, and I hope it goes the way I want it to go. I want Drew—any way I can have him. Where in the hell did that that come from? I do want him? Oh, who am I fooling? Yeah, he might tire of me after a few months, but I'll still have a part of him forever. I touch my stomach and feel the little bump that's starting to show.

"Where is your father?" I say to him or her.

I hear a cell ringing and I glance at mine, but the ringing comes from another room, so it's Jeff's phone. I hear his muffled voice and then nothing. A feeling of dread like I've never felt before comes over me. I know a call this late at night isn't good.

His door opens. The first thing I notice is that he's fully dressed and pulling on his jacket. His face is grim as he looks down at me. I know something really bad has happened, and I know it affects me.

"Dora, I'm going to get your coat. That was Liam. We have to go to the hospital. Drew's been in an accident."

My stomach rolls, and I don't make it to the bathroom. Jeff rubs my forehead and holds back my hair as I dry heave into the kitchen sink. When I feel that I'm in control, he lets me go. I turn around as he brings me my coat. I'm numb. Jeff kisses me on the forehead, helps me with my coat, takes my arm, and leads me out of the apartment.

The car is toasty, but I'm still shivering with a deep cold inside me. I'm praying that Drew is okay and he'll smile at me when he sees me and we will live happily ever after, or until he gets sick of me.

"It's my fault. I called him and he said he would come right over. Oh, Jeff, what if he …" I can't continue as uncontrollable sobs tear through me. Jeff grabs my hand tightly.

"Stop it, Dora. Liam didn't say, but we have to think positive. It's not your fault. If anything, it's mine. I made you call him."

He squeezes my hand, and I turn, trying to control my sobs. I see a tear roll down his cheek. If this is a nightmare, I want to wake up. Please don't let this be real. With my free hand, I pinch myself and it's real. It's so fucking real.

We arrive at the ER a few minutes later. The bright lights of the foyer sting my eyes, or it might be the salt from my tears. Jeff drops me at the front door and leaves to park the car. I immediately see Liam and Colin as I walk through the automatic doors. Again, my legs turn to rubber as I see the looks on their faces. They rush forward and both reach for me before I sink to the floor.

Liam picks me up and moves to the waiting room, putting me down on an overstuffed sofa. He takes a seat beside me

"How is he?" I whisper. Please, please let him be okay.

"We don't know. Nobody has come out to talk to us. We called his dad, his sister, Emily, and we tried reaching his mom, but she's somewhere out of the country," Colin answers, his face as white as a ghost.

"It's my fault. He was coming to see me," I say, feeling numb and exhausted.

"How is it your fault? He was like a little kid after he got off the phone. He …" Liam chokes up and I pat his hand and lean into him, closing my eyes and letting the beat of his heart try to soothe me.

"How is he?" Jeff's voice sounds close, but I have no energy to look at or answer him. I hear Colin mumble a few words and then nothing but Liam's heart beating and an annoying TV that's blaring from somewhere close by.

An hour later, Drew's father joins us, looking worried. He worry turns to anger when Colin tells him we haven't been told anything. He storms off. I let Liam's heartbeat take me away again. I must have fallen asleep, because when I open my eyes, Emily is there, and so are a bunch of people I've met and some I've only seen in magazines.

Liam explains the late-night news had reported the accident, and people just started showing up. The agency also sent over private security to keep the press at bay. And there is still no news on Drew's condition.

Emily sees me talking to Liam and comes over, making Jeff move so she can sit beside me. Her face is tear-streaked. She grabs my free hand and draws me into a hug. My stomach starts tumbling, and I stand up quickly. Jeff is right there, guiding me away from the crowd and into a secluded hallway. I want to see Drew. I have to see Drew.

"Jeff, I have to see Drew. Please help me. I can't stand not knowing if he's okay." I cling to him and he pats my back and then seats me in a chair that he grabs from an open empty room.

"I'll be right back," Jeff assures me, and I let my head fall into my hands. I hear him on the phone, and then he's back with a slight smile on his face.

"What did you do?"

"I called my dad. He's calling the CEO of this hospital. In a few minutes, we should have some action. Let's go back to the waiting room. I know it's crowded, but they need to be able to find us."

The room is just how we left it, except everyone is silent. A harried-looking man in a long white coat with a stethoscope slung around his neck enters a few minutes after Jeff and I sit down. All eyes focus on him.

"I need to talk to the immediate family of Drew Johnson." I zero in on his father and Emily, who for some reason grab my arm and take me with them. We follow the man down another hallway and into a small room, really more like a large closet.

"I'm Dr. Morely, and I've been attending to Drew. The crash was pretty serious and so are his injuries. We lost him a few times, but he's stable enough now to undergo surgery. He's bleeding internally, and we have to find the source. His right leg is broken, but we'll fix that after we get the bleeding under control. We need you to sign the forms so we can take him to the OR. We're sorry we haven't come out sooner, but it was touch and go, and my team and I were very busy." He sounds exasperated, but I don't feel guilty. We were in the dark.

Emily and I go back to the waiting room, arms around each other. Her father follows the doctor to sign the papers. I know how the doctor felt, because as soon as we walk into the room, it's like a spotlight is on us.

"Well?" Jeff comes up to me and holds my hand.

"He's going to surgery because he's bleeding internally and they don't know where, so they have to stop it."

Emily starts crying and Liam and Colin move in to comfort her.

444

Time seems to stand still, but the hands on the clock say differently. It's been four hours since we last talked to the doctor. In that time, the head of the modeling agency showed up, followed by a catering service handing out coffee, tea, and pretty much anything you can think of as far as drinks and sandwiches and pastries. A few people eat. I notice the models passing on the food but consuming flavored waters.

"Dora, you should eat something. You didn't have dinner. And lunch and breakfast weren't much either."

I shake my head at Jeff. I definitely don't want a vomiting session in front of this crowd. He insists I drink a cup of hot tea and it warms me up a little.

"Are all of you here for Drew Johnson?" A petite woman in scrubs is standing in the doorway looking us all over. We nod our heads like sheep. "I'm Dr. Galena and I'm the surgeon. We found the site of the bleeding, and we had to remove Mr. Johnson's spleen. While we were in the OR, a scan revealed some swelling in the brain. We've had to place him in a drug-induced coma in hopes it will give the brain time to heal on its own. Only time will tell. We were able to repair the damage to his leg once the bleeding was under control, and he's now in intensive care. Only immediate family members are allowed to visit, one at a time, for a few minutes every hour. Even though he's in a coma, it's believed that patients in his condition can still hear you. We encourage you to talk to him in a positive manner. Please no negativity. A nurse will be in shortly to take family members back to the ICU waiting room." She turns and leaves quickly before anyone can ask questions. But what else can she say? We know what she knows.

"Come on, Dora, the nurse is here." Both Emily and Drew's father are waiting for me. I'm shocked why they're still including me, like I'm family or something. Before I have the chance to wonder anymore, Jeff kisses me on the cheek and gently pushes me to join them in pursuit of the nurse down the hallway.

ICU is a scary place. I'm in total shock as Emily and her dad let me go first. It's like walking into a tomb, but with little beeping and whooshing noises. The nurses walk quietly from one room to another. Rooms are laid out in a semicircle, with a large island in the middle where other nurses sit observing monitors. The nurse who came to get me gestures to a room in the middle of the semicircle, and I prepare myself for what lies beyond the door.

"Now remember," she says quietly, "he will look different. He's hooked up to machines by many tubes, and has some bruising." She made this speech earlier in the waiting room. How could I have forgotten?

I turn the corner into the room, and I don't recognize the person in the bed. Drew's face is all bruised and swollen. His leg is in a cast, and there are so many tubes, I can't begin to count. I wipe the tears from my eyes. I have to be brave. This is the man I love, and I have to help him pull through this.

"Hi, Drew." I say, taking hold of his hand, hoping against hope that he'll squeeze it back. I kind of feel silly for talking to him like this, but if they think he can hear me, I don't care how ridiculous I look. "I'm sorry I ran out on you in Florida. I just felt out of my league. If it makes any difference, my heart has been broken ever since. I think and dream about you. I've never in my life ever felt so happy and loved. Yes, I said the L word. I love you, Drew, and deep down I knew it was you on Halloween but I thought you were a bad boy, and the parade of women I've seen you with in the magazines, tabloids and on TV made me believe you were a player. I'm so sorry I judged you. I'm wrong, and I want another chance if you'll let me. Please forgive me. I love you, Drew. I'm not just saying that because you're in here, and we're supposed to only say positive things. I really do love you, and I want to be with you until you get tired of me. Please get better soon so we can talk like we were supposed to before this happened. My mom says things happen for a reason, but I don't understand the reason behind this. I love you, and I'll keep saying it until you wake up. I love you, Drew."

"Sorry, time's up," a nurse says. "Can I make a suggestion?" She looks at me with kind eyes. "Go home and get some rest and then come back. I promise I'll call you if anything changes. You have to take care of that baby."

"How do you know?" I ask, thinking whether I've said anything. I'm so tired it could be possible.

"I was watching you on the monitor, and you've been rubbing your abdomen the whole time you've been talking to him."

"Nobody knows except my best friend." I feel a little panicked that my secret will be out before I'm ready.

"I won't say a word." She pats my hand and then lets me out of the room. I lean up against the wall, not sure if I can take another step. Just as the thought goes through my mind, I look up and see Jeff standing there waiting for me.

"Come on, we're going home to get some rest. I've told Emily and Mr. Johnson, and they're going back to the loft to stay a while," he says while I let him lead me down the hallway.

Twenty-Six

The morning after the accident, my mom showed up at Jeff's door. I was sound asleep and didn't wake up until late afternoon, feeling like I had been hit by a truck.

I check the bedside table. My cell is missing. I slowly get out of bed, in deference to my sensitive stomach and crazy equilibrium. That's when I hear voices and I open my door to see my mom at the kitchen table with Jeff. She gets up and meets me halfway with open arms.

"Mom? What? How?"

"Henry told me. I know he's supposed to keep quiet about family matters and problems, but I knew something wasn't right and he gave in after I told him I would start ignoring him all together. I kept getting your voice mail, so I drove down this morning. He told me along the way. No, I didn't get stopped by the police, and no, your dad didn't know I was coming. Why didn't you call me? I'm your mother." She's hugging me tightly. I feel like I did when I was a little girl and she would hug away my fears. "Jeff has filled me in. Drew's going to pull through. From what I've found out, he's in love with my daughter and she's in love with him too. So with my connections to the other side, I'm pulling out all the stops. My grandbaby will not be fatherless." She kisses the top of my head as I realize what she just said.

"How do you know? Henry?"

She nods her head. "Of course, I would have known anyway. I'm your mother, after all." She pulls back and wipes the tears flowing down my cheeks and then gently rubs my abdomen. "Now, pull yourself together. No more crying. Jeff says you haven't eaten since yesterday morning, so we have to feed you. It's an old wives' tale that you're eating for two. You're just eating for yourself. That baby will take whatever it needs."

"You're not mad?" I ask in disbelief.

"Of course not. You love Drew and he loves you, and you will both love this baby. That's all that matters."

From that point on, my life changed. I felt more positive—okay, except for today, the two-week anniversary after the accident.

I make my way into the ICU and see Drew's doctor having a discussion with his dad and Emily. They look up when they see me through the doors. I walk through, not sure what is waiting for me.

"Ah, Ms. Phillips. I've just been telling the Johnsons that we feel it's time to bring Drew out of the coma. The swelling in his brain has resolved. He should wake up soon. There's no timetable though. It just depends on how his body shrugs off the remnants of the drugs. We'll see when he wakes up what, if any, damage was done," the doctor explains and then leaves us to talk amongst ourselves.

"Dora, you go first. Dad and I will go down to the cafeteria. We haven't eaten breakfast yet." Emily kisses my cheek and Drew's dad pats my back awkwardly. We have come to know each other these last weeks, and we've had long talks on why I left the photo shoot that day. I haven't told them that I'm pregnant yet, or that I love Drew, but they have said he's loved me from the first minute he saw me. I've cried many tears over the time I've wasted being so stubborn through all of this. But these two have made me feel like I'm family. Drew's mother never showed up though. Apparently, she calls Emily once a day for progress reports, but has no plans on coming. Emily and her dad were relieved at the news, and I get the feeling if I met her, I would feel the same way.

How could a mother abandon her children? I touch my stomach. *I will never leave you*, I say silently to our precious bump.

I walk into Drew's room and the first thing I notice is there are fewer lines leading into his body. The bruises have turned yellow, and over the last few days, the swelling has drastically diminished. He looks like Sleeping Beauty, except a male version, of course. I wish a kiss would wake him up. A nurse walks in behind me and moves around me to the bed.

"As you can see, the doctor has removed the breathing tube and before you know it he'll be waking up soon," she says, turning to look at me. She didn't say "if," and I'm so grateful for that. "I'll leave you two alone." She quietly makes her exit.

"Hi, Drew. It's me again. Hope you're not getting sick of me, and if you are, too bad. The doctor has cut off your sleeping meds, so you'll be awake soon. I can't wait to see your beautiful eyes. I've so missed them so much. When you wake up your throat will be a little sore. The doctor says you're healing wonderfully and that if you keep this up, you could go home soon. I know you'll want to go as soon as you can once you taste the food. It's horrible. As soon as you can, we'll go to Papa's. They send their love, as does my family. Even my grandma now believes you're not gay because I told her I love you, and that I have firsthand knowledge of that. It went completely over her head, of course. I have a secret to tell you, but I won't tell you until I can see your eyes and you can speak. Or maybe I should wait until you've completely recovered because you might not like my secret. I'm hoping that you do though." I look at my watch. I've been in here more than an hour, and I smile at the kindness of the nursing staff.

Jeff's waiting for me when I come out of the room and we sit in the waiting area, watching the morning talk shows. Life goes on.

444

"Dora. Dora, wake up." I look up and see Emily standing over me. She's smiling and laughing. I'm lying on a couch and I sit up when she grabs my hands. "He's awake and I asked him questions and he blinked once for 'yes' and twice for 'no,' or was it the other way around? The nurse says a doctor is on his way up to check him out."

She's jumping up and down. I stand up and she hugs me like she will never let me go. Yes, I'm happy, but anxious too. After weeks of talking to him, I'm scared I won't know what to say.

"She'll come and get you after it's done. Now remember, you promised you wouldn't tell him I told you he's quitting the modeling gig, or that he's opening a children's center and the shelter for battered women. I want him to be the one to tell you, okay?"

"I won't forget."

When Emily first told me about Drew's plans, I couldn't believe he would give up his career. She told me that he started thinking about this in September, and she felt it was because he met me. As we wait for the nurse, I try hard not to rub my stomach to calm my nerves. I want to tell Emily, but I think Drew should hear it first. Okay, so he's not the first, but I don't think he'd like the fact that I told Emily the day he woke up from a coma before I told him. I hope he's happy about it.

"The doctor's finished with his exam," says the nurse as she enters. "Now, he'll be hoarse and his throat will be sore, so he won't feel like talking much. Who's first?"

Emily pushes me forward and I follow the nurse, dread sitting like a rock in my stomach. I reach the door and then step over the threshold and look to the left. Drew is sitting up … well, as high as he can due to his leg, but he watching me as walk in. I smile, wobbly, but a smile nonetheless. I can't believe the relief I feel seeing his eyes open.

"Hi, Drew." That's it, you idiot? The love of your life is sitting there and that's all you can say?

"Hi." He swallows as if that one word has caused him great pain. I rush over to his side and put my fingers to his lips.

"Don't talk. It's going to hurt for a while."

He's still staring at me like—I don't know what it's like. What the hell is he thinking? His hand reaches up to my fingers and he pulls my hand down and just holds it. Okay, so I get teary-eyed and so does he. He smiles and so do I, sans the wobble.

"I love you, Drew."

"I love you too, Dora," he whispers.

I do something I know is taboo, but I crawl up beside him, watching out for all the wires and tubes, and snuggle next to him. His arm cradles me, and I feel his lips caress the top of my head. As I listen to the gentle thump of his heart, I close my weary eyes for some much needed rest.

I don't know how long I slept, but I wake up next to Drew, who is snoring lightly, and I feel like someone is watching me. I turn my head and see it's the nurse who guessed I was pregnant.

"I'm sorry," I say, but I'm not. I know I've probably broken a major hospital rule, but I'm not going to budge until I know. Drew is going to completely recover. I'm the mother of his baby, and I love him, and they'll just have to deal.

"We can move in a cot for you to sleep on," the kind nurse whispers.

"I'd rather lie here. I'm being careful of his leg and the wires. I need to hear his heart beating." I wait for her answer, praying that she won't make me move.

"Okay. Let me know if you change your mind." She smiles and leaves the room.

"I can't believe I'm holding you. I never want to let you go. Why did you leave the shoot and ignore my calls and then block them? I tried to see you but Jeff told me that you needed space and that if I pushed too hard you wouldn't ever want to see me." I look at his face and see the pain in his eyes.

"I left the shoot because seeing you with Angela made me think two weeks were all I was going to get with you. You acted like you were so into her. It wasn't until I got home, that

I realized the steamy kissing scene was all an act. And when I called your room and Angela answered …"

"What do you mean when Angela answered? She was never in my room. When I came back and found out you left, I flew back home to talk to you. Oh, wait I gave her the key so she could have a few friends over."

"She told me you were in the shower and that you guys were going out and it might be late when you returned my call. I'm so stupid, I fell for her lies."

"I should've ignored Jeff and just made you talk to me," he whispers."

"I'm so sorry Drew, can you forgive me?"

"Only if you will swear that you'll never leave me again." He sounds tired and I gently kiss him.

"I promise." I lay my head on his chest and smile as he starts to nod off.

4 4 4

"What's the secret?" I hear Drew's raspy voice whisper next to my ear. I look at the clock and see we've been asleep for a couple of hours.

"You heard me? They said you might be able to." I tilt my head to look at him smiling at me. He squeezes my side gently and tilts his head, obviously awaiting my answer.

"Maybe I should wait until you're out of here," I say quietly, "when you feel better." I watch as he smiles crookedly due to the minor swelling still left around his mouth. He slowly shakes his head. My heart melts, then starts racing as I realize he's not going to wait. "But I think I should. You might not like what I have to say." I bite my lip nervously and he squeezes me again.

"As long as it's not that you don't love me, and don't want to be with me, I'll be okay," he whispers as his eyes bore into mine. I know I have to tell him.

"Remember New Year's Eve?" I ask, and watch as he nods, sending me a wicked smile. "Well, we didn't use any protection, which was my fault because I attacked you and …" I take a deep breath. "I'm pregnant," I blurt out, and he squeezes me hard.

"We're pregnant," he says, his eyes filled with excitement. "New Year's right?" He tries to sit up straighter and I curl into him and gently press him back down.

"Yes, New Year's, now behave. You're supposed to be resting and staying calm. Do you want to get me thrown out of here?" I say, giggling at the huge grin on his face.

"We're pregnant. You know what that means?"

"Yes, it means I'm going to get fatter and then in five months we're going to have a baby."

"Yes, that of course. But I need to get out of here so we can get married." He excitedly whispers.

"Wait, you don't have to do that." I say biting my lip hoping that he ignores what I've just said.

"Are you kidding? I love you and you love me so why wouldn't we get married? Okay, so I can't get down on one knee, but Pandora Ann Phillips, will you marry me?" I look at him and tears fill my eyes.

"Yes! Of course I will." I feel his arms surround me and his lips touch mine.

Epilogue

Waking up, I look at the clock. It's three a.m. I listen for a sound, but nope, no crying. I do hear a muffled voice, so I get out of bed, putting on my slippers and satin robe. I move quietly to the nursery where I hear the voice coming from. Drew is standing by the changing table, expertly putting a diaper around our sweet baby girl.

So much has happened this past year: Drew and my wild week of passion, our separation, his accident, his recovery, Julie and Kevin's bundle of joy arriving in July, our wedding, Liam and Jeff off in Australia for a few months, and the birth of our twins, Amanda Lynn and Jason Edward, two of the most beautiful babies in the world.

"Now, we have to be quiet. Mommy needs her sleep and we don't want to wake up your brother either. At least not until I have your bottles fixed up. You know how impatient he is when he wakes up hungry. But you, my little angel, you're the patient one, and you're such a good girl, aren't you? Of course, I love you both equally, but I hope you understand that I love your mom the best. She is, after all, the one who gave you guys to me. How was I to know the necklace I gave her last Christmas was a Mexican pregnancy ball?"

My hand reaches up to my neck to hold the little silver ball that chimes softly when I move.

"I guess it worked pretty well, huh? We got two for the price of one. Today is going to be a busy day, as it's your first Christmas. You probably won't enjoy it much this year, but just wait until next year."

I see Mandy watching her father as he talks to her as if she understands every word.

"We're going to see all your grandparents and great-grandparents today. Your aunts and uncle too. Now let's be super quiet and we'll go get the bottles ready, because I hear your brother moving in the crib."

He picks Mandy up and kisses her cheek and she giggles. She keeps on giggling the more he shushes her. He turns and sees me standing in the doorway and his smile—yes, his smexy smile—totally makes me melt. Here we are, our own lucky group of four, and I couldn't be happier. As I continue watching him tend to our children, a warm sensation washes over me. There's really nothing hotter in my opinion than a gorgeous man who's wonderful with kids. I know exactly what we'll be doing once he finishes feeding our twins—yes, I do.

444

There she is, the woman of my dreams, the love of my life. We truly are our own 'Lucky Number Four'. Judging by her beautiful warm smile, I have a feeling I know what we'll be doing after I finish up here, and frankly I can't wait.

The End

About the Author

Amanda Jason is the pen name for Carol Kunz's New Adult romance novels. She is the C part of the mother and son author duo, C.A. Kunz. The pen name Amanda Jason actually has a special meaning to Carol because it is a tribute to the set of twins she lost many years ago. Carol began her dream of writing when her son, Adam, asked her to write a young adult fantasy novel back in 2011. She couldn't have been happier to embark on this wonderful journey into the literary world with her son because it was #1 on her bucket list.

Carol currently lives in sunny Florida with her hubby and her two four-legged fur babies. She takes comfort in the fact that her amazing daughter and son live close by. When she isn't writing, you can find her walking her yellow Lab or reading a good book. Lucky Number four is the debut novel of Amanda Jason, and it's been a long time coming. If you would like to find out more about Amanda Jason, please visit the links below:

Author's Twitter Account- @AmandaJason13

Author's Facebook Page- www.facebook.com/AuthorAmandaJason

Author's Email- amandajason13@aol.com

29926189R00221

Made in the USA
Charleston, SC
29 May 2014